THE PRICE
OF FREEDOM

www.rbooks.co.uk

THE PRICE
OF FREEDOM

Mary Jane Staples

BANTAM PRESS

LONDON · TORONTO · SYDNEY · AUCKLAND · JOHANNESBURG

TRANSWORLD PUBLISHERS
61–63 Uxbridge Road, London W5 5SA
A Random House Group Company
www.rbooks.co.uk

First published in Great Britain
in 2007 by Bantam Press
a division of Transworld Publishers

A CIP record for this book
is available from the British Library.

ISBN 9780593058619

Addresses for Random House Group Ltd companies outside the UK
can be found at: www.randomhouse.co.uk
The Random House Group Reg. No. 954009

The Random House Group Ltd makes every effort to ensure
that the papers used in its books are made from trees that have been
legally sourced from well-managed and credibly certified forests.
Our paper procurement policy can be found at:
www.randomhouse.co.uk/paper.htm

Typeset in New Baskerville by
Kestrel Data, Exeter, Devon.

Printed and bound in Great Britain by
Clays Ltd, St Ives plc.

2 4 6 8 10 9 7 5 3 1

THE PRICE
OF FREEDOM

Chapter One

Crash!

Beer glasses smashed as they hit the sawdusted floor.

It wasn't that the pub on Brixton Hill was open, and that some drunken customers had dropped their glasses. No, it was just that a tray of them had slid off the counter, due to having been pushed.

'Here, what's the bleedin' game?' shouted the proprietor, who had been preparing for the morning opening time.

'Sorry about that, Stan,' said Muscles Boddy, as beefy Dan Boddy was known. He was five feet ten inches tall and five feet wide. 'Me hand slipped.'

'What for?' demanded the rageful proprietor. 'I've paid me monthly dues, haven't I?'

'And so you should, seeing your pub's kept nice and quiet for you and yer customers by me guv'nor's firm,' said Muscles. 'But according to a dicky bird that whispered in me lughole,

7

you've been talking about complaining to the rozzers. Dear oh Lor'.' A sad sigh seemed to issue from his inappropriately jovial if knobbly countenance. Such a cheery expression was most incongruous on a man who dealt in bone-crushing violence. 'I don't want nosy bluebottles coming round to see me, do I? I ain't on friendly terms with any of 'em, and me guv'nor wouldn't like it no more than I would. He's worked himself near to death building up a business in Brixton. So I thought I'd come and let you know he's upset. What upsets me guv'nor upsets me as well, and ain't I said so before?'

'Would I complain, would I?' said the shaken proprietor.

Muscles Boddy reached over the counter and took hold of the man's collar, twisting and tightening it until he had his victim turning blue in his fight for breath.

'Well, here's hoping you won't, Stan,' he said, 'but suppose you had a rush of blood, eh?' He released the publican's collar in case the bloke had a fatal choking fit. 'Don't do it, or you might get taken to hospital with a leg off. Well, that's all, Stan, see you next month. No, wait a tick, if the flatties come and mention me monicker any time, let 'em know I'm your best friend, which I am, ain't I?'

'They'd believe that, wouldn't they?'

'Don't answer me back, Stan, it ain't what I

8

like,' said Muscles, and left, his boots crunching shattered glass.

A heavy East End gang had moved from Shoreditch into Brixton a year ago, in 1935, and established a lucrative protection racket. The people of Shoreditch would have been glad to see them go if it hadn't meant they'd been forced out by an even heavier mob.

In a house in Baytree Road, Brixton, Mrs Hilda Jones had just informed her youngest daughter that she intended to live a life of her own.

'Mum, what d'you mean?' asked the daughter, Mrs Olive Way.

'Just what I said, that I'm going to live me own life,' stated Mrs Hilda Jones.

'I wish I knew what you were talking about,' said Olive. 'How can you live your own life? There's Dad.'

'Well, he can live his own life too,' said Mrs Jones. 'He'll have to.'

'You can't mean you're going to leave him,' said Olive, shocked.

'That's exactly what I do mean,' said Mrs Jones.

'What?' Olive couldn't believe her ears. Twenty, she had been married six months, and she and her husband had set up home in this house in Baytree Road, off Brixton Hill. An attractive brunette, she was a likeable young woman who enjoyed helping her husband to apply new paint and new wallpapers to the rooms. There was nothing enjoyable, however, about the feeling that her mother had gone bonkers. 'Mum, you're not serious, you can't be.'

'Well, I am serious, and that's it,' said Mrs Jones. Forty-three, she was still comely in looks and figure. 'Now that I've seen all of my daughters married and settled, I feel I've done my duty as a mother, and I know I've done more than my duty as a wife. I've given your father the best years of me life. Twenty-five, I might point out, and now I'm going to enjoy the rest of my years by meself.'

'Mum, are you sure you know what you're saying?' asked Olive, incredulous.

'I've been thinking about it since your wedding day,' said Mrs Jones, 'and that's given me time to be as sure as I can be. I don't know how many socks I've washed or shirts I've ironed or meals I've cooked for your father. Thousands, I should think, and it's going to be a pleasure only doing things for meself.'

'I'll go dotty in a minute,' breathed Olive. 'I mean, are you talking about getting a divorce from Dad?'

'No, I don't want any messy divorce business,' said Mrs Jones. 'Well, I don't know, do I, if a woman can get a divorce on account of wanting to live her own life. The law's mostly on the side of men. Well, men make it, don't they? I'm just after a separation. I'm hardly likely to want to marry again and find meself washing some other man's socks. No, I want to be free to please meself how I spend my time, and to take up some lively interests.'

'I still can't believe you're serious,' said Olive. 'What's Dad going to say and what's he going to do?'

'He'll have to fend for himself for a change,' said Mrs Jones, 'and as for what he's going to say I don't suppose it'll be anything much. Well, he's never said anything much all his life.' Mrs Jones was a very talkative person herself, and forthright with it. If she wasn't as well spoken as Olive or her other daughters, that was because they'd had the benefit of a grammar-school education while she'd only had an elementary one, having been born of hard-up Camberwell parents. 'In fact, I don't know your dad's ever managed to hold a single decent conversation with me in all the years I've known him. I might as well come right out with it, Olive. Your dad is a boring old sod.'

'Why did you marry him, then?' asked Olive.

'I thought marriage would liven him up a bit, didn't I? It livens up other men, so I've heard.'

'But Dad's not a bad old stick, and he's sort of harmless as well,' said Olive, 'and you did marry him for better or worse.'

'Yes, but twenty-five years of being married to

someone that's about as lively as a doorpost, well, that's more than enough years for any woman,' said Mrs Jones.

'I know he's never been much of a talker,' said Olive, 'but he's never come home drunk or run after other women or been a rotten dad. And he did find money to make sure Madge, Winnie and I had a good education.' Madge and Winnie were her sisters. 'Mum, he's just the kind of man that's naturally quiet.'

'I've sometimes wondered if he's actu'lly alive,' said Mrs Jones. To Olive, her mother had seemed resigned to her father's quiet ways, apart from moments when irritation surfaced and she'd tell him he didn't even know how to listen, let alone know how to talk. Now she seemed a challenging woman, sprightly and active in her look and manner. 'Anyway, after all these years of having to put my fam'ly first, I'm going to start putting meself first.'

'But Dad's had to do the same,' protested Olive, 'he's had to put you and us first.'

'He's put the shop first,' said Mrs Jones. 'He should've married it instead of me. Olive, I've waited till you followed your sisters into wedlock, and now that you and Roger have settled in here, I'm going to get settled meself in a new home, a flat in Stockwell Road. That part-time job I've been doing is going to be full-time from next Monday, so what with the wage and what

12

savings I've made, I'll live quite comfortable. Mr Burnside, the manager, has been a lot more appreciative of what I'm worth than your father ever was. He's taken me for granted since the day I married him. Well, lots of women are beginning to feel their feet these days, and I'm one of them.'

'Mum, I don't like this,' said Olive. It was true, of course, that her dad was hardly the liveliest bloke in the world. It was also true that now she and her sisters were all married, her mum was entitled to enjoy a bit more freedom. But leaving Dad, separating from him, well, that was hard to take. 'Look, stay and have some lunch with me, and we'll talk about it some more.'

'I can't stay, I've got to be in the office by one o'clock for me afternoon's work, and I had a sandwich at home,' said Mrs Jones. Her part-time job, in the office of a Stockwell factory, filled her afternoons. It dovetailed with the morning work of another part-timer, who was leaving. 'Staying wouldn't change my mind, in any case, especially as I've been invited by Mr Burnside to join the Stockwell Amateur Dramatic Society, which he's president of and which'll take up a lot of me evenings. I quite fancy meself on the stage, and I think I can hold my own with younger women when it comes to being costumed a bit glamorous. In fact, if it turns out I've got a gift for the stage, I've been promised a part in the society's Christmas pantomime. My, when I think of all the years I've spent living with a doorpost, I know it's been wasted years except for the times I've enjoyed with you girls.'

'I don't see how you can say wasted years,' said Olive, 'and, anyway, Dad wouldn't stop you joining the society.'

'I don't suppose he would, or even notice that I'd joined,' said Mrs Jones. 'I don't suppose, after I've left him, that he'll even notice I've gone.'

'Of course he will,' said Olive. 'Mum, you're upsetting me something rotten.'

'You'll get over it,' said Mrs Jones, who felt a new and more exciting life was going to open up for her. It was May 1936, and she was looking forward to being free and independent for the first time since marrying Herbert in 1911.

She went on about her happy prospects until it was time for her to be on her way to her job. By then, Olive was almost glad to see her go. It was a relief to her ears. Her mother could get carried away sometimes by her gift for sounding off. That was when her father had most of his un-listening moments by going deaf.

The shop on the corner of the little Brixton street close to the borders of Streatham sold newspapers, periodicals, tobacco, cigarettes, confectionery and some simple grocery items such as tea, sugar, condensed milk and Camp coffee. It was a boon to local people, and was owned and run by Mr Herbert Jones. The freehold of the property had been left to Herbert by his father, who had run the shop before him. Above the shop was a flat that has been occupied for many years by an old lady, Mrs Goodliffe.

Oddly, the fourteen terraced houses extending from the shop in a solid row were all empty. The landlord, Walter Duffy, had sold the whole row to building contractors for development into attractive maisonettes, currently in favour with newly retired people who had a bit in the bank, and all tenants had been given notice to quit six months ago. The plan embraced the corner shop as well, but Herbert shocked the developers by refusing to sell, despite the original offer of a thousand pounds for the property and its prime site being upped to a thousand and five hundred. That, in the eyes of the developers, was a small fortune for any piddling corner-shop proprietor. Herbert said what good was one and a half thousand pounds to him when it would leave him without a business, without its turnover and without any property? Besides, he said, old Mrs Goodliffe had been his tenant for years, and his father's tenant previously. What was going to happen to her if he sold the place?

The developers said they'd find her a flat somewhere else, but Herbert didn't think much of that. They kept on at him, but he remained steadfast in his refusal to sell. Mind, he was forty-eight and beginning to think frequently about a new kind of life in which he wouldn't have to get up at six every morning, including Sundays, and work right through until six every evening, except Sundays, when he shut up shop at one o'clock. Nothing, however, would induce him to give old Mrs Goodliffe notice to quit. The flat was hers until she died. He had promised his father that. And he had let the developers firmly understand that the three-roomed abode was her own little world in her fast-declining years.

He'd lost some regular customers since the terraced houses had been vacated, but the shop still had a good turnover. He had money in the local branch of Barclays, and had always given Hilda, his wife, a generous housekeeping allowance to enable her to save a bit on her own account. Women needed something behind them in case they were left widowed. A widow's pension by itself didn't amount to much.

Hilda was a good wife. A bit of a gasbag at times, and always inclined to wear the trousers, but still reliable. And now that all the girls were married and settled, he'd made arrangements for her to enjoy a really posh holiday with him in the Isle of Wight come July. Two weeks and all, with Mrs Binns looking after the shop. Mrs Binns usually worked from seven thirty in the mornings until one in the afternoons, giving him needful assistance. From seven thirty until about eight, the paperboys and papergirls arrived to pick up their bundles of newspapers for delivery before they went to school.

It would come as a nice surprise to Hilda, two weeks holiday in the Isle of Wight at a posh Shanklin hotel.

At the moment, however, he was in a sorrowful state, a state that had come about two days ago, when old Mrs Goodliffe had gone at last, dying peacefully in her sleep. He'd known there was something wrong, because she hadn't come down for her pint of milk in the morning. He was the one who'd discovered her dead in her bed. A nice old lady, she deserved to slip away peacefully. If her going still saddened him, it was also giving him food for thought.

Mrs Nell Binns, a widow of forty-two and an invaluable help, interrupted his thoughts.

'It's half twelve, Herbert, time you had your sandwiches and your lunchtime cup of tea.'

'Be all right for a bit, will you, Nell?' said Herbert. He always said that. He was not a man of verbal versatility.

'Course I will,' said Mrs Binns. The shop being empty of customers for the first time that morning, she added, 'By the way, I've got to tell you I'm thinking of moving to Forest Hill, to keep house for an uncle of mine, a widower that's getting on a bit. It'll be board and lodging for me, and an allowance as well, and security for when I'm getting on a bit meself, so I'll probably say yes. It means I'll have to give you notice, Herbert, which I'll be sorry about.'

'I'll be sorry too, Nell,' said Herbert, 'but I can see you'd be wise to take up the offer.'

'I knew you'd be nice about it,' said Mrs Binns, 'and I'm sure you won't have any trouble getting someone to take my place, except now that old Mrs Goodliffe has passed on, will you be changing your mind and selling out to them builders?'

'I'll give it a bit of thought,' said Herbert, and went into the back room to put the kettle on for a cup of tea and to eat the sandwiches Hilda had prepared for him, as usual and as always. Someone came into the shop as he placed the kettle on the gas ring. A moment later, Mrs Binns called to him.

'Herbert, Mr Cawthorne wants to see you.'

Mr Lawrence Cawthorne, presumed Herbert. Joseph Cawthorne & Son (Building Contractors) Ltd was the firm that, having bought up the terraced houses, had been after his shop for ages. Their persistence and perseverance were still ongoing, and it was the son, Lawrence Cawthorne, who regularly came down from up on high to project his important self into the shop in repeated attempts to persuade Herbert to sell.

'Tell him to come in, Nell,' called Herbert.

Mr Lawrence Cawthorne entered the room, a little retreat from the shop. A brisk man with an engaging smile, he was in his element when negotiating for a contract on terms favourable to the firm, but he had found the quiet obstinacy of shopkeeper Herbert Jones difficult to break down.

'Here I am, Mr Jones, I've turned up again, but not like a bad penny, would you say?'

'Good morning to you,' said Herbert.

'Same to you,' said Mr Cawthorne. 'What's your present frame of mind?'

'I like to think it's tidy,' said Herbert.

It's still a hard job getting anything out of this character, thought Mr Cawthorne. Never speaks more than one sentence at a time, and never puts himself at a disadvantage.

'Mr Jones, is there no way we can overcome the one stumbling block, that of your tenant and the loyalty you owe her?'

Herbert could have said at once that his tenant was being prepared for burial at the undertakers, but paused to reflect on the matter before replying. Honesty winning out, he murmured, 'I'm sorry to say Mrs Goodliffe passed away two days ago.'

'She's dead?' said Mr Cawthorne not un-happily.

'I can't say it's surprising considering she was eighty-one,' said Herbert.

'That's a good run for anyone's money,' said Mr Cawthorne. 'Does that make you more willing to sell?'

'I wouldn't say I'm more willing,' said Herbert.

'But more open to a new offer?' suggested Mr Cawthorne. The firm was going to lose money unless work began on knocking the houses and the shop down within the next three weeks. The board had had to consider putting the houses back on the market unless the corner shop was acquired before the month was out. As it stood, the shop would be quite out of keeping with the superior quality and design of the maisonettes, whose proximity to the superior facades of Streatham would be emphasized. Further, the shop's site had always been necessary to the project.

'What d'you call a new offer?' asked Herbert.

'Well, look here,' said Mr Cawthorne, 'you've got us by the short and curlies, and you know it as much as we do. All right, then, what d'you say to us doubling the offer to three thousand? That'll look after you for the rest of your life. It's a more than generous amount as far as we're concerned, but it's on the table, ready to be picked up, providing you'll sign the contract inside a week from now.'

'Let's see, three thousand,' said Herbert, showing no signs of what the offer was doing to him. If he added his savings to it, he'd have three thousand eight hundred and fifty pounds in the bank. Invested in government stocks at four per cent, he'd collect interest of just over a hundred and fifty quid a year, a good three pounds a week. He and Hilda could sell their present house and buy one with a garden, and he could do what he'd always wanted to do, grow roses, sweet peas and vegetables.

'Come on, old chap,' said Mr Cawthorne.

'What with the shop, the flat, the wide frontage and the yard behind, I wouldn't say three thousand is overdoing it,' said Herbert. 'By itself it might be, but as part of what you've already bought, I'd say you'd still be getting a bargain.'

Mr Cawthorne blinked. All that was at least twice as much as this shopkeeper had ever come out with in one go, and what was more it meant he had a bit more up top than one gave him credit for.

'I'd say the bargain's more on your side than ours, Mr Jones, since frankly the yard's an eyesore.'

'You mean the people buying your maisonettes wouldn't like seeing it from their back windows,' said Herbert.

Mr Cawthorne blinked again. The shopkeeper

was proving that he wasn't simply an obstinate blighter.

'You've got a point, Mr Jones,' he admitted, 'but there's no chance of us offering a penny more. Three thousand is definitely the limit. In fact, old chap, that amount is going to make us feel skint.' Which statement was a bit of a porkie.

'Well, from where I am, the sale is going to make me feel I've lost my daily labours,' said Herbert, 'which could make me unsatisfied.'

'But a lot richer,' said Mr Cawthorne. 'Tell you what, we'll promise to pay all exes, such as solicitors' fees, yours as well as ours.'

'The kettle's boiling,' said Herbert, 'd'you want a cup of tea?'

'Not at this time of the day, thanks,' said Mr Cawthorne. 'All I'd like is an answer. In the affirmative.'

'Let me have the offer in writing,' said Herbert, 'and the day after I receive it I'll let my solicitors know I'll sign the contract. Can't say fairer, can I, Mr Cawthorne?'

Mr Cawthorne smiled. The man was almost loquacious today.

'I'll have the letter hand-delivered to you to-morrow, Mr Jones.'

'That'll do,' said Herbert, filling the teapot.

'Shall we shake hands on it?' asked Mr Cawthorne.

'Seems we ought to,' said Herbert. He put the teapot down and they shook hands on the deal, Mr Cawthorne thinking about a starting date for the demolition work, and Herbert thinking about delivering the good news to his wife.

Chapter Two

Herbert entered the kitchen when he arrived home. He and Hilda lived in their own house in Vining Street, Brixton. It seemed a bit of a hollow dwelling now that all their daughters were married and away. It wouldn't be a bad idea at all to move into a smaller house. There were some in the area east of Effra Road, two-storeyed terraced houses, three up, three down, with gardens – neat, compact and respectable-looking dwellings.

'Had a nice day, Hilda?' he said.

Hilda Jones looked at him. He had a sort of stolid, dignified appearance, with never a hair out of place, nor a tie ever creased, nor a button ever undone. And every evening of their married life he had said the same thing to her on his arrival home from the shop. Had a nice day, Hilda? Sometimes she didn't bother to answer, and he never pressed the question.

'Oh, in and out, up and down,' she said

now. She knew what he'd say to that. And he did.

'Oh, well, look on the bright side.'

It was a wonder she'd never thrown saucepans at him. She'd been a saint, really, in the way she'd put up with his dull and unimaginative character. She couldn't remember the last time he'd been an excitement to her in any way. In fact, she couldn't remember if he ever had been, even in bed, although she knew she'd always had a good body and still did. The marital act had probably been a sort of routine to him, and she wouldn't have been surprised if during his performances his thoughts had all been of his shop and his customers. He'd gone to work in that shop when his father owned it, since when he'd never been out of it, so to speak.

'Well, sit down, the supper's ready,' she said, and it occurred to her that that was how she'd responded to him every evening for many years. A born doorpost, that's what he was, and all she knew now was that if she didn't get away quick she'd turn into one herself. Mr and Mrs Doorpost, that's how they'd end up if she stayed.

Herbert sat down and she served rabbit stew.

'Well, this is tasty,' he said, which was more or less what he always said about any meal.

'There won't be many more,' she said.

'By the way, Hilda, I've got some news, I—'

'I said there won't be many more.'

'Many more what?' asked Herbert.

'Many more suppers cooked by me.'

'Pardon?' said Herbert, thinking supper was the right occasion for delivering good news, not for listening to remarks that didn't make sense.

'I'm moving to Stockwell next Monday, into a flat that's got its own bathroom,' said Hilda.

'Pardon?' said Herbert.

'Don't keep saying pardon, try and listen for once.'

'Did you say—'

'Yes, I did.' Hilda spoke positively. 'Now that all our girls are married and settled, I don't feel I'm obligated any more as a wife and mother. I've had twenty-five years fully obligated, so next Monday I'm moving out to live me own life. D'you understand me, Herbert Jones?'

'Well, no, I don't,' said Herbert, pretty sure he was either dreaming or not hearing her properly.

'I said I'm moving out on Monday. I want some fresh air and new faces in me life. We've come to a parting of the ways, you and me, Herbert. You take me for granted, you don't talk, you live for that blessed shop, you've got no real life in you, and you're about as exciting to a woman as a suet pudding. I'm leaving you before I go into a decline and lose me health and strength on account of aggravated depression.'

'Hilda, are you all right?' Herbert felt she was saying things that could only come from a woman who was suffering not depression but a serious attack of mental instability. 'I mean, d'you feel a bit ill or something?'

'No, I don't,' said Hilda, 'I happen to feel quite perky, like I've got a new life dawning, that's what. Look at you, always in the same suit, always saying the same things every day, and doing the same things every year. You wouldn't have noticed the difference if you'd married an empty flour sack or a bag of potatoes. Well, you can get hold of one to take my place. I'm packing me wherewithals on Sunday, and moving on Monday, like I said. The van will take part of the furniture, enough for what I'll need in the flat, and no more than I've worked and slaved for. I'll have me Savings Bank account, and I'll be working full-time instead of part-time, so you won't have any worries about having to keep me. I want to be independent, anyway.'

'Hilda, I don't understand, I've always been myself—'

'Don't I know it,' said Hilda. 'You've always been in need of having some fireworks tied to your coat tails, Herbert Jones. Still, just keep on being yourself and you won't miss me, you won't even notice I'm gone. And you'll always have the shop and your customers.'

Herbert, who had stopped eating during these last few minutes, looked down at his meal, then looked up at his wife, his brow furrowed beneath his handsome mane of iron-grey hair, his eyes dark with emotion new to him.

'I'm sorry, Hilda, about being, well, inadequate, I suppose, but I never thought—'

'I'm sorry too if I'm upsetting you a bit, but it's got to be said.' Hilda tried to look sorry for him. 'It's not your fault, I suppose, that you were born without any go. When we first got to know each other, I thought you were just a nice quiet type that I could help liven up, but after all these years I can't help thinking I ought to have seen my married life was going to be all work and no play, like. You ought to have sold the shop to the builders, treated me to some nice new outfits, put the rest of the money in the bank for both our benefits, then gone out into the world and got yourself a lively job that would've woken you up a bit, like with the Fire Brigade. Mr Murchison down the street is a fireman, and no-one could say he's not lively; he keeps Mrs Murchison in fits, so she says. Well, that's it, Herbert, I've said me piece, and now we're going to live separate lives. It won't hardly affect you, except you'll have to do your own washing and cooking, and I daresay you could soon learn what the gas cooker is for when—'

'Stop.' Herbert stood up. His placidity had taken one sharp arrow too many. 'I'm sorry for you, Hilda, I'm sorry for any woman who sees a husband like you see me. I never offered myself to you as anything but what I was at the time. After all you've said to me, I ought to throw you out here and now, and save you any more of your married suffering, but I can't do that, it's not in me nature. So I'm going out, I'm going to take a long walk and try to work out why you had to feed me salt and vinegar after all my years as a husband and father.'

'It wasn't easy,' said Hilda, 'but I had to speak my mind, and I'll tell you this much, Herbert, you've just said more to me than you've said in six months. That ought to make you think a bit.'

'It's doing that all right, Hilda, believe me.' Herbert was stiff with shock and flushed with humiliation. 'But if you don't mind, don't say any more, I've got the picture, thanks very much.'

The front door closed behind him a few minutes later, and it closed quietly, not with a slam.

Well, I've got that over with, thank goodness, said Hilda Jones to herself. I ought to have spoken to him years ago about the way he was turning me into a cabbage. If it hadn't been for the girls and the neighbours, I'd have felt buried alive. I did myself a really good turn when I went after that part-time job, it's been the making of a new life for me. All these years that I've put up with him and the same old suits, how did I manage to? Boring old sods shouldn't be allowed into women's lives.

During his long walk, Herbert made up his mind about what he wanted to do.

On his return, Hilda said, 'We don't have to act uncivilized to each other for the few days we've got left together.'

'No, we don't,' said Herbert.

'We can talk, if you want,' said Hilda.

'Better than that, I could let off a few fireworks,' said Herbert.

'That sounds a bit sarky,' said Hilda.

'Yes, I'm trying to put some sparks into me conversation,' said Herbert.

'You're too late,' said Hilda.

'Bloody shame, then,' said Herbert.

'Yes,' said Hilda.

'Sorry,' said Herbert.

'You'll be all right,' said Hilda, 'you don't really need anybody, not while you've got your shop.'

'Maybe,' said Herbert, keeping quiet about business events.

Hilda's other daughters got to know from Olive what was in the wind, and called on their parents the following evening. Their mother explained at length.

'Well, you can talk all night, but none of it makes sense to me,' said Madge, the eldest daughter. Twenty-three, she was buxom, healthy and assertive. She was also a lover of cats. She had three. She'd been married two years and her husband Brian Cooper kept wondering why his virility hadn't yet helped her to produce a child. Madge could have told him what the teachings of Marie Stopes had done for her, but didn't. She was happy with her cats. Cats weren't as messy or demanding as kids, and Brian would come to love them as she did. 'Does it make sense to you, Win?' she asked.

'No, it doesn't,' said Winnie, who was twenty-one, the mother of a year-old son by her husband Victor Chance, and a bit weird in her liking for standing at her open front door on a clear night and looking at the stars. She had a feeling that somewhere in the Milky Way was her own star. Victor, of course, often asked her how she was going to recognize it. She'd know, she said, as soon as she saw it. And then what? Victor asked. I'll come into a fortune, she always replied. And I'll come into a state of lumbago from all the draughts you're letting in, said Victor once, but that was as much as he did say in the way of a complaint. However barmy Winnie was about the Milky Way, she was a loving woman and couldn't be faulted in bed on Saturday nights. That was when she liked a kind of free-for-all beneath the sheets, on Saturday nights, give or take the occasional miss for one reason or another. 'Mum, you've had an over-forty brainstorm,' she declared now.

'Well, p'raps I have,' said Hilda, 'and if it surprises you, it doesn't surprise me. I wonder I haven't blown up ages ago.'

'Have you talked to her, Dad?' asked Madge.

'Not a great deal,' said Herbert.

'Talked to me?' Hilda laughed. 'He's never properly talked to me in twenty-five years. I could've been just an ornament. When he does open his mouth, it's only to say something he's said a hundred times before.'

'You don't have to be that unkind, especially not in front of Dad,' said Winnie.

'She can't help it,' said Herbert, 'it comes from her years of suffering.'

'Help, that's not like you, Dad, saying something like that,' said Winnie. 'You were born under a good-natured star, I've always said so.'

'Well, it must've just fell on me and knocked my brains about,' said Herbert.

'Being sarcastic won't help, Dad,' said Madge in her strong assertive voice, 'and you've got to face the fact that Mum's right about one thing. You hardly ever get sociable and talkative, and every woman ought to be able to rely on her husband to be good company to her.'

'D'you mind speaking a bit quiet?' said Herbert. 'Only I've got a slight headache in the region between me ears.'

His daughters stared at him, and his wife rolled her eyes.

'Dad, you're coming out with some unusual words,' said Winnie.

'He's had a shock,' said Hilda. 'Still, it's a change, a few unusual words from him.'

'Don't go on at him like that,' said Winnie. 'Being bitter won't help. But I must say, Dad, you could have taken Mum out and about a lot more than you have. I mean, how often have you taken her to the cinema or theatre?'

'Periodically, I have,' said Herbert.

'But how often is periodically?' asked Madge.

'Once a year,' said Hilda.

'A bit more than that, I'd have thought, but I've always wanted to save as much as possible for our old age,' said Herbert, looking apologetic. 'For when I retired from the shop and had time for us to be a bit more active together.'

'Not so we could live it up a bit, I bet,' said Hilda. 'As for that shop of his, he could've sold it months ago, and treated me to a trip to some-where exciting like Paris without the expense hardly noticing. As it is, my mind's made up, I'm moving on Monday so's I can live a free and independent life. Your dad's accepted it, and you two girls and Olive have got to accept it as well.'

'I think the pair of you have got to act your age and have some sensible talk about it,' said Madge crossly. 'Winnie and myself, and Olive, don't agree with any separation, and we're not going to take sides, either.'

33

'I hope you all understand I've got justified reasons for wanting to live me own life,' said Hilda.

'The trouble is you and Dad don't have a lot in common,' said Madge. 'Now if you had a nice cat to look after, you could share the pleasure.'

'I don't like cats,' said Hilda, 'and are you sure your Brian does?'

'Brian has a natural liking for them, the same as I have,' said Madge.

'Well, your dad's natural liking is for his shop,' said Hilda.

An argument developed about shared interests, in which Herbert did not participate. He got up after a while and left his wife and daughters talking across each other.

They were so absorbed in making their points that they didn't notice he'd disappeared. Well, one could have said he'd always existed unnoticed in the background of their family life.

The argument didn't solve anything. Hilda remained adamant about having the right to be free after twenty-five years of slaving. Madge said she was out of her mind. Winnie said she'd come to regret it. Not me, said Hilda.

Chapter Three

The contract having been quickly prepared for signature, Herbert took time off on Friday to visit his solicitor in company with Mr Cawthorne, leaving the reliable Mrs Binns in charge of the shop for an hour or two. Mrs Binns was pleased for him. He was going to get a really handsome sum for his property, and the builders had allowed him two weeks to close the shop down. He was offering his customers a whole range of items at cost price, and every customer was being given a Roneo'd copy of a letter expressing his thanks and appreciation for their support over the years. Herbert Jones was a nice man, that was the firm opinion of Mrs Binns, even if he wasn't exactly electrifying. So it had shocked her all over to have him tell her his wife was leaving him. She'd had quite a conversation with him about it.

'But what for, Herbert? Is she having a fling, then?'

'A what?'

'You know, is she having it off with some man somewhere?'

'I'll have to ask you to choose your words a bit more careful, Nell.'

'Well, I wouldn't want to insult Hilda, no, nor you, Herbert, but I can't think why else she's leaving you.'

'It seems I'm not very exciting.'

'What?'

'It seems I'm a stodgy old bugger, Nell.'

'Hilda told you that?'

'That and more on the same lines,' said Herbert. 'She's right, of course, I'm no talker, and don't go in for playing a piano or doing a knees-up.'

'Well, you're a quiet man, Herbert, I won't say you're not, but that's better than being loud, rowdy and drunk, and there's plenty of that kind about when the pubs shut of a Saturday night. I don't want to say more than I should, like, but what's so exciting about Hilda that she thinks she's the cat's whiskers compared to you?'

'I won't talk about it, if you don't mind, Nell.'

'Well, let me just say I'm on your side, Herbert. Is she going to get half the money from the sale of the shop?'

'That's a private matter, Nell.'

'Oh, beg pardon, Herbert.'

'Still, after Hilda's left, I'll take you out for a

treat somewhere before you go and housekeep for your uncle. I couldn't have done without you in the shop these several years.'

'It's been a pleasure, Herbert, you've always treated me very friendly and fair, and as Hilda's leaving you and I'm a widow woman, why shouldn't you take me out before I go off to me uncle?'

'There's no strings, Nell.'

'Well, there wouldn't be, would there, Herbert, you're not that sort of man.' Nell mused on the matter for a moment or two. Then she said, 'Still, out of respect for the occasion, I think I'll wear me best hat and costume.'

Herbert and Hilda said their goodbyes to each other on Sunday night. Herbert had been sleeping in daughter Madge's old room since being advised by his wife that he wasn't much to write home about. And as he was always up very early, well before Hilda came down, he thought Sunday night the right time to say goodbye.

Hilda had done her packing. All her clothes and personal possessions were in a large trunk, and she had placed a slip of paper on each item of furniture she needed, which the removal men would collect. She had offered to discuss her furniture requirements with Herbert, but he said no need, she could take whatever she wanted. She said she felt she had earned ownership.

'Yes,' said Herbert, 'I appreciate you have.'

'Men don't always appreciate what their wives are entitled to,' said Hilda.

'No, apparently not,' said Herbert, 'especially us dull old buggers. Sorry I've been a bit negative.'

'Not as sorry as I've been,' said Hilda. 'Still,' she added, 'I don't want to go on at you any more, best if we say our goodbyes friendly like.'

The definitive goodbyes began at ten on Sunday night.

'Well, I'll say so long now, and then go up to bed,' said Herbert.

'All right, goodnight, then,' said Hilda. 'Oh, I suppose it's only fair to say not every day of our marriage has been dreary. More like a bit quiet, and I might remark there's even been them pleasant times, when the girls were young and you read bedtime stories to them. One thing I'll admit is that you weren't ever a neglectful father.'

'Just a bit of a stodgy one,' said Herbert.

'Well, even about that, no-one can help the way they're born, like I mentioned before,' said Hilda. 'If you're not born to set the world on fire, it's not your fault. I did try to buck you up a bit, but it didn't work.'

'There was no meat on the bone, I suppose,' said Herbert.

'What?' said Hilda.

'Not much for you to go to work on,' said Herbert.

'You're coming out with some surprising remarks lately,' said Hilda.

'No good me asking if you're likely to change your mind about going, I suppose?' said Herbert.

'No, I'm not going to change my mind, not now, thanks very much,' said Hilda. 'Anyway, I know you're not all that helpless, I know you'll be all right on your own. Well, it's not as if you've ever needed anyone to talk to, so I don't have to worry about you, which is a bit of a blessing under the circumstances.'

'Would you like me to come and see you once in a while?' asked Herbert.

'Yes, once in a while you could come,' said Hilda. 'Say for a cup of tea on a Sunday afternoon now and again. I'll drop you a line to invite you each time. Oh, I hope you won't forget to go and visit your daughters fairly frequent, Herbert.'

'I know I've got daughters, Hilda,' said Herbert.

'Yes, three of them, Madge, Winnie and Olive, and they're all married now, don't forget,' said Hilda.

Herbert nodded, looked at her with the eyes of a man who still didn't quite know what had hit him, and said, 'Well, I've got to thank you, Hilda, for being a good wife and mother all these years, even if I don't understand how you could come to say all those things to me, or the way you said them. I suppose you had good reason, but it's fair knocked me sideways, I can tell you.'

'It was best for both of us, Herbert,' said Hilda, 'we'll both be better off living on our own, and I don't want you to feel sorry for yourself. It'll only make you brood. Why don't you take up darts at one of the local pubs? That's the sort of thing you need, a bit of activity, a lively atmosphere and some sociable company.'

'I'll go for some walks,' said Herbert. 'Well, goodbye, Hilda.'

'Goodbye, Herbert, and don't forget you've got to do shopping for yourself.'

'I won't forget,' said Herbert. 'By the way, I'll be gone, of course, before your removal van comes.'

'Yes, I know,' said Hilda, 'you'll be in the shop.' She rarely went there herself. That shop was something she'd been fed up with for years, mainly because she was sure he thought a lot more of it than he ever did of her.

'Goodbye, then, Hilda,' said Herbert.

'I'll tell you something,' said Hilda.

'What?' asked Herbert, halting on his way to the door.

'We've actu'lly just done some talking to-gether,' said Hilda.

*   *   *

40

In the shop on Monday morning, Nell Binns kept giving Herbert inquisitive glances. She was sure he must be suffering a bit, seeing his wife had just left him. But he didn't seem fraught about it. At one point, when he was attending to two ladies who had dropped in to pick up their weekly magazines, he sounded very much like his normal self.

'Mr Carraway in the pink still, Mrs Carraway?'

He always asked that question of Mrs Carraway, a jolly woman with a jolly husband.

'I'll say he is, we went to a party Saturday evening where they gave us gin and tonics,' said Mrs Carraway. 'Gus had heard about gin and tonics, but never thought people outside of Noel Coward and his London toffs actu'lly drank them. Nor did I, but it seems they do in Streatham, which was where the party was. Well, the gin put Gus in the pink all right. There was a lot more of it than tonic. He's still got spots in front of his eyes, and I don't know how he's managing his greengrocer's shop this morning, or if I'm seeing any straighter meself than I was yesterday. You sure this is *Woman's Weekly*?'

'Quite sure, Mrs Carraway.'

'Well, I believe you, Mr Jones, you've always been a man to trust.'

'Yes,' said the other lady, Mrs Robbins, 'and I don't know what we're going to do now you've sold the shop, Mr Jones.'

41

'I hope none of my customers feel I've let them down,' said Herbert.

'Of course not – oops – ' Mrs Carraway let go an involuntary hiccup. 'Would you believe, that gin's still getting at me. I'll stick to port and lemon in future. No, we'll miss you and the shop, Mr Jones, but we don't feel you've let us down, especially if it means you and Mrs Jones can enjoy a nice retirement. Oh, and while I'm here, I think I'll have four packets of tea, three tins of evaporated milk and four pounds of sugar at the cost price you're offering.'

'I'll have the same,' said Mrs Robbins, 'and a jar of raspberry jam as well.'

'A pleasure, ladies,' said Herbert. He always expressed himself in that way over any purchases made by lady customers, and Nell Binns thought his wife just couldn't help seeing him as a middle-aged stick-in-the-mud. But what about his good points, his honesty and reliability? And he was still manly in his looks.

He caught her glance then and gave her a slight smile.

That's the stuff, Herbert, she thought, grin and bear it.

'Well?' she said later on, when the shop was empty at last.

'Well what?' said Herbert, his handsome mane of hair well brushed, his plain brown tie looking neat and tidy.

'Hilda's gone?' said Nell.

'As far as I know,' said Herbert.

'Hurting a bit, is it?' said Nell.

'I won't talk about it, if it's all the same to you,' said Herbert.

'I'm a friend, y'know,' said Nell.

'And a good woman,' said Herbert.

'Thanks,' said Nell. She was no beauty, but her features were pleasantly homely. 'Hope I'll be just as good as a housekeeper for me elderly uncle.'

'Bound to be,' said Herbert. 'I'd bet on it. Probably make the old lad sit up and take notice.'

'Complimented, I'm sure,' said Nell. 'And it's a nice change, hearing you say things like that.'

'Well, I suppose some of us can learn a few things, even if we're getting on a bit,' said Herbert.

Nell might have said he still looked in his prime, but a customer came in.

Muscles Boddy put in an appearance at the shop on the stroke of six, just as Herbert was closing. He always chose that time. It meant there were no nosy parkers about.

'Evening, 'Erbert old cock.'

'You're on time as usual,' said Herbert.

'Didn't want to miss you,' said Muscles Boddy. Strangely, he had a soft spot for Herbert. Well, he never gave any trouble, nor handed out any lip. Muscles Boddy didn't like lip, not from people whose shops or pubs or other business premises were under the protection of the guv'nor. Herbert Jones, who ran a very profitable shop, according to the guv'nor, had seen the sense of being protected when it was put to him seven months ago. The opening conversation had been very agreeable to Muscles.

'Do I understand,' said Herbert, 'that protection means my shop won't catch fire or get smashed up or burgled?'

'Have yer been burgled, then?' asked Muscles.

'I've had three break-ins these last twelve months,' said Herbert. Old Mrs Goodliffe, a bit deaf, hadn't heard a thing, and if she had she'd have collapsed, poor old lady. Of course, he was insured against fire and burglary, which cost a bit, but it did cover shop and flat.

'Three break-ins? Dear oh Lor',' said Muscles, 'that's a cruel lot of dishonesty. Painful, I call it.'

'What did you say protection costs?' asked Herbert.

'Well, you ain't running a pub nor the Locarno ballroom, mate,' said Muscles, 'and me guv'nor's got a reputation for being fair. Ten bob a week suit yer, paid monthly?'

'Calendar months?' said Herbert.

'Eh?' said Muscles, his bulk taking up nearly half the cosy back room. 'Is that your lips moving?'

44

'It's January, February, March and so on,' said Herbert.

'Blind me, I think I've heard of them,' said Muscles, 'but two smackers a month means every four weeks on the dot.'

Twenty-six pounds a year is a lot, thought Herbert, but he could recognize what the alternative might mean. He knew all about the gang that had moved in, and he reckoned they'd had a good guess about the extent of his turnover.

'Sounds fair,' he said. He was a practical man, and his visitor was half the size of a mountain.

'Pleasure to do business with yer,' said Muscles.

'I'll be protected against break-ins?' said Herbert.

What a decent cove, thought Muscles, he's talking sweet. What a change from all the argufying he usually had to put up with from piddling shopkeepers. Break-ins? Well, they could be taken care of. It only needed for the word to be put around that the guv'nor required tuppenny-'a'penny operators to lay off this corner shop or else.

'You got my word, mate, that there won't be no smashed winders nor break-ins, providing you contract to me guv'nor. Mind, it won't be no written contract, just word of honour between gents. The guv'nor don't go in for a lot of writing, except to his loving ma on picture post-cards.'

45

'Good enough,' said Herbert.

'Let's see yer mitt,' said Muscles. Herbert put out his hand. Muscles smacked it. 'Done,' he said. 'Mind, payment in advance.'

'Of course,' said Herbert.

'Well, bugger me,' said Muscles, 'I like your style, 'Erbert.'

Herbert handed over two pound notes, then said, 'Like a nip?'

'Eh?' said Muscles.

'Scotch?' said Herbert.

If there was anything Muscles liked more than a pint of foaming wallop, it was a finger or so of Scotch.

'Sod me, I do like your style, 'Erbert,' he said, and Herbert took a bottle of whisky from a cupboard, together with two glasses. He poured two fingers into each glass. Muscles drank the health of his new client in two mouthfuls. Herbert drank his more slowly. Tomorrow he would give the insurance company notice to cancel coverage of burglary, break-ins and the like. He'd retain fire coverage, just in case. Allowing for the dues paid to this gorilla, he'd actually be in pocket.

Muscles considered the contract very agreeably settled. Corner shops generally couldn't come up with more than a measly quid a month, or even only fifteen bob. And some the guv'nor didn't even bother with. Clients like publicans or car dealers had to agree to ten quid at least.

46

Commission for Muscles was ten per cent of all collections.

He parted from Herbert on very friendly terms. Since then good old Herbert had paid up promptly and with never any lip. And there was always a nip or two of whisky offered. No wonder Muscles liked the bloke.

Today, however, the collector of dues looked sorrowful.

'Listen, 'Erbert, I heard this morning that you've sold the shop.'

'Yes, I have,' said Herbert.

Muscles took off his brown bowler and placed it over his heart.

'Well, I'm grieving, 'Erbert,' he said gloomily. 'I don't grieve much, having been brought up the hard way in a Borstal college, but I ain't above feeling sad sorrow for the end of our happy business relationship. Got a drop of reviver handy, have yer? It'll ease me sorrow a bit.'

'You've got a dubious way of earning a living, y'know,' said Herbert. 'I'm not sure you deserve a nip.'

'Here, come off it, 'Erbert,' protested Muscles, 'that ain't like you, giving me lip. Ain't it a bleedin' fact that since I've been keepin' me protective eye on your shop, it ain't ever caught fire, been burgled or had its winders broke?'

'It's a fact,' said Herbert.

'There y'ar, then,' said Muscles.

Herbert took the bottle of whisky from the cupboard, and poured a generous measure into one glass, and a modest amount into another. He paused, then added more.

'I think I'm in need myself,' he said.

'That's better,' said Muscles, 'that's more like it. What's friends for, eh, except to share a bottle when it comes to a sad parting?'

'Funny kind of friends,' said Herbert, handing the bruiser a glass. Muscles enjoyed a swig, then peered at Herbert.

'What's up, 'Erbert? You ain't your usual prime self.'

'My wife's left me,' said Herbert in a moment of bitterness, and took a mouthful of reviving Scotch.

'Eh?' said Muscles.

'After twenty-five years, she's walked out on me,' said Herbert. He owed this racketeer nothing except a kick in the crutch for crooked extortion, but there it was, an involuntary need to confide.

'She's done what?' said Muscles.

'Called me a boring old sod and left me,' said Herbert.

'Well, not having had the pleasure of meeting the lady, I ain't formed no opinion of her,' said Muscles, 'but calling you that and then walking out after all them years of you providing for her, well, she don't sound like my idea of an appreciative woman. I hope you ain't been soft enough to split the proceeds with her.'

'Proceeds?' said Herbert.

'Come to, 'Erbert,' said Muscles. 'What you sold the shop for. I heard it was a tidy sum, sort of mouth-watering.'

'Before I could tell her anything,' said Herbert, 'she came out with all her complaints about me imperfections, besides letting me know I was on a par with a sack of potatoes. So I didn't say a word to her.'

'Good on yer, 'Erbert mate,' said Muscles with an admiring grin. 'A tight north and south is a wise one, according to me guv'nor. But she's upset you, I can see that, plain as a sparrer on a lady's titfer. I ain't known you with a long face before. Below the bleedin' belt, that was, calling you names and walking out on you after twenty-five years. Listen, have you thought about pushing her under a bus accidental, like, and marrying again? There's always a welcoming widow woman somewhere about, ready and willing to get hitched to a steady bloke like you. I married one meself once. Pity she went and got drowned off Southend Pier one night, poor unhappy woman. Still, that needn't put you off marrying some other one that'll be more appreciative than yer present trouble and strife.'

'I'll be all right on me own,' said Herbert.

'No, that ain't for you, 'Erbert, you're a bloke

49

that needs his natural home comforts,' said Muscles, finishing his whisky. 'And you need a friend, don't you, matey? Well, you got me. Could you squeeze another tot out of that there bottle?'

'Don't know why I should,' said Herbert, 'not after what you've had out of me.' But he poured more whisky into the gangster's glass.

'Bless you, 'Erbert,' said Muscles. 'I ain't too fond of too many people, but I've always had a liking for you. You want a good turn done any time, you can rely on me, I promise yer.'

'You've got a good side, have you?' said Herbert.

'I ain't a cherub, I'll grant you that,' said Muscles, 'but I ain't been known to let a friend down. Cheer up, 'Erbert, you ain't lost nothing that counts. I suppose she ain't told you where she's gorn, has she?'

'She kindly left her address on a postcard on the kitchen mantelpiece,' said Herbert.

'That was kindly, was it?' said Muscles. 'Ruddy condescending, I call it. Gorblimey, 'Erbert mate, no wonder you ain't yourself.'

'I can go and see her now and again, if she invites me and if I feel like it,' said Herbert.

'I'm buggered if I'd feel like it meself,' said Muscles. 'Well, it's been sad, listening to you, matey, but there's always tomorrer, and you never know what tomorrer might bring, eh? A

50

welcoming widow woman to start with. You got a notice in your winder, I see, advising customers your shop's closing down at the end of this here week. I ain't feeling too cheerful about that. Still, I'll collect your final donation while I'm here. Say a fiver.'

'It's two quid, the usual,' said Herbert. 'It's not even that, considering I'm closing down come Saturday.'

'Now, 'Erbert, we ain't going to conclude this pertic'ler relationship in an argufying way, are we?' said Muscles. 'You ain't even going to notice a fiver, not now the sale of your shop has earned you a sackful.'

'I think you're talking about bashing my head in,' said Herbert. Muscles grinned. Herbert, having emptied his till, took five one-pound notes out of his small canvas money bag, and handed them over. 'Meeting and relationship closed,' he said.

'Business relationship, eh?' said Muscles. 'We still got friendship, so I won't forget you, course I won't. Good luck to you, matey.'

Off he went, wide and big, and whistling.

Chapter Four

The following evening, Herbert kept his promise to give Mrs Nell Binns a treat. He took her to the Streatham Hill Theatre, and to a late supper after the show. It let her know how much he appreciated the job she had done for him in the shop. And Nell let him know she honoured his appreciation by putting on her glad rags, in which she looked very nice.

They had a very friendly chat over the meal, and it brought forth a lot more talk from Herbert than he was wont to produce. But an evening of mutual appreciation called for a fair amount of sociable exchanges.

That same evening, Brian Cooper took his wife Madge, Herbert's eldest daughter, to the Gaumont Cinema in Streatham. At the end of the programme they walked to a bus stop amid the night lights of Streatham. On the way, Brian emitted a low whistle.

'What's that for?' asked Madge.

'Cop what's on the other side of the road,' said Brian.

Madge looked. For the moment her view was blotted out by a moving tram. It passed on and she spotted a man and woman on the opposite pavement and level with her.

'Well I'm blessed,' she breathed.

'Your dad and friend?' said Brian.

'It's Dad all right, and she's Mrs Binns, who works in his shop,' said Madge, turning her head to follow their progress. Herbert and Nell were on their way to their late supper in a classy Streatham restaurant. 'I can hardly believe it.'

'He's found quick consolation,' said Brian. 'Didn't think the quiet old lad had it in him.'

'Wait till I get a chance to talk to him,' said Madge.

'Leave it alone, Madge,' said Brian, 'it's his own affair now your mum's left him.'

'It's not decent, neither is it right, not when the separation has only just happened,' said Madge.

'Point is, does the lady – Mrs Binns, you said? Yes, does she think like that? Your dad still looks a very healthy specimen, and the lady might fancy him in his nightshirt. Is she a widow, by chance?'

'Yes, she is,' said Madge. 'And look here, you clown. Dad doesn't wear a nightshirt, he wears striped pyjamas.'

'Well, she's free to fancy him in striped pyjamas, then,' said Brian, 'and he's free to oblige her, so good luck to him, even if he isn't any live wire.'

'Don't talk like that,' said Madge, 'it's not decent, especially when we're all hoping he and Mum can get together again. Which they will when they've come to their senses. All this nonsense at their age, it's ridiculous.'

'That's not much of a hope, their getting together again,' said Brian. 'I can't see your mother going back to someone she calls a doorpost, particularly now all you girls are off her hands. Listen, lovebird, isn't it time you and I started a family?'

'We've got a family,' said Madge firmly, 'you, me, Pinky, Floss and Fluffy.'

'Shoot Pinky, Floss and Fluffy,' said Brian.

'You don't mean that,' said Madge.

'Wait till I get you home in bed,' said Brian, 'I'll show you exactly what I do mean.'

'Well, I'll have to wish you luck, I suppose,' said Madge.

Herbert took some daily walks to keep himself occupied. One evening, after he had prepared and eaten a simple supper, he referred to the postcard propped against an ornament on the kitchen mantelpiece. There it was, Hilda's new address, written in her neat hand and plain

54

for all to see. He read it, not for the first time. The Flat, 25, Stockwell Road. He knew Stockwell Road. Some shops, some houses, some flats.

He didn't think he'd get invited too often. After all, he'd always be a boring old codger to her. His best bet was to turn up uninvited and give her a surprise. She wouldn't like that, she always preferred to have tidy arrangements. Still, it might be useful to get a picture of her new background. See if she'd bettered herself and if her plans for herself were working out. He had his own plans.

Olive popped in to see him later that evening. She wanted to know if he was all right and how he was getting on. Herbert said he wasn't all right, she couldn't expect him to be under the circs, but he wasn't going to put his head in the gas oven or anything like that. He'd soldier on, he said. Olive said she just couldn't get over the shock of him and her mum separating. It simply wasn't right, she said. One thing about Olive, she was pretty normal, he thought, not a cat-lover like Madge or a stargazer like Winnie.

'Dad, I can't help thinking it wouldn't have come to this if Mum had felt you cared a bit more for her than for the shop,' she said.

'What I cared for was making sure the shop takings gave the family enough to live decently,' said Herbert, 'to see you girls had the advantage of grammar-school educations, that you didn't go short of anything and always had nice clothes. Yes, and to see your mother was able to save for herself out of her housekeeping money.'

'Dad, wives and mothers need something more than their housekeeping allowance,' said Olive. 'They need to know they're appreciated and not taken for granted. I'd be very upset if I felt Roger didn't appreciate me.'

'What about husbands and fathers?' said Herbert.

'What d'you mean?' asked Olive.

'Well, don't some of us like to be appreciated, or is it something sort of exclusive to wives and mothers?' replied Herbert. 'I feel now that I was short of being appreciated meself. Your mother told me I'd taken her for granted for years, and it came to me only today that what I provided for all of you from me long hours in the shop, well, that was taken for granted too. I don't know that your mother or any of you girls ever said thanks.'

'That's not fair,' protested Olive.

'I paid out handsome for your schooling and for the weddings of all you girls, and I paid out with a good heart, like any decent dad should, but none of you gave me any special blessings. You took me paternal obligations for granted, just as your mother took all that generous house-keeping allowance for granted. But it didn't

56

make me walk out on me family, it didn't even bother me a lot, because I don't believe in people having to go around thanking others for this, that and everything else. All I'm saying is that if I wasn't perfect as a husband, and I know I wasn't, it wouldn't do your mother any harm to take a look at herself in her mirror. Yes, that's all I'm saying.'

'You're saying quite a lot. Dad, considering you've never said very much before.' Olive put a hand on his arm. 'That was what got Mum really going in the end, that you hardly ever talked to her.'

'Well, that was a pity, and I'm sorry,' said Herbert, 'but I've never been much of a talking bloke. I admit your mother had a good reason there to pull me to pieces, except I always felt she liked the sound of her own voice much more than mine.'

'Dad, that's not fair, either,' said Olive. 'That's mean.'

'Yes, not very nice, I suppose,' said Herbert apologetically.

'Anyway, I don't think Mum meant everything she said to you, Dad, and I'm sure she's sorry about calling you boring.' Olive patted his arm consolingly, although she had agreed with her sisters that their father hadn't ever been an entertaining husband to their mother.

'Well, I never heard any woman complain

more than she did about me when she went for me,' said Herbert. 'I know I wasn't a talker, I've admitted that, but I could have said your ma was the other way about, a gasbag.'

'Dad, that's not a bit nice, talking about her like that,' said Olive. 'Look, I know what you mean, but don't mention it when you go to see her. Try your best to make it up with her.'

'I'm not going to make it up with her,' said Herbert.

'Yes you are,' said Olive.

'Not me,' said Herbert.

'Yes, you,' said Olive. 'You're both to blame, but you've got to be the one to make the first move. When you do see her, take her lots of flowers and make a kind of speech to let her know you can use plenty of words when you have to.'

'Turn myself into a talking husband, is that it?' said Herbert.

'Yes, that's it,' said Olive.

'I suppose you mean a gasbag,' said Herbert, and laughed.

'That's it, married gasbags making it up together,' said Olive, and she laughed too.

The door knocker sounded. Olive answered it and found Madge on the doorstep. In she came, and there was a brief family preamble before Madge enquired what her father had been up to just lately.

'Me?' said Herbert.

'Yes, you,' said Madge, 'you were out in Streatham a couple of nights ago with your shop assistant, Mrs Binns.'

'With Mrs Binns?' said Olive.

'Brian and I saw them together as large as life after we came out of the Gaumont,' said Madge.

'Did you?' said Herbert.

'Yes, we did,' said Madge in her meant-to-be-heard voice.

'Well I'm blessed,' said Olive, 'is that right, Dad?"

'It's right I was out with the lady that's been working several years in the shop,' said Herbert.

'Yes, you were on the other side of the road,' said Madge, 'and if I hadn't been so dumb-founded I'd have crossed over and spoken to you.'

'What about?' asked Herbert.

'About your being out with Mrs Binns,' said Madge. 'You're still married to Mum, you know.'

'I don't feel I am,' said Herbert.

'Don't be silly,' said Madge. 'How can you not feel married after twenty-five years?'

'It's a new feeling, I admit,' said Herbert, 'but it's risen up in me these last few days.'

'Something else has risen up in you,' said Madge.

59

'Has it?' said Herbert. 'What, might I ask?'

'Fretful talk,' said Madge.

'Can't be helped,' said Herbert.

'Yes it can,' said Olive, 'and then there's going out with Mrs Binns. Dad, you silly, you won't get Mum back if you start carrying on with other women.'

'Should I try to get your mother back?' asked Herbert.

'We insist you do,' said Madge.

'But what's the point?' asked Herbert.

'What d'you mean, what's the point?' asked Madge.

'Of getting your mother back,' said Herbert.

'Well, you don't really want her to live on her own, do you, Dad?' said Olive. 'You could go and see her, and promise to be more companionable to her, and a little more lively.'

'Stand on my head?' said Herbert.

'Do what?' said Madge irritably.

'Wear a funny hat?' said Herbert.

'I hope you're not going peculiar,' said Madge. Then, after a thoughtful moment, and an impatient jerk of her shoulders, she added, 'Well, even that might help to some extent.'

'It might,' said Herbert, 'but it's not me. I'm still the way I was born, I don't go in for funny hats or sawing a fiddle.'

'But you're going in for taking Mrs Binns out,' said Olive, 'which isn't your style, Dad. Heavens,

I hope it doesn't mean you're thinking of committing adultery.'

'Mrs Binns is a respectable widow,' said Herbert.

'It's not respectable being seen out with a married man,' said Olive.

'Especially as it looked to me as if she was wearing her best Sunday hat,' said Madge.

'Does wearing a Sunday hat on a weekday evening mean adultery's just round the corner?' asked Herbert.

'No, but wearing it for a man must mean she fancies him,' said Olive.

'I've just thought,' said Madge, 'have you been carrying on regularly with Mrs Binns, Dad, while she's been working in the shop?'

'I don't like that question,' said Herbert, 'it's a liberty.'

'That's not much of an answer,' said Madge.

'It occurs to me that as your mother's now calling herself a free woman, can I be called a free man?' asked Herbert.

'No, you can't,' said Madge, 'because all your daughters want you and Mum to get back together again. I think you'd better act your age and tell us if there's anything going on between you and Mrs Binns.'

'It so happens Mrs Binns has been invited by an old uncle of hers to be his housekeeper,' said Herbert. 'Which invite she's accepted. That shows she's sensible, not flighty.'

'She's leaving the shop?' said Olive.

'It's been a long time,' said Herbert.

'You can easily get someone else,' said Olive.

'The point is, I felt beholden to show my appreciation of her years in the shop by taking her to the theatre and then to supper,' said Herbert. 'I'm doing a bit of appreciating, which it seems I didn't do much of before.'

'I can't believe the way you're almost making speeches these days,' said Madge. 'Look, Olive and I won't quarrel with what you felt beholden to do for Mrs Binns, but you could have told us that five minutes ago.'

'I didn't feel I had to,' said Herbert. 'Still, you are my daughters, so I have told you. I'm sorry, mind, that I've been a dull old dad to you.'

'We've never called you that,' said Madge.

'No, but I know my faults,' said Herbert. 'And I realize now only too well that your mother would have liked a more entertaining husband. Someone like Max Miller, I suppose.'

'Dad, some of these things you're saying aren't like you at all,' said Olive.

'Must be because some heavy bricks dropped on my head,' said Herbert.

'Stop being silly,' said Madge. 'Come and have dinner with Brian and me on Sunday. Perhaps I could get Mum to come as well.'

'Very nice of you, Madge, but Mrs Binns has already invited me,' said Herbert. 'By the way, now that she's leaving and old Mrs Goodliffe has passed on, I'm giving up the shop.'

'You've sold it at last?' said Madge.

'Thought I might as well,' said Herbert.

'You'll be lost without it unless you get a job,' said Olive.

'Your mother suggested I might think about joining the Fire Brigade,' said Herbert.

'I'm not sure they'll take you at your age,' said Madge. 'Listen, are you giving Mum anything out of what you sold the shop for?'

'Well, she always made overnight sandwiches for me to take to the shop every morning,' said Herbert, 'so I'm thinking about a decent present for her.'

'How decent?' asked Madge.

'A set of new saucepans for her new abode,' said Herbert. 'Oh, and a bracelet for each of you girls.'

'Wait a minute, a set of saucepans for Mum?' said Olive.

'She'll throw them at you,' said Madge,

'I'll get the store to deliver,' said Herbert, 'and she can throw them at the carrier.'

'Well, I never,' said Madge in astonishment, 'I think you've just said something funny.'

'Not me, not my style,' said Herbert.

'Dad, a set of saucepans?' said Olive. 'You're not really serious, are you?'

'I'll buy the best quality,' said Herbert.

'You're joking,' said Madge.

'Never been a joker since the day I was born,' said Herbert, 'you all know that.'

'What I know now is that you're suddenly getting impossible,' said Madge.

'Sorry about that,' said Herbert.

'I can't stay arguing with you any more,' said Madge, 'I've got to get back to our cats.'

'You and your cats,' said Olive, but she departed in company with her sister. Both of them left feeling sorry for their father in his deplorable mood. It was shocking he wasn't going to do anything about getting their mother back, and very upsetting that he was only going to buy her some new saucepans out of what he got for the shop.

Things were quite different for Hilda that same evening. She was in very close company with a very close friend.

'Oh, you saucy devil, Rupert.'

'Can't help myself, can I, Hilda? And I can't tell a lie, either. You've still got a handsome body, my stars you have. You're an eyeful.'

'Oh, I can't hardly credit what you're up to, getting me all undone like this.'

'You should be like this, Hilda. I frankly admire you when you're all done up, but I admire you even more when you're not. It's all right to keep your proud bosom hidden when you're out

64

shopping, but not when you're up here in private with me.'

'Lord, I didn't know you were going to take this kind of liberty.'

'Didn't you?'

'If I had known, I wouldn't have—'

'Yes, you would, you teasing woman. And it's not taking advantage, Hilda, it's doing what comes naturally, even if we're both past forty.'

'Rupert, stop that. Oh, I can't remember the last time I blushed, but I'm blushing all over now. Me at my age too.'

'You're no age, Hilda, not with your kind of body, and don't get worried. I mean, I'm not blushing myself, I can handle everything without getting embarrassed. You just relax.'

'Relax? I can't even get my breath – you're near to indecent.'

'Is that good or bad?'

'Oh, I've got to admit it's an exciting change.'

'From what old stodgy bones never did?'

'Don't let's talk about him, just mind what you're doing to my modesty.'

'Well, let's try your bed for an hour, you'll feel happier under the sheets. That's it, up you come. My word, you're a fulsome woman, Hilda, a warm weight in my arms, but it'll be what you might call a labour of love, carrying you to your bedroom. Off we go, then, in for a penny, in for a pound.'

'Oh, help, you don't care what you say, do you?'

'It's time we found out if we suit each other, Hilda, and we can't complain about the circumstances. The shop below is closed, and there's no-one above, except the Almighty.'

The bed sighed and sank a little as he laid her on it. She gasped a faint protest.

'Lord, I don't know I'm ready for this.'

But it happened, all the same, and afterwards he told her what a warm and exciting woman she was, then said, 'Is the old sod really coming to see you now and again?'

'Only when I invite him, and I suppose I'll have to, or my daughters will go on at me.'

'Will he take advantage of you, Hilda?'

'Him? Don't make me laugh.'

'Well past it, is he?'

'He was well past it ten years ago. But he's still got his shop to cuddle up to. Listen, you'd better go now, I don't want you staying all night, I don't want anybody talking.'

'Well, seeing we've found out we suit each other, I'm not going to complain about being sent on my way. After all, Hilda, there'll be other times.'

'Yes, I'm a free woman, but you mind you don't take me for granted.'

*   *   *

She went out the following evening to visit her eldest daughter in Streatham. Madge and her husband were pleased to see her, although suspecting she might already be regretting leaving the comfortable home she'd known for years. On the contrary, however, she was obviously enjoying her new-found freedom, and let them know how much she'd liked meeting all the members of the local amateur dramatic society and being enrolled.

Madge and Brian decided not to tell her that they'd seen Herbert out with Mrs Binns, but they did acquaint her with the news that he'd sold the shop.

'Go on, he hasn't, has he?' said Hilda.

'So he told Olive and me when we saw him last night,' said Madge.

'How much did he get for it?'

'He didn't say and we didn't ask,' said Madge.

'Didn't ask?' said Hilda. 'Well, you should have.'

'Must have got a few hundred at least,' said Brian, eyeing his wife's two potted plants on the window ledge. The leaves were a bright shining green. Madge being a healthy type, she liked everything around her to look healthy too. That included her cats. Her mother didn't spoil the picture. She looked blooming, and she had a remarkably good figure. So did Madge, a buxom and attractive young woman. 'Say five or six hundred.'

'Oh, I think the builders were offering a bit more than that,' said Hilda. 'Well, whatever he got, some of it's mine. My twenty-five years looking after him earned it for me. I'll speak to him about it when he visits. I might ask him to come Sunday week, say. Just for a pot of afternoon tea and a currant bun. I've got to say I wouldn't want him for longer. Well, it's always been painful trying to get him to make conversation. You'd think, wouldn't you, that he'd at least be able to talk about the Government, like most men can. Most men can talk their heads off about the Government. Or football. I don't care myself for talk about governments or football, but it would be something to hear Herbert talk about anything. I feel really sorry for him, not having any trouble myself in being entertaining. It's being entertaining that got me invited to join the amateur dramatics in Stockwell. I'm going to a reading evening soon, it's when I'll be asked to read from a play. I'm looking forward to it, I've got a nice feeling I'm gifted.'

Brian managed to get a word in at that point.

'How are you off for kitchen utensils and suchlike in your new flat?' he asked.

'Oh, I've got all I need,' said Hilda, 'I took what I wanted, and Herbert didn't complain.'

'What about saucepans?' asked Brian, and received a little kick from Madge. He'd roared with laughter when told that her father, in the

68

money from the sale of his shop, was going to present her mother with a set of new saucepans. 'Got enough of them, have you?'

'Enough saucepans?' said Hilda. 'Yes, of course I have. What makes you ask?'

'Well, Madge and me like to think you're not short of anything in your new kitchen,' said Brian. 'D'you think you'll stay where you are, or d'you think you and Madge's dad might have second thoughts about any permanent separation?'

'He might, I shan't,' said Hilda, 'I like being free and independent, and I'm not giving that up. Were you thinking about making a pot of tea now, Madge?'

'I'll just give our cats their evening milk, then I'll put the kettle on,' said Madge.

'I've never heard of evening milk for cats,' said Hilda disapprovingly.

'In this house,' said Brian, 'there's morning, afternoon and evening milk for cats.'

'It's only what they need,' said Madge.

'They'll get fat,' said Hilda.

It was dark when she left, and a bus took her to Stockwell, and from the stop she walked down Stockwell Road. Halfway into her walk, she had a sudden feeling she was being followed. She looked back over her shoulder when she reached the light of a street lamp. But she detected no-one. Imagination, that's what it was, and having Herbert on her mind. He'd said some impertinent things to her and shown a bit of spite, and she thought now that he might be taking it on himself to come and watch her at times, and see if he could catch her out at something. No, but of course he wouldn't, he didn't have that kind of go in him. She wondered if he was even aware she was gone. She'd told him he wouldn't be.

Yes, that was it, she must have imagined there was someone a little way behind her. All the same, she hurried on, used her key to open a door at the side of a shop, closed it behind her and went up to her flat. It comfortingly embraced her and she murmured with pleasure that she didn't have to think about making over-night sandwiches for Herbert. She must have made a thousand in her time, always sandwiches, never anything else. It was a wonder he hadn't turned into something like a corned-beef sandwich himself. Well, perhaps he had because even if he didn't look like one, he had about as much up-and-go as one.

She laughed to herself.

Herbert was also late to bed that night.

Chapter Five

On Saturday, Herbert said a personal goodbye to every customer who came into his shop, and he also, by arrangement, had all his papergirls and paperboys call at ten thirty, when he delivered a few words to them.

'I've been very appreciative of your reliability, so here's a pound each for all of you.'

'Crikey, a pound? Ain't you a sport, Mr Jones?'

'We're ever so sorry you're closing down, Mr Jones.'

'I'm sorry too. Still, look on the bright side, that's what I always say.'

'Yes, you've told us that hundreds of times, Mr Jones.'

'Good luck, all of you, and if you want any sweets, Mrs Binns will weigh them for you at half-price.'

'Between you, you can have all that's left at half-price,' said Mrs Binns, and the boys and girls surged around the counters to make their choices from the depleted confectionery stocks.

At six that evening, Herbert helped a dealer load all that was left of his stock into a van, received the agreed price for it, then closed the shop for the last time and went home.

Nell Binns travelled to Forest Hill to see her elderly uncle, the one who wanted her to keep house for him. She needed to have a talk with him.

Hilda spent a thrilling evening with established members of the local amateur dramatic society. She was given excerpts from a play to read, and guidance from the director. She must have acquitted herself commendably, for listening members clapped her, bringing a flush of pleasure to her face, especially as she received handsome praise from Mr Burnside. Mr Burnside, the manager of the factory where she worked, was the society's president. He was also the director. A good-looking man of forty-seven, with a lot of self-assurance, his enthusiasm for amateur dramatics could bring out the best in a cast. Hilda felt he had already done wonders for her in the way he had made her approach her readings.

Having congratulated her on her first efforts, he addressed the company.

'I think we're all agreed that Mrs Jones has the makings of a good character actress.'

'Hear, hear,' said some.

'Well, I must say I've always had a feeling for going on the stage in a modest way,' said Hilda, 'and I do appreciate everyone's encouragement. It's kind of heart-warming.'

'Um, there's a subscription of five pounds a year,' said a young man, the society's treasurer. 'I should have pointed that out when you enrolled.'

'Never mind, and I can afford five pounds,' said Hilda. 'I can pay now, if you like.'

She paid and her membership was confirmed. She was delighted. What a lovely new life she was going to lead.

The evening ended at ten, when she had an escort to see her home to her flat. They conversed on the bus.

'If your husband divorced you, Hilda, you could marry again.'

'Not likely I couldn't. I'd end up washing socks and shirts again every Monday. When people talk about women's work never being done, they mean married women.'

'You'd escape that as far as I'm concerned, I'm not the marrying type.'

'Nor am I now.'

When they reached her door in Stockwell Road, a question arrived in her ear.

'Would you like me to come up with you, Hilda?'

'No, not this time of night, thanks. Someone will notice, and I don't want my new neighbours talking.'

'There's no-one about.'

'Might I ask what you want to come up with me for?'

'Well, together we could do what comes naturally again.'

She laughed.

'I never met anyone with more sauce than you,' she said.

'I like to feel I'm an exciting change from old stodgy boots.'

That made her laugh again, but she still didn't invite him up to her flat and her bed. A free woman could please herself what she did, she could have an intimate man friend even at her age. But it still wouldn't do to be careless about that in case her daughters found out. She felt she had a long way to go before the pleasures of independence made her indifferent to what her family thought of her. Just now, she especially didn't want details of her private friendship with Rupert to come to Herbert's ears. He might come round and act like a wronged husband. He really had been very impertinent and spiteful about being told his faults, and he might get extra spiteful about her having a fling. He was never going to understand that a woman was entitled to be free after twenty-five years as a slaving wife and mother. He simply didn't have any imagination.

Just before going to bed, Olive spoke to her husband Roger.

'I really don't know what's got into Dad.'

'So you keep saying,' said Roger, a personable young man of twenty-four. An engineering draughtsman, he wasn't advancing up the ladder as quickly as he'd have liked, but he was fairly happy-go-lucky about it, although he could have done with a salary increase. Olive had discovered that, with his easy-come easy-go nature, he had a tendency to let money slip through his fingers. During the last week of their fortnight's honeymoon in Devon, he'd asked if he could borrow some from her. They'd spent all that he'd brought with him, he said. Olive said she didn't think much of a bridegroom who had to borrow honeymoon money from his bride. Roger said he'd pay her back. She'd given him a pound, and he hadn't paid it back. She was having to watch his pockets for him, just in case they were empty when bills came in.

'Well, he was very upset about Mum leaving him, of course,' said Olive, 'but I didn't think it would make him go peculiar.'

'Peculiar?' said Roger.

'It's the things he says.'

'Are you surprised?' asked Roger. 'I'm not.'

'I can understand him being down in the dumps,' said Olive, 'especially now he's got a bee in his bonnet about not being appreciated himself.'

'He might have something there,' said Roger. 'Well, for a start, I'd like to know how much your mum's got in her savings account. That could tell us if your dad was generous or not in what he doled out to her. Generosity's worth some appreciation.'

'Well, yes,' said Olive, 'but saying he's going to make Mum a present of a set of new saucepans out of the money from the sale of his shop, and that she can chuck them at the carrier if she wants to, well, that's not like him at all.'

Roger grinned. He'd heard the story.

'I don't call that peculiar,' he said, 'I call that a bit of a laugh at your mum's expense.'

'Perhaps it is,' said Olive, 'but there's something about him that makes me feel uneasy.'

'D'you mean you feel he might be thinking about blowing his head off?' asked Roger.

'Roger, what a thing to say. That's awful. And no, I don't mean that, anyway, I mean I think he's got something up his sleeve that might come as a nasty shock to Mum.'

'Well, that'll make them even,' said Roger, 'he's had his own nasty shock.'

'Yes, I suppose he has,' said Olive. 'But I do feel that Madge, as the eldest, ought to keep her eye on him. That's if she can forget her cats for a while.'

'Brian might help.' Roger grinned again. 'He might drown them one day.'

'Roger, really,' protested Olive, although struggling to keep a straight face. 'I don't think you ought to be as unkind as that. Remember, what's said unkindly often comes to pass.'

'Someone had better warn the cats, then,' said Roger.

For the first time for years, Herbert enjoyed the experience of not having to open the shop on a Sunday. He'd planned a bus ride and a walk for the afternoon. Nell Binns had accepted an invitation to go with him after they'd had dinner together, he having discovered that with no shop to run, he actually fancied a bit of company.

Let's see, he thought, shall I take round a bottle of Guinness and share it with Nell over the meal? Does she like Guinness? I know a lot of working women enjoy a glass of same with their Sunday dinner, and no-one could say Nell isn't a working woman. She'd said she was going to do roast mutton with roast potatoes and garden peas. Not greens. A welcome change, garden peas would be. Hilda had put greens in front of him nearly every Sunday of their married lives.

The door knocker sounded. He answered it.

Muscles Boddy grinned at him from the door-step.

'Watcher, 'Erbert, how's yerself, matey?'

'To what do I owe the pleasure?' asked Herbert.

'To me good nature,' said Muscles, 'and me liking for sharing a couple of bottles of Sunday wallop with you.' He produced two pint bottles of Watney's stout from somewhere about his capacious person. 'Drink stout on a Sunday, do you, 'Erbert?'

'Not often,' said Herbert.

'Just occasional, like?' said Muscles. 'That'll do.' He stepped in. 'You lead the way, old cock.'

'All right, come in,' said Herbert, and took the affable crook through to the kitchen. The square room wasn't small, but Muscles Boddy's bulk made it look a bit undersized.

'Well, you keep a tidy place here, 'Erbert.'

'It's been kept that way by a tidy woman,' said Herbert.

'I take it you mean your ungrateful trouble-and-strife,' said Muscles, placing the bottles on the table.

'We won't talk about her,' said Herbert.

'Painful, eh?' said Muscles, and twisted free a rubber-washered stopper from one bottle. The black-looking stout sprang to life in reaction to the entrance of oxygen. It foamed, and the head spilled. 'Glasses, 'Erbert old cock?' Silently, Herbert brought two glasses from a dresser shelf,

78

and Muscles filled them slowly, the foam rising to create a creamy froth. 'There y'ar, 'Erbert.' He handed Herbert a glass. 'Here's to your prosperity, matey.' He downed half his own stout in one swallow.

'Kind of you,' said Herbert, and took in a mouthful of the rich brew.

'I'll sit down, shall I?' said Muscles, and lowered himself into a chair, which emitted a sigh beneath his weight, followed by a creak of suffering wood. Herbert showed a small smile, then sat down himself on the opposite side of the kitchen table. He considered it wise to be able to look Muscles Boddy in the eye.

'All alone now, are you, 'Erbert?' enquired Muscles.

'Yes.'

'Gone, has she?'

'I'm bearing up,' said Herbert.

'Well, good on you, cully,' said Muscles, 'but as I mentioned previous, it ain't natural for a bloke like you not to have some home comforts. Looking around for a welcoming widow woman, are you?'

'Not so's you'd notice,' said Herbert.

'I know one or two meself that might take your fancy,' said Muscles.

'Well, you hang onto them,' said Herbert, 'I'm still a married man.'

'Got principles, have you?'

'Some,' said Herbert.

'Bleedin' crippling, that is, 'Erbert, having them kind of principles,' said Muscles, downing the rest of his stout. He refilled his glass from the second bottle, and topped up Herbert's. 'Me guv'nor's got principles.'

'Has he? What kind?' asked Herbert.

'The kind that stretch a bit,' said Muscles. 'Elasticated, like. More convenient, y'know, them kind. Still, you being a gent, they ain't your style. Strictly hon'rable, you are, matey, and gen'rous with your Scotch.' He rattled on in his gravelly voice about honourable blokes needing the help of friends, and Herbert said he was very appreciative of friendship as long as one half of it didn't relate to extortion. 'Here, that's a funny word,' said Muscles, 'I ain't heard of that one before. What's it mean?'

'That some friends need to be watched,' said Herbert.

Muscles grinned. It made his rough, craggy countenance look like that of a good-natured gargoyle.

'Well, I ain't one of that kind,' he said, and poured most of what was left in the second bottle of stout into his glass. He paused, then, as a good friend, he poured the meagre remains into Herbert's glass.

'Actu'lly,' said Herbert, 'I'm not one for making too many friends, I'm a bit of a loner.'

'I'm the same, y'know,' said Muscles, 'but you and me hit it off swell, 'Erbert, and I ain't the sort to let you down.' He made short work of the rest of his drink, then stood up. 'Got to see a bloke about a dog now, old cock. Nice to have talked to you. Just wanted to know how you was doing. I got the picture. Keep the bottles, there's tuppence back for the pair at the off-licence. See you again sometime.'

Herbert, relieved that the visit had been fairly brief, saw him out. Muscles shook his hand vigorously, and Herbert felt thankful he didn't end up with broken fingers. He hoped, quite naturally, that the bloke wasn't going to make a habit of calling on him.

On his way to Nell's flat, he bought a pint bottle of Guinness from the Jug and Bottle department of the local pub. Nell expressed pleasure and appreciation.

'Well, I do think a nice drop of Guinness with Sunday dinner's a treat, Herbert. How kind.'

They shared the pint along with the roast and the lush green garden peas. Nell talked, and Herbert said several words himself from time to time, which encouraged Nell to say she couldn't think why Hilda had complained that he wasn't much company. Herbert said he'd rather not talk about Hilda, and Nell said she could understand that.

After he had helped her with the washing-up,

he took her for the planned bus ride to the upper reaches of Streatham, and they enjoyed a long saunter all over Streatham Common. Herbert didn't have to say a lot, Nell being the kind of woman who didn't ask to be entertained. Like most chatty women, she was more in favour of a good listener, and Herbert was proving to be just that. She could tell he was, from his comments.

'Well, you don't say, Nell.'

'Go on, is that a fact, Nell?'

'Tell me more about getting caught with your skirts up in front of a young bloke at the Hampstead funfair.'

'Oh, I couldn't, Herbert, I'm already embarrassed, and I'm sure I don't know what made me say as much as I have. Seventeen's a very blushing age for a girl, and I could see that the young gent in question could hardly take his eyes off me frillies.'

'Girls of seventeen do go in for frillies,' said Herbert.

'Well, so they do,' said Nell, 'fancy you knowing that, Herbert. When we're that age, it's the pretty look of things that count most, even if you only get to show them accidental at a funfair.'

'Well, even showing them accidental, Nell, makes you a good sport,' said Herbert.

Nell laughed.

'I suppose it was a bit of a lark,' she said, 'and

82

the young gent, having near lost his eyesight, did help me to forget me blushes by treating me to a plate of cockles.'

'Worth all of that, I bet,' said Herbert.

'Beg pardon?' said Nell, dressed in her best costume and hat.

'Probably worth a plate of cockles and some fish and chips as well,' said Herbert.

'Herbert, you cheeky man,' said Nell. 'My, all the time that's gone by since then, with me pretties a thing of the past. Look at me now, I'll be near to being a middle-aged widow in a few more years.'

'Well, you don't look it yet, Nell.'

'Well, I hope I don't, not yet.'

They talked on and became very confiding and involved. It was really a very pleasant afternoon for Herbert.

It was also very pleasant for Hilda. Up to a point, that is. Her close private friend had taken her out into the country on a Green Line bus, and walked with her to a lovely quiet spot where there were only trees and chirping birds to observe them. Then everything became alarming.

'Rupert, oh, not here.'

'Here seems all right to me.'

'But supposing someone sees us— Oh, don't do that.'

'This, then?'

'Oh, that's worse.'

What was alarming became exciting, and of course she'd been starved of excitement for years. So she gave in to it, and considering she was in her early forties and he was in his late forties, no-one could have said either of them was short of health, strength and aptitude. The chirping birds, hopping from branch to branch, turned to twittering in their astonishment.

When it was over, and the surrounding countryside still looked empty of people, Hilda expressed faint words of indignation at having been treated like a tarty village girl.

'You didn't feel like one, Hilda, you felt a lot more like a wild woman.'

'Well, I was wild, I could hardly believe what was going on, all my respectability being disrespected like that in public.'

'There's not much public around here, Hilda, just a handy collection of beech trees.'

'Now you know what I mean, Rupert.'

'I know what you're like, Hilda, you're a woman and a half.'

'And I know what you're like, you just can't be trusted.'

'Makes a change, though, does it, Hilda?'

'You can say that again,' said Hilda.

Chapter Six

Hilda was busy in the factory office on Monday morning. Her main job was to write out orders which arrived by letter or over the phone. She wrote them out on dockets, a docket for each order, with two carbon copies. The top docket was for the factory manager, who checked it and passed it to the foreman. The first carbon copy went to the invoice clerk, and Hilda was responsible for filing the second copy.

The factory made items for the hardware trade, like hammers, chisels, screwdrivers, drills, padlocks and so on, including many thousands of different-sized nails and screws.

The factory manager, Mr Burnside, popped into the office mid-morning. Hilda's desk was in a corner, well away from the typist and the clerk, both women.

'Morning, Mrs Jones.'

'Oh, good morning, Mr Burnside.'

He leaned over her, smiling. He had a winning

smile, as befitted a man who was both president and director of the Stockwell Amateur Dramatic Society.

'Write me out a docket for a dozen three-inch paintbrushes, two dozen four-inch, and two dozen hand drills, will you?' he murmured.

'Who for?' asked Hilda.

'Timms Hardware Stores of Mitcham.'

'My, they're real regular customers of yours, Mr Burnside,' said Hilda. The pad of dockets was in front of her. She put the carbons in place, and wrote the order out with a hard-leaded pencil. Mr Burnside was taking a lot of orders over the phone himself lately.

At the end of the day, when the factory was quiet, the workers on their way home, Hilda waited at the gates. Mr Burnside emerged from the door that led to the office.

'Hello, standing about for something, Hilda?' he said, informal now that they were out of the factory.

'I was waiting for you,' said Hilda, and he began to walk with her.

'People will start talking,' he smiled.

'They will if they get to know what I've just found out,' said Hilda. 'There's no copies on the file of all those orders I've wrote out for you, and I know I did file them. And there's no copies in Miss Taylor's invoice tray of today's order from Timms. I think someone's been making a habit of going into the office after work and taking the file copies and the copies I put in Miss Taylor's invoice tray. I'm talking about just the orders from Timms. It's upset me.'

Mr Burnside lost his smile.

'You bitch, you've been snooping,' he said.

'Here, watch your tongue, if you don't mind,' said Hilda, 'I didn't say I was going to tell the boss, did I? But you'll have to stop. I'm not going to write out any more dockets for Timms unless I know the carbon copies won't just disappear. In all me born years, I've never done anything dishonest, and I'm surprised to find I can't say the same about you.'

'Now look here, Hilda, you keep on doing as I tell you,' said Mr Burnside, far more nettled than discomfited.

'Not likely,' said Hilda, 'and don't come it over me, not now I know what I do know.'

'Just forget what you know.'

'You've been making money on the side,' said Hilda, 'and the firm could put the police on you.'

'Don't talk like that,' said Mr Burnside.

'If I went back to the office, I suppose I'd find the carbon copies of that docket for the Timms order today had gone missing,' said Hilda. 'Still, I'm not going to say anything.'

'Of course you're not,' said Mr Burnside.

'I was thinking,' said Hilda. 'The society's doing that play by Oscar Wilde in September.'

'Which one? Oh, *The Importance of Being Earnest*, you mean.'

'Yes, that's it,' said Hilda. 'I went up West once to see it with my eldest daughter. It was really good. I'd be ever so pleasured to play the part of Lady Bracknell.'

'Lady Bracknell?' Mr Burnside was sour. 'You couldn't play that part any more than my aunt's cat could. You can't even act yet. '

'You could coach me,' said Hilda.

'But the casting committee wouldn't give you the part.'

'You could use your influence,' said Hilda.

'Damn that, you monkey,' said Mr Burnside.

'You could think about it,' said Hilda.

'I get it, it's the part or else, is it?'

'No, of course not,' said Hilda, 'it's just that one good turn deserves another, like they say.'

'Well, sod me,' said Mr Burnside, 'there's more to you than meets the eye, Mrs Hilda Jones.'

They reached a bus stop, and there they parted, Mr Burnside to board a bus with the expression of a man trying to digest something that violently disagreed with him, and Hilda to walk on with a little smile on her face while thinking of the thrill of playing Lady Bracknell, and discounting any possibility that she'd be hopeless at it.

*   *   *

The following day. Muscles Boddy enjoyed an hour or so in a corner of a Brixton pub with a long-time crony from the East End. They shared a plate of cold beef sandwiches and each drank a couple of pints of the publican's best draught ale. They also exchanged a lot of chat without talking out loud. Well, most of Muscles' verbal exchanges with cronies were of the kind that shouldn't be overheard. It had been like that since he'd started his career of illegal activities with a crooked East End boxing promoter years ago. It hadn't taken him long to learn how to talk out of the corner of his mouth. His old-time crony had acquired a similar aptitude.

Eventually, taking a new tack, Muscles said, 'Well, I'll see you again tonight, then, in the Red Lion.'

'Look, we don't need to break the place up,' said his crony, nearly as big as Muscles himself, but not half as loud when at work.

'Well, course we don't,' said Muscles, 'we'll do it nice and quiet. The guv'nor says it's time we handed Alf some personal injuries.' Alf was the landlord, and Alf had been playing up lately.

'OK, I got you,' said his crony, 'soon as last orders is over, right?'

'Right, and you mind you keep a sharp look-out,' said Muscles. 'I don't want the rozzers interfering with the guv'nor's contracts.'

'You and me both,' said his crony.

'Them flatfeet have got a nosy way of turning up uninvited when the Red Lion's customers is leaving,' said Muscles.

'I dunno sometimes why coppers can't mind their own business,' said his crony.

'I tell you, they've been interfering with me all me ruddy life,' said Muscles.

'Me heart's bleeding for yer, Muscles.'

'Eh what?' said Muscles.

'Er, nothing.'

'That's better,' said Muscles, 'I thought for a tick you was giving me lip.' He came to his feet. 'Well, see you sometime tonight.' And off he went, larger than life.

'Roger, you're not short of money again, are you?' said Olive that evening.

'Me?' said Roger. 'No, of course not.'

'Why were you going through your wallet, then?' asked Olive.

'Just to see if I've got enough to stand my round after the meeting,' said Roger. He was a member of a cricket club and due to attend a meeting this evening. 'I'm covered.'

'Well, all right,' said Olive, 'I don't like thinking you're broke again. We don't want to end up as pawnshop customers.'

'Not a chance,' said Roger breezily.

'That's good,' said Olive. 'Don't be too late home, love.'

*   *   *

Later that same evening, Hilda arrived back at her flat after visiting her second daughter Winnie and Winnie's husband Victor Chance. She had enjoyed a glimpse of her little grandson before he went to bed.

After undressing for bed, she went to the bathroom. She found the bath full of water. It was right up to the waste pipe, and the tap was trickling a mixture of hot and cold. Well, that's funny, she thought, I don't remember running the bath before I left for Winnie's. I wasn't thinking of having one, anyway. Did I do it absent-minded or something?

She pulled up the right sleeve of her night-dress, bent over the bath and dipped her hand deep into the lukewarm water to release the plug.

At that moment, someone came up silently behind her.

It was an unfortunate evening for someone else. A little while after closing time the landlord of the Red Lion in Brixton lost some teeth, which happened when they made contact with Muscles Boddy's fist. The police weren't informed.

Chapter Seven

The factory boss entered the office at nine thirty the next morning.

'What's happening to the dockets?' he asked. 'Where's Mrs Jones?'

'She's not come in yet, sir,' said the typist, a Miss Simmonds.

'How's that?' asked the boss, Mr Richards. 'Do we know why?'

'No, she hasn't phoned or anything,' said the clerk, a Miss Taylor.

'Taken sick, I suppose,' said Mr Richards. 'Well, leave the invoicing, Miss Taylor, and take over the job of filling in the dockets. Mr Burnside and the shop floor are waiting for the first of them.'

'Yes, Mr Richards,' said Miss Taylor.

Mrs Hilda Jones remained absent all day.

During the evening, Olive and her husband Roger called on her mother by arrangement. But

92

there was no answer to their several knocks on the door at the side of the shop.

'That's funny,' said Olive, 'she must have forgotten we were coming and gone out.'

'She's not a forgetful woman,' said Roger.

'No, she's not, especially about family arrangements,' said Olive.

'Perhaps she's just popped out to the corner shop.'

'It's not open this time of an evening,' said Olive. 'Perhaps she's already made friends with a neighbour and is having a chat. She'll remember in a minute about us. Let's go for a walk and then come back again.'

They did that and returned twenty minutes later. Roger knocked loudly. No answer.

'Wait a tick,' he said, 'perhaps she's been taken ill.'

'Or perhaps Dad's been round and they've gone out somewhere to make it up,' said Olive.

'Ruddy long shot, that one,' said Roger, 'and I'm not buying it. She wouldn't have gone out with anyone, not when she knew we were coming. Olive, I'm opting for trying to get in.'

'Oh, you can't break the door down, Roger,' said Olive.

'If she's been taken ill, we'd better do just that,' said Roger, 'we can't just walk away. Wait here a tick.'

Off he went to a neighbouring house, and

from the residents there he was able to borrow a crowbar. With it, he forced open the door at the side of the shop, and he and Olive went up to the flat.

A few moments later, Olive screamed and collapsed.

Roger stood staring. His mother-in-law was in the bath, fully immersed, a tablet of soap on the bottom of the bath and against her right hip. She was naked, and as dead as any woman could be.

Just after ten, Herbert, who was enjoying a quiet read while listening to some music on his wireless, heard a brisk rat-a-tat on his front door. He answered the summons. Two men were on his doorstep, one a good-looking bloke in a trilby hat and grey suit, the other a rugged type in a bowler and blue serge suit. They regarded him sombrely.

'Mr Jones? Mr Herbert Jones?' said the one in grey.

'That's me,' said Herbert.

'I'm Detective Sergeant Tomlinson of the Stockwell station, and this is Detective Constable Fry. Might we come in, sir?'

'What for?' asked Herbert.

'To talk to you, sir,' said Constable Fry.

'I can't think why, and it's a bit late, but all right,' said Herbert. They came in. He closed the door and led them into the living room. There wasn't much furniture. Half of what had been

94

there now reposed in Hilda's flat. 'What's it about?' he asked.

'Your wife, sir,' said Sergeant Tomlinson.

'My wife? What about her?'

'I'm afraid it's bad news, Mr Jones.'

'Bad news about my wife?' said Herbert. 'Why, what's happened to her?'

'Something very unfortunate, sir.' Sergeant Tomlinson braced himself to deliver the news. 'I'm very much afraid I have to inform you she's dead.'

'What?' Herbert blinked. 'Dead? Hilda?'

'She was found dead in her bath earlier this evening by your daughter, Mrs Olive Way, and Mr Way.'

'I don't believe it,' breathed Herbert.

'D'you want to sit down for a bit, sir?' suggested Constable Fry.

'I want to disbelieve what you're telling me,' said Herbert.

'I'm sorry, sir, but it's true,' said Sergeant Tomlinson. 'Your daughter identified her. At the moment, all we know is that, according to the police surgeon, she died between about nine and ten thirty last night, and that your daughter and her husband discovered her at eight this evening after Mr Way had forced the front door.'

'Good God,' breathed Herbert, and he did sit down then, heavily. 'Hilda?'

'We understand, sir, that the two of you were separated, that she took up residence in the Stockwell Road flat last Monday week,' said Sergeant Tomlinson. 'D'you think that would have affected her to the point of committing suicide?'

'Never. Never, not Hilda.' Herbert sounded as if it was difficult to find words, any words. 'No, not Hilda. Is that – is that what she did, committed suicide in her bath?'

'We can't say, sir,' said Sergeant Tomlinson.

'But you said—'

'We don't know if it was suicide or not,' said Sergeant Tomlinson. 'We could say it looked like it. If it was, then a state of depression about the separation could have been the reason.'

'No. No.' Herbert kept swallowing. 'She wasn't depressed, she wanted the separation and couldn't have been happier about it, which hurt me, I can tell you. I can't believe she drowned herself in her bath.'

'We didn't say she'd drowned, Mr Jones,' said Sergeant Tomlinson, 'just that she'd been found dead. The cause of death hasn't been established yet, only the approximate time she died. We mentioned the possibility of suicide only because her separation from you might have badly affected her.'

Herbert looked as if he was trying to believe the unbelievable. It took him a little while to respond to the sergeant.

'My daughter Olive, the one you say found her, could have told you her mother wanted the separation far more than I did,' he said. 'I didn't want it at all. I don't believe in separations or divorce, only in trying to work things out. God, this is bloody awful. What did Olive say to you?'

'I'm afraid your daughter was too shocked to answer any questions,' said Constable Fry, 'but her husband did tell us your wife seemed all right in herself the last time he and Mrs Way saw her. But you'd have known her better, sir.'

'The day she left you, sir, was she upset or emotional?' asked Sergeant Tomlinson.

'I wasn't here when she actu'lly left,' said Herbert, 'I was at work in my shop.'

'She was here on her own when she went off, Mr Jones?' said Sergeant Tomlinson.

'Yes,' said Herbert, and wiped his forehead with the back of his hand.

The two CID men looked at each other.

'That would've upset her a bit, wouldn't it?' said Constable Fry. 'I mean, you not being here when she left. You'd had quite a few years together, hadn't you, sir?'

'I'd said goodbye to her on the Sunday night.' Herbert's face looked stiff now. 'She'd told me more than once she was looking forward to being on her own, and she told me again then. She was even excited about it, saying she'd be a free woman at last. Would you believe a wife could say that to a husband of twenty-five years?'

'I suppose she gave you her reasons,' said Sergeant Tomlinson. 'D'you mind telling us what they were?'

'Yes, I bloody well do mind,' said Herbert, 'but what's the point of keeping it to myself? Her main reason was that I was a boring old bugger.'

Constable Fry coughed.

'That upset you, Mr Jones?' said Sergeant Tomlinson.

'What do you think?' said Herbert, staring at the floor.

'Made you angry as well, I daresay,' said Sergeant Tomlinson.

'Shocked me to my core, I can tell you that,' said Herbert.

'Understandable, sir,' said Constable Fry.

'Shocked and angry, were you, sir?' suggested Sergeant Tomlinson.

'Well, of course I was annoyed when she kept on about my faults,' said Herbert, 'so I went out and walked it off.'

'That cooled you down, sir?' said Sergeant Tomlinson.

'Yes.'

'Could I put it to you, Mr Jones, that when you lost your temper you hit her, p'raps?' suggested Constable Fry.

Herbert raised his head, his expression one of disgust.

'Who said I lost my temper?' he asked. 'I didn't, and even if I had, I wouldn't have hit her, I wouldn't hit any woman for any reason. So don't make any more suggestions like that.'

'Didn't mean to upset you, sir, only trying to find out if your wife had cause to be in a bit of a state when she left you,' said Constable Fry.

'Give over,' said Herbert, 'I was the one in a bit of a state. Well, I ask you, after twenty-five years of working and providing for her and my daughters, what sort of a reward was it to be told I was about as useful as a doorpost?'

'It would have made some men furious,' said Sergeant Tomlinson.

'I daresay it would, but it only left me feeling like I was unconscious,' said Herbert. 'So stop trying to suggest I was in her flat last night, that I knocked her senseless and then drowned her in her bath. Last night I went out for a walk up to about eight thirty, when I called in on a friend of mine and got back here a little after eleven. You can check if you want.'

'We haven't said anything about your wife showing signs of having first been knocked senseless, sir,' said Sergeant Tomlinson.

'You've said enough to worry me,' said Herbert, wiping his forehead again.

'You're living here alone now, sir?' said Constable Fry.

'Yes. My three daughters are all married.'

99

Herbert bit his lip. 'Look, when d'you expect to know about the cause of my wife's death?'

'Tomorrow, sir,' said Sergeant Tomlinson. 'Well, that's all for the moment, thanks for putting up with us, and you can believe me when I say we didn't like having to bring you the bad news.'

'We'll see ourselves out, Mr Jones,' said Constable Fry.

Herbert didn't move from his chair or say anything as the CID men left.

'I'd be interested now to hear if his wife was asphyxiated, not drowned,' said Sergeant Tomlinson when he and Constable Fry entered their parked police car.

'Strangled before she was put into the bath?' said Constable Fry.

'What would you feel like doing to a wife who called you a boring old bugger and a useless doorpost before walking out on you after twenty-five years of marriage?'

'I'd feel like knocking her head off,' said Constable Fry.

'We should have asked him if he'd seen her since the day she left him.'

'And if he had a key to her flat,' said Constable Fry.

'Would she have given a spare key to someone she was glad to be shot of?' mused Sergeant Tomlinson.

'Well, that may be,' said Constable Fry, 'but in

my book, twenty-five years have got to mean something.'

'I tell you this much,' said Sergeant Tomlinson, 'if it wasn't suicide, then someone was with her in the flat last night. Someone who was well away from the place by the time Mr and Mrs Way arrived.'

'The husband, you remember, told us he was with a friend,' said Constable Fry. 'Should we check?'

'Now?' said Sergeant Tomlinson. 'It's too late for that, to get people out of bed, but once we've reported on our interview with Jones, we'll get orders to start checking tomorrow, you can bet on it.'

'Well, I know the form,' said Constable Fry.

'My guess is that what looks like suicide or accidental drowning is going to lead to an inquiry into suspicious circumstances,' said Sergeant Tomlinson. 'There was no sign of a break-in, so we're looking at how Jones felt about what his wife said to him. And did to him by walking out. I've got my doubts about suicide. It doesn't fit, not for a woman who sounds as if that was the last thing she had on her mind.'

'Could've been a sudden heart attack,' said Constable Fry.

'That's a thought, laddie, except it didn't occur to Jones, which it might have done if his wife was known to have had a weak heart.'

'Well, we'll get to know when the post-mortem's been done,' said Constable Fry.

The car carried them away then.

Herbert, watching from a window, went and poured himself a stiff whisky.

By now, having been told the terrible news, Madge and Winnie and their husbands were in the house of Olive and Roger. Olive was on her bed, still in a state of collapse, and Madge and Winnie were numb with shock. The three men were doing all the talking. Victor, Winnie's husband, wanted to know if his mother-in-law was lying flat in the bath when she was found. He pointed out that not many baths could take the full length of an adult.

'This one could,' said Roger.

'And did, apparently,' said Madge's husband, Brian.

'Listen.' Victor spoke quietly, not wanting Madge and Winnie to hear. The two women were seated on a settee, and Roger had found some brandy for them. 'Listen, do either of you think she simply got into the bath, laid herself flat under the water and then let herself drown?'

'I've asked myself that,' said Roger.

'So have I,' said Brian.

'In my opinion, the answer's no,' said Victor.

'Same here,' said Brian.

'There's got to be another answer, then,' said Victor.

'Too bloody right,' said Brian, 'considering Roger mentioned there was a cake of soap lying beside her. She wouldn't have bothered with any soap if she was going to drown herself.'

Madge spoke in a painful voice.

'What're you men saying?'

'We're just going round in circles, Madge,' said Victor.

'Haven't you thought Mum must have had a heart attack?' said Madge.

'It's on my mind,' said Brian.

'It's the only answer,' said Roger. 'The police will let us know tomorrow. If anyone would like some tea, put the kettle on, Brian, will you, while I just go up and see Olive again.'

Up he went, to find that Olive had recovered enough to come down. The atmosphere of the full gathering was of prolonged shock and lingering disbelief, and a large pot of tea was all that anyone could think of in the way of help. With Winnie's infant son asleep in his pram, they sat around the pot into the small hours. Introspective moments of silence were broken by verbal spasms of incredulity.

'How's Dad going to take this?'

The three daughters kept asking each other that question.

Chapter Eight

The following morning, the shocked typist carried to Mr Richards, the factory boss, a copy of her daily paper to let him see why Mrs Jones hadn't been at work yesterday and why she would never reappear. The Stop Press column announced that a Stockwell woman by the name of Hilda Jones had been found dead in her bath. That was all, but it was more than enough.

Mr Richards, who had Mr Burnside with him, drew a breath.

'Unbelievable,' he said.

'Let me see,' said Mr Burnside, and took hold of the paper, while the office typist looked on palely. He read the announcement, then breathed, 'Jesus Christ, her of all women.'

'Dying in her bath, a woman as healthy as that?' said Mr Richards.

'Lord, it must've been a weak heart and the water too hot,' said the typist, Miss Simmonds.

'Did she have a weak heart?' Mr Richards

asked the question of Mr Burnside. 'Did she ever mention she had?'

'Why ask me?' said Mr Burnside.

'Well, you had as much to do with her as anyone, she being the docket clerk,' said Mr Richards, 'and didn't I hear she'd just joined your drama group?'

'True,' said Mr Burnside, 'but I never discussed her state of health with her. I wouldn't have thought it necessary to, not a fine-looking woman like her.'

'I suppose a woman could faint in her bath if the water was too hot,' said Mr Richards.

'Yes, she could, sir,' said Miss Simmonds.

'And she wouldn't need to have a weak heart?' said Mr Burnside.

'No, she probably wouldn't, Mr Burnside,' said the shaken typist.

'Well, I'm damned sorry,' said Mr Richards, 'and I'll see to it that the firm sends a wreath for her funeral. Perhaps you'd like to represent the firm, Burnside?'

'Someone should,' said Mr Burnside.

'Thanks,' said Mr Richards. 'Meanwhile, I'll have to ring the Labour Exchange to see if we can get a replacement fairly quickly.' He shook his head. 'Poor bloody woman,' he said.

Miss Simmonds hesitated, then said, 'Did you know, sir, that Mrs Jones had just separated from her husband?'

'No, I didn't know,' said Mr Richards. 'Not my business, in any case, but I suppose it'll be as much of a shock to him as anyone.'

'I'm sure, sir,' said Miss Simmonds.

'I wonder now, could she have committed suicide if the separation was forced on her?' murmured Mr Richards.

'I couldn't answer that,' said Mr Burnside.

'But she didn't act or look or talk as if she was suffering,' said Miss Simmonds.

'True enough,' agreed Mr Burnside.

'People don't always show their innermost feelings,' said Mr Richards.

'That's true too,' said Mr Burnside. He rubbed his chin. 'Tragic,' he said. 'We'll miss her, and the drama group will be shocked.'

'Oh, I'm sure you thought a lot of her, Mr Burnside,' said Miss Simmonds, essaying a sidelong glance.

'We all did, didn't we?' said Mr Burnside, who could take or leave sidelong glances from pettifogging typists.

The post-mortem examination had been finished. The slab was cold, so was the body. The pathologist covered it up just as Detective Sergeant Tomlinson arrived.

'What's the verdict?' asked the CID man.

'Death by drowning.'

'Following a heart attack?'

'A reasonable assumption, Sergeant, but no, her heart was in first-class condition. She could have fainted and slid under, perhaps, but I can't say that that possibility is a fact.'

'We've probably got a suicide, then?' said Sergeant Tomlinson.

'That's for the coroner to decide when he's had all the relevant information. But certainly she drowned.'

'Then it's more a matter for the coroner than the police?' said Sergeant Tomlinson.

'I'm not so sure,' said the pathologist. 'There are slight bruises around her ankles. Look.' He lifted the sheet and Sergeant Tomlinson took note of faint marks around both ankles.

'Now how could they have come about?' he asked.

'Good question, Sergeant.'

Sergeant Tomlinson, a keen and incorruptible arm of the law, gave the point some thought.

'She wasn't touched until the ambulance team lifted her out of the bath,' he said, 'and I can't say I noticed those marks at that particular time. Would prolonged immersion in the water have temporarily reduced the signs of bruising?'

'Very possibly,' said the pathologist.

'Christ, you don't think she could have been tied up, do you?' said the CID sergeant.

'You're thinking of foul play? I wouldn't have said so. The marks would have been more definite, even allowing for the effects of immersion, and, in any case, there are none about her wrists or arms. Just her ankles. Worth a little thought, I suppose.'

'Yes, I'd say so,' said Sergeant Tomlinson, suspicions very much aroused, 'and I'll have to land it in Inspector Shaw's lap. Incidentally, I've just remembered, she had a tablet of soap in the bath with her.'

'That's news to me,' said the pathologist, 'but it's consistent with her deciding to take a bath, although not with any decision to drown herself, unless she had a sudden death wish.'

'Suicide on the spur of the moment? I don't go much on that, with or without any cake of soap,' said the sergeant as he left.

'You're talking about an enforced drowning?' growled burly Detective Inspector Shaw. 'On account of slightly bruised ankles? Reason? Motive? Method?'

'Haven't got a reason or motive yet,' said Sergeant Tomlinson, 'but method, sir? Held down in the bath?'

'That would mean two buggers, wouldn't it? One holding her ankles and one pressing her shoulders?'

'Might be on, sir, if the motive was a bit serious,' said Sergeant Tomlinson.

'A bit serious?' The growl was deeper. Inspector Shaw was noted for imitating irritable bears. 'I see. Two possible suspects make the motive a bit serious, do they? One would be enough to make it bloody serious to me. What're you offering me, might I ask?'

'Suspicion of murder, sir?'

'Don't make me cry for you, Sergeant.' Inspector Shaw regarded Tomlinson pityingly. 'All you're offering are faint marks around the ankles. Shoes, man, shoes.'

'Shoes, sir?'

'With ankle straps. Women wear them. They're fashionable. Go back to the flat and see if you can find the pair Mrs Jones was wearing that particular evening. They'll probably be on the floor of her bedroom. If they've got ankle straps, let the pathologist have a look at them. Then he'll let you know if the marks were caused by the straps. I don't want to be bothered by flights of fancy. I'm busy.'

'What?' Nell Binns goggled at Herbert. They were in the kitchen of her Brixton flat. 'Hilda's dead?'

'Drowned in her bath,' said Herbert.

'Gawd Almighty,' breathed Nell, 'you're standing there telling me that?'

'Be all the same if I was sitting down,' said Herbert.

'Herbert, I don't know how you can be so calm.'

'I'm not,' said Herbert, 'I'm out of my wits, I can tell you. It looks like it could have happened while I was on my way home from my evening with you. Well, the police said between nine and ten thirty. What time was it I left? Was it about nine thirty?'

'Was it a bit earlier?' said Nell.

'Might have been,' said Herbert. 'Anyway, the news was a real shaker, Nell, and still is, believe me.'

'Oh, you poor man,' said Nell, 'imagine the police bringing word of it to you at that time of night. You couldn't have slept a wink. Here, sit down, and I'll make us some Camp coffee, and you can talk to me about what the police told you.'

Herbert seemed to fold his firm frame limply. It put him into the holding security of a kitchen chair.

'I still can't believe it,' he said. 'I'm actu'lly on the way to my daughter Olive, but I stopped to call on you. Hope you don't mind, Nell.'

'Course I don't mind,' said Nell, and while she bustled about he recounted details of his conversation with the police. Nell was all shocked and astounded ears, but she produced two cups of hot coffee made from Camp, and then sat down with Herbert. He drank his coffee scalding. She talked to him, trying to console him, and of course, like others, she suggested Hilda had

had a heart attack. Herbert said it might have been that, but the police hadn't mentioned the possibility. Nell said well, a police doctor would find out fairly quick, wouldn't he? There'd be a proper examination, wouldn't there?

'Yes, I suppose so, yes,' said Herbert.

'Well, I'm sure it'll show something was wrong with her heart,' said Nell. 'But I can see that's no consolation, I can see you're sorely grieving, Herbert.'

Herbert, finishing his coffee, said, 'I'd better go, Nell, but it's helped a bit, talking to you.'

'Come in again this evening, if you want,' said Nell, 'you shouldn't be alone, not at a time like this.'

'Thanks,' said Herbert, 'you're a good woman, Nell, and a good friend too.'

Roger had taken the day off from his work to stay with Olive, who was a rag of a young woman after a sleepless night. They were expecting Herbert, both quite sure he would call since the police had said they were going to inform him of his wife's death and of who found her. Olive cried on his shoulder when he arrived, and Herbert gave her some embarrassed pats.

'It can't be helped, Olive, things like this do happen to people,' he said awkwardly.

'Old people, yes, they can sort of collapse in a bath, but not Mum, not when she was still such a healthy woman,' said Olive, 'not when she was still young compared to the old. Oh, if only she hadn't been by herself in that flat, if only you'd stopped her leaving you, which you ought to have, Dad. You ought to have stood up to her instead of standing aside.'

'No, your dad can't be blamed, Olive,' said Roger, 'he and your mum came to an agreement about the separation. They could have chucked things at each other and had an almighty row, but I don't think that would have stopped your mum doing what she wanted. I knew her well enough to know she liked having her own way.'

'All the same, she'd still be alive if Dad had put his foot down for a change,' said Olive.

'I'll take the blame,' said Herbert.

'No, I didn't mean that,' said Olive, red-eyed and pale.

'Nobody's to blame,' said Roger. 'Listen,' he said to Herbert, 'I'd go back home now, if I were you, because the police will probably have been told by now the exact cause of death, and I suppose they'll let the family know. If so, you're bound to be the one they'll call on, you're the nearest next of kin.'

'I ought to go and see Madge and Winnie,' said Herbert.

'I'll see to it that they come and see you,' said Roger. 'You must be as hard hit as anyone, and Madge and Winnie'll recognize that. You're done in. Go back home, and stay there for the time being.'

'Yes, that's best, Dad,' said Olive shakily, 'and I'll come and see you myself as soon as I feel a bit better.'

'Perhaps I'd better go back,' said Herbert, 'I don't want to be out if the police do call.'

'Yes, push off, old man,' said Roger, 'and if there's anything I can do any time, just let me know.'

'Thanks, Roger,' said Herbert.

After he'd gone, Roger said, 'He's a walking question mark.'

'What d'you mean?' asked Olive.

'He can't understand that it's actually happened,' said Roger, 'and he's asking himself all the time if it really did.'

'Well, I'm the same, I'm asking myself the same question over and over,' said Olive.

'I agree with what everyone else in the family thinks,' said Roger.

'What's that?' asked Olive tiredly.

'Heart attack,' said Roger.

'Yes, it's got to be that,' said Olive, refusing even to think about an act of suicide.

'I've just thought,' said Roger, 'the front door's still broken. It's open to anyone, so's the flat. Your mum had quite a few decent possessions, and there might be a bit of money around as well.'

'Oh, there wouldn't be a lot,' said Olive, 'except what's in her handbag. She kept all her real money in the Post Office Savings Bank.'

'And where's her savings book, I wonder?' asked Roger. 'Would you know where she kept it?'

'No, and who cares, anyway?' said Olive.

'Still, some petty thief could pinch her handbag and whatever little valuables she had by sneaking into the flat,' said Roger. 'I'd better go round, Olive, and at least get her handbag. And I ought to do something soon about getting the street door repaired.'

'All right, go and fetch her handbag, Roger,' said Olive, 'I can't get worried about her little possessions myself. Nothing seems important to me except her death.'

'You'll be OK till I get back?' said Roger.

'Yes, I'll be all right, but don't be long,' said Olive.

There was a uniformed constable guarding the damaged door by the side of the shop, a shop that sold pictures and picture frames. Roger, arriving, explained to the constable that he was the dead woman's son-in-law and had come to check up on her possessions. The constable, however, had a duty to ensure all such possessions remained intact and that entry was allowed only to authorized persons. Accordingly,

114

he was dubious about allowing Roger entry, since there was no way of proving his relationship with the dead woman there and then.

Roger said that while it was jolly decent of the police to be keeping an eye on the place, he really was the unfortunate lady's son-in-law. In fact, he and his wife had been the ones who'd discovered her dead in her bath last night. He described the discovery in detail, and pointed out he himself had been responsible for telephoning the police. He gave the constable a description of Detective Sergeant Tomlinson, the investigating officer. The constable re-laxed.

'Right you are, sir, you can go up, then,' he said.

The door that had been jemmied open by Roger showed splintered wood by the forced lock. Its damage was evident to any passer-by, and although it was closed it swung inwards as Roger pushed it. He stepped in, closed it again, and went up to the flat. The entry door wasn't locked and he went in. All three rooms were empty and had an air of brooding quiet. He didn't go into the bathroom. He made a careful survey of the kitchen and living room, both of which seemed undisturbed, and then went into the bedroom. He began a search of the dressing-table drawers.

A voice from the doorway startled him.

'Hello, what's the idea? My constable informed me a relative was here. Who are you and what're you up to?'

Roger swung round. Detective Sergeant Tomlinson eyed him suspiciously for a second, then he gave a nod of recognition.

'I know you,' said Roger, 'and you know me.'

'You're Mr Way, of course,' said Sergeant Tomlinson, 'you had the nasty experience of finding Mrs Jones.'

'Yes, I'm her son-in-law, you remember,' said Roger. He made a face. 'Or was, I suppose. I don't know, I'm still a bit out of sorts. I came to look for her handbag and to see if anyone had sneaked in. Well, it was on my mind, the possibility that the wrecked door meant the place was wide open to wrong 'uns, and my wife and I thought her mother's handbag and any little valuables might get pinched. I'd no idea a constable was on guard.'

'As a precaution, Mr Way,' said Sergeant Tomlinson. 'Incidentally, is that it, what you were looking for?' He pointed. 'The handbag there, on the bedside chair?'

Roger smiled faintly.

'Can't see for looking, can I?' he said. 'Shows I'm still in a state. It's OK for me to take it?'

Sergeant Tomlinson considered the request. He was still not in favour of a suicide verdict.

'D'you mind if I have a look at it first, sir?'

116

'What for?' asked Roger, picking up the hand-bag.

'Just a formality, sir,' said Sergeant Tomlinson, who had already seen what he himself had come for, a pair of shoes, with ankle straps, next to the bedside chair.

'Wait a bit,' said Roger, 'd'you know the cause of death now?'

'We know at the moment that she did drown,' said Sergeant Tomlinson, 'but not why. There's one or two loose ends.'

'What loose ends?'

'Oh, only the kind that need tidying up before the inquest,' said Sergeant Tomlinson. 'Shouldn't take long. Regarding the inquest, your father-in-law Mr Jones will be informed of the date. And so will you and your wife, sir.'

'Hold on,' said Roger, 'drowning means – well, suicide or a fatal heart attack, doesn't it?'

'That's for the coroner to say,' said Sergeant Tomlinson.

'There was nothing like a heart attack?' said Roger.

'It seems her heart was as sound as a bell, sir.'

'The family's not going to believe it was suicide,' said Roger. 'Still, if it looks that way—?'

'Very sad, sir,' said Sergeant Tomlinson.

'Could I ask why you're here yourself?'

'I'm doing what you might call a bit of the

tidying up,' said Sergeant Tomlinson. 'The hand-bag, sir?'

Roger gave it to him. Sergeant Tomlinson opened it. He also opened up an inner compart-ment, then turned the bag upside down and shook the contents out on the bed. Out came a compact, a handkerchief, a comb and various other little items indigenous to most women's handbags. He ran a well-trained eye over all of it.

'There's no purse,' said Roger.

'So I note,' said Sergeant Tomlinson, and won-dered when it had gone missing and who had it now. 'Has someone sneaked in under the eyes of our constable?'

'I shouldn't think so,' said Roger.

'So where's the purse?' said Sergeant Tomlin-son.

'You tell me,' said Roger, flicking glances here and there in hopeful search.

'Well, it's a fact that some women living alone like to keep their money out of sight. Let's see.' He crossed to the bed. The covering sheet and blanket were turned down at one corner, exposing part of the pillow. He lifted the pillow and revealed a purse and a brown envelope about six inches by four. 'There we are, sir.' He picked up the purse and handed it to Roger, then took up the envelope. There was something in it, something that might represent a clue to a policeman disbelieving of suicide. The envelope wasn't sealed and he took out what was in it.

'Well, look at that,' said Roger.

'I am looking, sir.'

'That's her Post Office savings book,' said Roger.

'Yes, so it is,' said Sergeant Tomlinson, leafing through it. He noted regular entries in the deposits column, and two recent withdrawals amounting to ten pounds. He made a guess that on leaving her husband, she'd treated herself. 'Savings aren't uncommon to some housewives.'

'No, but that book's valuable if there's much in the account,' said Roger, ready to take care of it. 'It's favourite with some petty crooks, getting their hands on Post Office savings books and fiddling withdrawals. I suppose my mother-in-law kept it in her handbag by day and under her pillow at night since moving here. I wouldn't keep a savings book in a handbag myself.'

'Nor would I, Mr Way, but neither of us is a woman,' said Sergeant Tomlinson. 'And your mother-in-law, by keeping it in an envelope as well, at least made sure it didn't show whenever she opened her handbag.' He looked over the collection of items again, but without any real interest. Whatever he might have expected to find to give him more food for thought, he'd found nothing. His suspicions were still fed by the marks around the deceased woman's ankles, which the pathologist thought odd, and which Inspector Shaw thought might have been made by ankle straps. Inspector Shaw might be right. 'Well, that little lot seems all right, Mr Way, though I suppose the savings book should be held by the nearest next of kin for the moment. The husband.'

'I'll see he gets it,' said Roger, taking the book and putting it into his jacket pocket.

'Um, what's in the purse?' asked Sergeant Tomlinson as an afterthought.

Roger opened it, and the CID man watched him count its contents, three pound notes, two ten-shilling notes and seven shillings and eight-pence in coins. The CID man thought that meant the deceased was pretty flush.

'Four whole quid plus seven bob and a bit,' said Roger. 'It would've pleased my father-in-law to know the separation hadn't put her into a hard-up state. Well, she had her job, in any case.' He returned the money to the purse, and then began putting everything back into the handbag, except for the savings book, safe in his jacket pocket.

'Just as well you came back, Mr Way,' said Sergeant Tomlinson. 'It would be a good idea, wouldn't it, to have the street door repaired pretty quick?'

'I'll see to it,' said Roger.

'Oh, when you do, let us have a spare key just

in case we need to do more tidying up,' said Sergeant Tomlinson. 'Don't touch anything in the bathroom.'

'Right,' said Roger. 'I'll get back to my wife now, I'm taking time off from my job to keep her company until she's over the shock.'

'Understood, Mr Way,' said Sergeant Tomlinson, and waited until Roger was out of the place before picking up the shoes. They were very nice shoes, of black patent leather. He looked them over, paying particular attention to the slender ankle straps. Then he dropped the footwear into a carrier bag.

Chapter Nine

The pathologist made an earnest examination of the shoes and their fashionable ankle straps.

'No,' he said eventually.

'Why not?' asked Sergeant Tomlinson.

'Because the straps are the wrong shape, Sergeant, and also not high enough. The marks describe a level circle around each ankle above the joint. The straps are angled downwards from the ankles below the joint.'

'Would you say, then, that the marks were more likely caused by gripping hands?' asked Sergeant Tomlinson.

'No, I wouldn't. They're not wide enough.'

'Cords, then?'

'No. I told you earlier, Sergeant, that the bruises aren't deep enough to point to tied ankles. Cord would have resulted in positive weals. But I'll admit I'm suspicious. That is, I will be if you or the coroner can find no reason why the deceased should have committed suicide.'

'I'll tell Inspector Shaw that,' said Sergeant Tomlinson.

'I see,' said Inspector Shaw, who looked as if he didn't see at all. 'You feel there's still a reason for an investigation into suspicious circumstances, do you?'

'It's a fact I do have a feeling, sir.'

'You can't wait for the result of the inquest?'

'That's not up to me, is it?' said Tomlinson.

'Are those the shoes?' asked the inspector.

'They're the ones.' Sergeant Tomlinson extracted the pair from the carrier bag and handed them to the inspector, who regarded them sourly.

'Well, they're a decent pair of shoes, I'll say that much, Tomlinson. But they've been ruled out, you said, so what am I doing holding them? You can return them. Here.' Inspector Shaw handed them back. 'I've seen the body while you've been out.' He then delivered some instructions that suggested he'd come round to puzzling about the faint ankle bruises himself. 'Listen, on account of your feelings, and on account of the deceased having left her husband, find out if she had a bloke on the side.'

'You mean – ?'

'She wasn't too old for an affair,' said Inspector Shaw. 'That might have been the real reason why she set up on her own. Women are deep,

Tomlinson, deep, even women over forty with twenty-five years of marriage behind them. Married women only a little over forty, in fact, sometimes try to make up for what they think they've missed. From my inspection of her corpse, I'd say Mrs Jones still had a good body.'

'I agree, sir.' Sergeant Tomlinson, of course, had seen the body as it lay in the bath.

'Get going, then.'

'Where do you suggest I start?' asked the sergeant, who knew he'd get a rollicking if he decided for himself and nothing came of it.

'Where?' Inspector Shaw growled. 'Where do you think, man? Among the people she worked with. Women talk to the people they work with, especially to other women. Then there are the daughters. Mrs Jones might have confided in them, or one of them. If you come up with anything, then I might take a hand myself. Until then, it's your job.'

'I'll take it on,' said Sergeant Tomlinson, twenty-nine, broad-shouldered, physically impressive, quick of mind, and in line for promotion.

'Have Constable Fry go along with you. D'you know Mrs Jones's place of work?'

'Yes, sir, Stockwell Tools Ltd.'

'Get going, then.'

'Right, sir,' said Sergeant Tomlinson, and left to pick up his colleague, Detective Constable Fry.

*   *   *

A brawl erupted in a Brixton pub, the publican
himself being on the receiving end. At the delivery
end was Muscles Boddy, whose manners and
behaviour never improved. Just three customers
were present, two of whom were looking the other
way. The third was a newcomer. A fairly naive
character, he couldn't understand why nobody was
doing anything about what was going on. He
couldn't do much himself, he was a shortie, a titch.
So, unseen by Muscles, he slipped out and almost
at once ran into what he hoped to come across,
two uniformed constables on their beat.

That proved unfortunate for Muscles, who
was only doing what he was paid to do to a
recalcitrant client. Usually, he delivered his
punitive assaults in quick time and without inter-
ference, and was away before trouble arrived
in the shape of the law. On this occasion, the
early and unexpected appearance of two hefty
bobbies not only flabbergasted him but caught
him behind the bar putting his boot in. He was
arrested, taken away, given a summary hearing at
Lambeth Magistrates Court, and awarded twenty-
eight days without the option of a fine. Muscles
Boddy was too well known merely to have his
wrist slapped.

Twenty-eight days upset him considerably. He
complained bitterly about the prospect of being
forcibly locked away from his friends.

'Miss you, will they, Muscles?' said an escorting copper on the way to Brixton Prison.

'Course they bleedin' will, you bugger,' said Muscles. 'They rely on me, don't they? To cheer 'em up and do 'em reg'lar good turns.'

'We know what kind of good turns. And what kind of friends. They end up in hospital.'

'You been misinformed,' said Muscles, lumpy countenance all gloomy undulations. 'I had a visit to a special friend all lined up for Sunday. Now you've been and messed it up.'

'Your special friend won't mind. Might save him a broken leg, in fact.'

'Don't come it,' said Muscles, 'I hate the lot of you, and I pertic'lerly hate you.'

'Why me?' asked the copper.

'I don't like your phizog. It ain't human.'

'Well, you're in luck, you won't see it for the next twenty-eight days.'

'I'll improve it for you one day,' said Muscles, who was at his gloomiest. Among other things, he'd proposed to call again on his friend Herbert on Sunday, just for a chat. He'd miss out on that. And then there was the fact that he knew he'd have to answer to his guv'nor for getting himself crimed when he came out. Not that he'd told the court exactly why he was sorting out the publican. But the bleedin' coppers knew, of course, and they'd be keeping a closer watch on his guv'nor, who wouldn't like it a bit.

'What's that?' asked Olive, returning to the living room after making herself a mug of hot Bovril. Roger was examining something.

'Eh?' He looked up. 'Oh, didn't hear you, thought you were still in the kitchen. Feeling better?'

'No, not much,' said Olive, 'but I hope this Bovril will help a little.' She sat down. 'Roger, what's that you've got?'

'It's your mum's savings book,' said Roger.

'I thought you'd only found her handbag and purse,' said Olive.

'Didn't I mention her savings book?' asked Roger.

'No, you didn't,' said Olive, 'so let me see.'

'It's—'

'Let me see.'

'Of course,' said Roger, and handed it to her. Olive opened it and looked at the current balance. It was quite a bit.

'Oh, well, it's not much good to poor old Mum now,' she said. She was unable at the moment to express any further interest, and she passed the book back to Roger.

'I'm glad I found it before any petty thief did,' said Roger. 'Can you believe that balance of eight hundred and eighty-three pounds?'

'Does it matter?' said Olive, still grieving. 'Who cares about it just now?'

'Well, even as things are,' said Roger, 'all that much money is still an eye-opener, Olive, especially as it's earning interest.'

'Is it?' Olive sipped the Bovril and sighed. 'Roger, I simply can't credit Mum taking her own life. Did that policeman say it was definitely suicide?'

'No, I told you he said it only looked like it, that we'll have to wait for the inquest,' said Roger. 'All the same, Olive, I think we're going to have to accept it. But God knows why she did it.'

'Yes, why should she, it doesn't make sense,' said Olive, 'especially as she kept saying she liked being a free woman, that she was already enjoying herself. That might not have been very fair on Dad, considering he felt he always did his best as a husband, but living her own life was what she wanted, so why should she commit suicide?'

'Beats me, Olive.'

'I'd rather she'd had a heart attack,' said Olive.

'Well, there's still a possibility she fainted,' said Roger, 'we both agree that could have happened. Christ, though, she had nearly nine hundred pounds savings. Look at all the monthly entries since 1911, one after the other and no withdrawals except two recent ones of five quid each.'

'What's there is all the money she saved out of her housekeeping allowance every year of her marriage,' said Olive flatly.

'Well, that's in your dad's favour,' said Roger, 'giving her the kind of housekeeping that enabled her to save this much in twenty-five years. It's an average of about thirty-five quid a year. No wonder the poor old bloke couldn't understand her walking out on him. D'you know how much housekeeping he gave her each week?'

'Roger, I can't get interested in this,' said Olive, 'but all right, it was two pounds five shillings.'

'As much as that?' said Roger.

'Well, Dad made a profit of about five pounds a week from his shop, and a lot more at Christmas-times,' said Olive. 'And he paid all the bills so as to make sure Mum could put more than a few shillings into her savings every month. And he put savings away himself for their old age.'

'Then she was a bit hard on him in the end, wasn't she?' said Roger.

Olive told him not to speak ill of the dead. She said her mum deserved extra housekeeping because of all she did for her family, and that she wouldn't have walked out if only she hadn't been taken for granted, and if Dad had been more sociable as a husband. Roger said he supposed her mother's savings would all revert to her father, unless her mother had made a will and given equal shares to everyone.

'Mum wouldn't have made any will,' said Olive, 'she never thought about anything like that. Only property owners and the gentry make wills, generally.'

'It'll all go to your dad, then,' said Roger.

'At the moment, Roger, I don't care what happens to it,' said Olive. 'I'm not good for anything except grief just now. You'll have to give me time to get over the shock before I can interest myself in Mum's savings.' However, she managed a few moments of concentrated thought, and came to the silent conclusion that if she did receive a share she'd open a savings account of her own with it. A savings account would guard against an empty domestic kitty, which Roger's spendthrift habits might bring about.

Madge and Winnie arrived then, wanting to talk and to mull repeatedly over everything, especially when told that according to the police their mother's death looked like suicide. That really got them going, and although Roger could understand it, the constant repetition of the same overworked questions and disbeliefs began to play on his nerves. So he brought the savings book up for discussion. Neither Madge nor Winnie were all that surprised by the recorded balance. They both said their mother was a good manager, and that she was able to save more each week when she started her part-time job a year ago. Roger said it all belonged to their father now.

'I don't see why,' said Madge, 'it all ought to be shared out.'

'Yes, so it ought,' said Winnie. 'It's what she'd have wanted.'

'I don't think money is what we should be talking about now,' said Olive, 'it's not the right time. I'm still hoping I'll wake up and find everything's just been a nightmare.'

'God, wouldn't we all like that,' said Madge, recovered enough to be her assertive self. 'But listen, I must say something about Mum's savings book. Don't let my father have it, Roger, not until we find out if he intends to divide the amount into fair shares.'

'Fair shares sound like a fair solution to me,' said Roger. 'You girls all had a special regard for your mother, and she appreciated that. You're all entitled to fair shares.'

'Roger, must you?' said Olive.

'Sorry, love,' said Roger.

'We can put that subject aside now,' said Madge.

'Actually,' said Winnie, 'the stars aren't right at the moment for money matters. Oh, Lord, and they couldn't have been right for Mum two nights ago. I still can't take it in.'

That, not unnaturally, brought the sisters back to their lamenting state, to a resumption of the sad whys and wherefores, with an emphasis on the fact that if only she had stayed with their father she would almost certainly still be alive.

Roger intervened to say their father had called earlier, but had been persuaded to go back home because he looked done in. Perhaps Winnie and Madge would go and see him sometime? Madge said they'd do that, of course they would.

'Well, I know one thing,' said Winnie, 'and that's that Mum didn't deliberately drown herself. She wasn't born under that kind of star.'

'Oh, leave off about stars,' said Madge.

'I expect it'll be called an accident,' said Roger.

Olive picked quickly and hopefully at that remark.

'Oh, d'you think she might've slipped, hit her head on the side of the bath and then fell in unconscious?' she said.

'She might, yes,' said Madge, 'but, look here, we can't keep on and on about what might have been. It's not doing us any good, and it's not getting us anywhere. Roger, did the policeman say anything definite at all?'

'Sergeant Tomlinson?' said Roger. 'About the cause? No, nothing definite, just that we'd have to wait on the inquest.'

'Well, the police ought to know something a bit definite by now,' said Winnie. 'I mean, if Mum did hit her head.'

'I don't think he thought anything like that happened,' said Roger.

'But it might have,' said Olive. 'You could go round to the police station and ask.'

'Yes, stop being negative, Roger,' said Madge.

'Roger's not being negative, just reasonable,' said Olive. 'All the same, go and ask, Roger.'

'All right,' said Roger. Although easy come, easy go as far as money was concerned, and not a stickler for principles, he had his good points, and was willing to humour his stricken wife.

'I'll come with you,' said Madge, 'let's go now.'

She and Roger went together. The desk sergeant at the station assured them that if there'd been any signs of a head bruise on Mrs Jones, it wouldn't have been missed during the post-mortem examination.

'Sure?' said Roger.

'Sure,' said the desk sergeant.

'Well, it just might have been missed,' said Madge.

'It might, but I don't think so, Mrs Cooper,' said the sergeant sympathetically.

'But you never know,' said Madge, 'and I'd like the doctor or surgeon or whoever did the examination to have another look.'

'Pardon?' said the sergeant.

'I do have a right to ask him to,' said Madge.

The sergeant realized argument wasn't the thing.

'I'll pass your request on, Mrs Cooper,' he said, 'and if you could come back tomorrow, I think I'd be able to give you an answer. Will that do?'

'Yes, all right,' said Madge, clutching at straws on behalf of the family. 'You can understand, I suppose, that none of us can believe it wasn't accidental?'

'I can understand, but, of course, I'm not at liberty to discuss it, Mrs Cooper.'

'No, I suppose not, and it's painful for me too, I assure you,' said Madge.

'You do have my sympathy, Mrs Cooper. A shock like that takes a long time to recover from.'

'Yes,' said Madge, 'I'm sure of that. Well, thanks, anyway, and I'll call in again tomorrow.'

That was all she and Roger could carry back to the others, the hope that an answer tomorrow would point to the possibility of an accident, which would be far more acceptable than suicide.

None of the daughters wanted to believe their mother had taken her own life.

Chapter Ten

Sergeant Tomlinson had a thought as he and Constable Fry left the station that afternoon. The thought made him suggest they should visit the Stockwell Road flat again.

'What's the idea?' asked Constable Fry. 'Aren't we supposed to be heading for the poor old girl's place of work?'

'There's something I want to find out first,' said Sergeant Tomlinson.

'Don't mind me or my aching feet,' said Constable Fry.

'I've got my own feet to worry about,' said Sergeant Tomlinson, who'd have liked the use of a police car. Inspector Shaw, however, had said do some old-fashioned plodding, too much use of cars is softening the force. Furthermore, he'd said, this isn't an emergency, it's a shot in the dark.

When they reached 25 Stockwell Road, there was a barrow parked at the kerbside, its painted boards advertising 'J.C. Meadowes – Carpenter – Stockwell Lane S.W.9'. The carpenter himself was at work, and about to take the damaged door off its hinges. The duty constable was standing by.

'Sorry, the bobby can't let no-one in,' said Mr Meadowes. 'Mr Roger Way was particular about telling me that.'

'We're police officers,' said Sergeant Tomlinson, and the carpenter looked them over. He nodded.

'That's different,' he said. 'Finding things out, are you, about the poor woman's accident? Mr Way told me about it. Imagine she finished up drowning. Talk about you never know what's going to hit you. Well, there we go, gents, the door's off.' Manhandling it, the carpenter rested it against the outside brick wall. 'You can go up now.'

'You're fitting a new lock when you've made the repair?' said Sergeant Tomlinson.

'Repair? That's a job for me workshop,' said the carpenter, 'and pricey too. And time-consuming. No, I agreed with Mr Way to fit a new door. There it is, in the passage.'

'Good,' said Sergeant Tomlinson. 'Got the keys for the lock?'

'A door lock ain't much use without a key, y'know,' said the carpenter. 'I've got three for that there new one.'

'Two spares? Let me have one. I'm Detective Sergeant Tomlinson of the Stockwell station.' The sergeant showed his card. 'You can take my word it's all right by Mr Way.'

'Well, if you say so, guv'nor,' said the carpenter. He dug into the pocket of his boiler suit, brought out three keys on a ring, released one and handed it to the CID man.

'Much obliged,' said Sergeant Tomlinson, 'you can let Mr Way know you've given me one, which I'll let him have in due course.'

'Fair enough,' said the carpenter.

The CID men climbed the stairs and went straight to the bedroom.

'Now what, seeing the key means you're thinking of coming here again?' said Constable Fry.

'Well, I'll tell you,' said Sergeant Tomlinson. 'It's assumed Mrs Jones was taking a bath before she went to bed. I don't suppose she intended to dress again. I suppose what she'd have put on after her bath was her nightdress. I don't recollect seeing it about. Nor did I see it when I lifted her pillow and uncovered the purse and savings book. So let's find out if she left it somewhere handy.'

'You've got a bee in your bonnet,' said Constable Fry.

'Yes, and it's buzzing,' said Sergeant Tomlinson, and crossed to the bed. The covering sheet and blanket were turned down at one corner, as before, showing part of the pillow. He lifted the pillow to confirm that, with the purse and savings book having been removed, there was nothing there. 'Don't women keep their nighties under their pillow?' he asked.

'Usually,' said Constable Fry. 'Lily does.' Lily was his better half.

'Well, Mrs Jones's isn't here, is it?'

'I can't see it, no,' said Constable Fry, 'but what I can see is that the bedclothes have been turned down. Was that to get at her nightie?'

'Or just to put her purse and savings book under the pillow?' suggested Sergeant Tomlinson. 'In any case, where is the ruddy nightdress?'

'Have you thought of trying the bathroom door? It might be hanging on the peg, ready to be put on.'

'Wouldn't we have noticed it when we were called out to investigate? And who'd use a night-dress damp with steam? But never mind that, take a look, Sidney.'

'That won't be too hard on me feet, Frank,' said Constable Fry, and went to the bathroom, while Sergeant Tomlinson moved around the bedroom. Back came Constable Fry. 'No luck, Sarge, no nightie, just an empty peg except for one of them thin waterproof bath caps.'

'Eh?'

'Fact. No nightie, only the cap, the kind some

138

women cover their heads with when they take a bath.'

'Well, ruddy hell, why wasn't Mrs Jones wearing it? Her head was bare.' Sergeant Tomlinson made a quick journey to the bathroom himself. He saw the cap on the peg. He looked around, and the bee in his bonnet buzzed louder. 'Something else,' he said.

'We've been here before, y'know,' said Constable Fry, 'so what's the something else that's on your mind?'

'Where's the ruddy bath towel?' asked Sergeant Tomlinson. There wasn't one, only a small hand towel hanging from a hook between the handbasin and the toilet.

'Listen,' said Constable Fry, 'this bathroom is as we left it.'

'I can see it is,' said Sergeant Tomlinson, 'and we should have made a note about no bath towel. But we were only interested in the bath and its corpse, and what looked like suicide or an accident. Now why didn't Mrs Jones put the cap on and bring a towel with her? And another thing, wouldn't she have worn some kind of a wrap or did she walk naked from the bedroom to here?'

'If she'd made up her mind to drown herself, she wouldn't have bothered with a wrap or a bath cap,' said Constable Fry. 'But I've suddenly got a bee in me own bonnet.'

'Listen, she'd left her old man, and we know from what he said himself and what Mr and Mrs Way said, that she was looking forward to a new and more exciting life.' Sergeant Tomlinson spoke firmly. 'No, I'm passing on suicide, so there's got to be a nightdress somewhere.' He went back to the bedroom. He pulled the covering sheet and blanket halfway down, but again only revealed the undersheet. 'Where the hell is it?'

'Any good suggesting she slept in the altogether?' offered Constable Fry.

'I'm not buying that, this is London, not the Sahara.' Sergeant Tomlinson opened up the wardrobe. It disclosed various garments, but nothing in the way of nightdresses or underwear. He advanced on the dressing table, and began to open its drawers. He found clean folded underwear in one drawer, and in the one below he found a pink nightdress on top of a white corset.

'That's it,' said Constable Fry.

'Is it?'

'Well, it's not an overcoat.'

'Don't let's get clever. Ten to one it's not the nightdress she was using. It's folded, it's clean, and uncreased. It's her spare.'

'You could be right,' said Constable Fry. 'So where's this week's one?'

'Is there an airing cupboard?' asked Sergeant Tomlinson. 'If so, she might have kept it there to put on warm each night.'

They discovered a small airing cupboard next to the bathroom, but it contained no nightdress. However, they did find two folded bath towels, the top one looking a little used. That's the one she would have taken to the bathroom, thought Sergeant Tomlinson. Now then, a drowned corpse, with the faint marks of a ringed bruise around each ankle. No bath cap or wrap worn, and no towel taken. And no nightdress visible. Was it an enforced bath? Had some lunatic got into the flat and jumped her at the moment she was fully undressed? If so, she'd have screamed and struggled. The flat overlooked the road, and someone could easily have heard the screams. And a violent struggle would have left its marks on her. He'd bet she was a strong woman: she was no little weakling – she had a fine physique. She wouldn't have gone quietly unless she'd been knocked out. But, in that case, the pathologist would have found traces of the blow.

And when it came down to the possibility of a lover, what reason would he have had to forcibly drown her? If there was a reason, if he had committed the crime, he'd done it in a way to make it look like suicide, a spur of the moment suicide after she'd got into the bath and picked up the soap.

He discussed the ifs and buts with Constable Fry. Sidney Fry wasn't exactly an imaginative plainclothes copper, but he could work a few things out.

'You know what we've got, don't you, Sarge? Pointers, but nothing else, not unless we can turn up a suspect, which would be a bloke with a motive. Such as her old man.'

'And what would have been his motive?' asked Sergeant Tomlinson.

'Blind fury. Seeing she dumped him, he could have told himself he had justifiable cause to drown her. Didn't you get the impression he was sweating a bit when we were talking to him? As if he was realizing an act of blind fury could land him in the dock?'

'It's a point,' said Sergeant Tomlinson. 'I wonder, did she have a lover? If she did, and Herbert Jones found out after she'd left him, that on top of having been dumped might've set him well alight.'

'Blazing,' said Constable Fry. 'And let's see, if he's as useless as a doorpost to a woman, then I don't suppose he's too bright generally. A cleverer bloke would've put the bath cap on Mrs Jones, and left a towel in the bathroom after drowning her.'

'He said he was with a friend that evening, remember?' Sergeant Tomlinson was thinking, thinking.

'Told you we ought to have checked on that,' said Constable Fry.

'I think we'd better do that now,' said Sergeant Tomlinson. 'I don't fancy presenting Inspector Shaw with what we've got if it doesn't include a check on Jones's alibi. But what we have got does make a call on Mrs Jones's place of work secondary at the moment. Not that I'm completely sold on what looks obvious, that Jones did away with his wife in a fit of blind rage.'

'You having second thoughts already?' said Constable Fry.

'Well, I think I'll allow for alternatives,' said Sergeant Tomlinson, tipping his hat back as if to let air cool his furrowed brow. 'All the same, let's find out if Jones is at home before we go back to the station. Listen, Sidney, how did we miss the marks around her ankles?'

'Easy,' said Constable Fry. 'She was right under the water, and the bath was as full as it could be. The tap was trickling, the water wasn't crystal clear and the body was a mite blurred. Seeing she was obviously as dead as a drowned sheep, we left it to the ambulance crew to get her out. They had a blanket over her in no time. You and me, we'd only have been interested in looking her over if there'd been clear signs she'd been knocked about.'

'Maybe, but I think at the time we took the possibility of an accident or suicide too much for granted,' said Sergeant Tomlinson.

'You can say so now,' said Constable Fry, 'but

at the time there was nothing to make us think there were suspicious circumstances.'

'That's true,' said Sergeant Tomlinson, 'and it's a fact that it wasn't until I was listening to Jones telling us how he'd been treated after twenty-five years of marriage that I started to think there might be more in that bathroom than met the eye.'

'Very upset husband and, all of a sudden, a dead wife,' said Constable Fry. 'Made us both think, didn't it?'

'Well, let's see if we can satisfy ourselves,' said Sergeant Tomlinson, and they left.

Chapter Eleven

Herbert was in. He wasn't surprised to see the CID men.

'Been expecting you,' he said, letting them in.

'Well, here we are, then,' said Constable Fry.

'You're going to tell me the cause of death?' said Herbert, taking them into the living room.

'Your wife drowned, sir,' said Sergeant Tomlinson.

'Well, I know that, don't I?' said Herbert, as tidy-looking as ever but showing strain. 'I meant what caused her to drown?'

'We can't say, Mr Jones,' said Sergeant Tomlinson. 'It's the coroner who'll deliver the verdict after the inquest has presented him with all the facts. But, from our point of view, there are one or two things to clear up.'

'Tidy up, you might say,' said Constable Fry. 'Like there's yourself, Mr Jones. The coroner'll want to know where you were at the time. I think you said with a friend, didn't you?'

'Oh, we're back to that, are we?' said Herbert.

'Back to what, sir?' asked Sergeant Tomlinson.

'To me,' said Herbert.

'It's a formality, y'know, sir,' said Constable Fry.

'I've heard about formalities,' said Herbert.

'We live with them every day ourselves,' said Sergeant Tomlinson. 'But we do have to tie up loose ends.'

'I'm a loose end?' said Herbert.

'Hardly, sir,' said Sergeant Tomlinson with a slight smile. It made him look more like Herbert's best friend than a policeman. 'As a matter of routine, we'd simply like to establish exactly where you were on the evening in question. So could you give us the name and address of your friend?'

'I'll be pleased to,' said Herbert, and gave Nell's name and address, which Constable Fry noted down. 'That's only a few minutes' walk from here. Oh, and give a double knock, her flat is upstairs.'

'Much obliged, sir,' said Constable Fry, 'that's all we wanted.'

'Fair enough,' said Herbert. 'And all I want is to know if my wife drowned because of a heart attack or because of some kind of collapse. It's got to be one or the other.'

'Well, sir,' said Sergeant Tomlinson, 'as I told your son-in-law, Mr Way, earlier today, the post-mortem showed her heart was sound, which could mean there was no obvious reason for a sudden collapse.'

'Bloody hell,' said Herbert, 'what you're saying could mean my poor old Hilda could have committed suicide. Not that I can believe it, but what else is there?'

'Good question, Mr Jones,' said Constable Fry.

'Well, we'll just make this routine call on Mrs Nell Binns, sir,' said Sergeant Tomlinson. 'Oh, and thanks for being helpful.'

'It's the inquest next?' said Herbert.

'That's right, sir,' said Constable Fry, and Herbert saw them out.

When they had gone he went into the kitchen and put the kettle on. He felt he needed some hot strong tea.

When he'd had it, he'd take a walk and call on Nell.

'You're what?' said Nell, having come down from her flat to answer a double knock on the front door.

'CID, Mrs Binns, from the Stockwell station. I'm Detective Sergeant Tomlinson, and this is Detective Constable Fry.'

'Well, thank you, I'm sure, and you look all right,' said Nell. 'Respectable, I mean. Me neighbours don't take much notice of respectable callers. It's the other kind that makes them talk.

Anyway, what can I do for you?' She had a good idea, of course, of why they had come.

'It concerns Mr Jones, Mr Herbert Jones – '

'Oh, you'd best come up,' said Nell. She took them up to her flat of three rooms, and into her living room, very neat, spruce and homely, with some potted plants on the wide window ledge. 'You can sit down, gents,' she said. They seated themselves. Nell brushed her skirt and sat down herself. 'Here we are, then,' she said, 'what d'you want to know about Mr Jones, poor man?'

'You're aware of his wife's death?' said Sergeant Tomlinson.

'Yes, and I was never more shocked,' said Nell. 'I expect Herbert – Mr Jones – has asked the same question, but did his wife have a heart attack in her bath?'

'No, the post-mortem examination showed her heart was sound,' said Sergeant Tomlinson, not for the first time that day.

'Was it suicide, then?' asked Nell.

'We can't say at the moment,' said Constable Fry.

'It's a bit of a mystery, then, is it?' said Nell. 'I knew Mrs Jones fairly well, although she hadn't visited the shop much these last two years. Oh, I worked in Mr Jones's shop for a good long while, I expect he's told you that. Anyway, his wife always looked very healthy, like, and I never thought she'd come to a mysterious drowning in her own bath, poor Hilda. It's been in the local weekly paper that come out this morning, but of course I already knew about it from Mr Jones, and I never saw him more upset. It's hard on him, coming at a time when he'd just sold his shop.'

'We understand he was with you on the night of his wife's death,' said Sergeant Tomlinson.

'Yes, so he was,' said Nell, 'and that's what really upset him, that he was here, spending a friendly time with me, when it happened. It made him feel guilty, made him feel that if only he'd gone to visit her that evening, she'd still be alive. I expect you know they were separated, that she'd moved out last Monday week, and that upset him as well. He did say he thought about going to see her, to find out how she was getting on, and now, of course, he wishes he'd gone that evening instead of being here with me.'

'You and Mr Jones are close friends?' said Constable Fry.

'Yes, course we are,' said Nell, too sensible a woman to dissemble. 'It comes from all the years I worked with him in his shop.'

'Mrs Jones didn't mind that?' said Sergeant Tomlinson.

'Beg your pardon?' said Nell.

'Mrs Jones didn't mind your close friendship with her husband?'

'Here, wait a minute,' said Nell, bristling, 'I

hope you're not making insinuations. Mr Jones is an upright and straightforward gent, and I'm a respectable widow. Like I've just said, I worked for more than a few years in his shop and we got on very nice together, but that's all. I don't want no-one being suggestive, if you don't mind. When poor Hilda left him, he needed someone to talk to, someone that could understand why he was so upset. I don't have to excuse meself for trying to cheer him up, nor for giving him me sincere sympathy when he told me what had happened to Hilda. If you think she left him because of me, and that she drowned herself on that account, you can think again, and I don't mind telling you so. There wasn't ever anything between me and Herbert except a nice friendship.'

'We simply want a clear picture of circumstances immediately prior to the unfortunate happening,' said Sergeant Tomlinson. 'Could you tell us how long Mr Jones was with you on the evening in question?'

Nell was no simpleton. It was obvious to her that these policemen were after something, probably something to do with Herbert because he'd been a wronged husband. Well, she wasn't going to say anything that would make them suspicious of him. Herbert would never lay a finger on any woman, not even on Hilda who'd said such terrible unkind things to him.

'I should think he was here most of the evening, from about half past eight,' she said. She paused. 'About what time did the police doctor say Mrs Jones died?' she asked, as if Herbert hadn't already told her.

The CID men looked at each other.

'If Mr Jones was with you most of the evening, can you say exactly what time he left?' asked Constable Fry.

'No, not exactly,' said Nell. 'I know I've got a mantelpiece clock, as you can see, but I don't look at it unless I need to know the time. I'd say that Herbert – Mr Jones – could've left sometime between ten and eleven. What I do know exact is that I went to bed just about eleven, which couldn't have been long after he'd gone.' Nell was being protective, simply because she was never going to believe Herbert had anything to do with his wife drowning.

Constable Fry thought the questions should have been asked of this witness immediately after they'd first talked to Jones about his wife's death, and before he'd had a chance to call on his lady friend. But at that time the police had no reason to begin an investigation into suspicious circumstances. Suspicious circumstances weren't evident then. But they were now.

Sergeant Tomlinson regarded the lady thoughtfully.

'Well, thanks for your time and your help, Mrs

Binns,' he said. 'Sorry to have bothered you.'

'Oh, don't mention it, I'm sure, you've both been nice and polite,' said Nell, altogether a very pleasant woman and disinclined to think ill of anybody. She'd shocked herself at what she'd thought of Hilda after her treatment of Herbert.

She saw the CID men out and said goodbye to them with a smile. Sergeant Tomlinson returned the smile, and she thought what a likeable man he was for a policeman. Most policemen, even the nice ones, could be very po-faced at times.

Inspector Shaw sat thinking. Tomlinson and Fry stood looking. Their interest in his ruminations made them search his broad countenance for signs of encouragement. But he hardly moved a muscle, and there was not even the slightest twitch as he finally glanced up at them.

However, he did say, 'I think there's the makings of a case.'

'You're taking charge, sir?' said Sergeant Tomlinson.

'Am I? I don't think so, I'm up to my eyes as it is, and you're doing well enough, Sergeant. So you can see this case through to the finish, if there's definitely a case. Up to you to get the evidence. It'll help your prospective promotion.' Inspector Shaw consulted his watch. 'The day's running away, I see, but there's still enough time for you to start getting your teeth into the case.'

'Right, sir,' said Sergeant Tomlinson.

'The bath towel, that's the main pointer,' said the inspector. 'Who takes a bath without having a towel handy?'

'Only forgetful old ladies or absent-minded inventors,' said Sergeant Tomlinson.

'Inventors?' said the inspector.

'If you know what I mean,' said Sergeant Tomlinson.

'Was Mrs Jones an inventor?' asked Inspector Shaw.

'A factory office clerk,' said Sergeant Tomlinson.

'Well, then?'

'Yes, do factory office clerks take a bath without a towel handy?' said Sergeant Tomlinson. 'No, I wouldn't think so, sir.'

'They're like the rest of us,' said the inspector. 'As for the nightdress that can't be found, you've got some thoughts about that, haven't you?'

Sergeant Tomlinson smacked himself on the forehead.

'I have now,' he said. 'Yes, of course. She was wearing it at the time, and it was taken off her.'

'Before or after she got drowned?' said Constable Fry.

'What do you think, Tomlinson?' asked the inspector.

'I think that if it had been pulled off her before, it would later have been put back in its natural place, under the pillow,' said Sergeant Tomlinson. 'Taken off after she was forced into the bath, it would have been soaking wet, and that would have meant having to disappear with it.'

'Someone's got a wet nightdress somewhere, unless it's been destroyed or hung out to dry,' said Inspector Shaw. 'Now then, Sergeant, go back again to the flat. Take Stebbings with you and have him collect what fingerprints he can find. Tell him to concentrate mainly on the bedroom and bathroom. He'll probably find any amount of the deceased's, but what you need are someone else's. By the way, what's the husband do?'

'Not much at the moment,' said Constable Fry, 'he kept a corner shop, but he's retired from that.'

'Has he?' asked the inspector. 'When did he retire?'

'Not long after Mrs Jones left him,' said Constable Fry.

'Sounds like a case of the angry sulks,' said the inspector. 'Mrs Binns is sure, is she, that he was with her up to about half ten?'

'Not sure, no,' said Constable Fry. 'She pointed out that she didn't consult her clock, so she made a guess at the time in question.'

'Well, I suppose a close lady friend of Jones's wouldn't want to quote the wrong time,' said the inspector drily. 'Have either of you got the impression that they were a lot more than close?'

'Personally, no,' said Sergeant Tomlinson.

'I'm a suspicious type meself about a close friendship when the woman's a widow and the man's not his wife's favourite bloke,' said Constable Fry.

'We could call Jones the obvious suspect, but for my liking he's a bit too obvious,' said Sergeant Tomlinson.

'You've got likings, have you?' said Inspector Shaw. 'That's dangerous. It can lead to catching a dose of intuition, which is a woman's complaint and nothing to do with tried and tested police work. Anyway, why is Jones too obvious?'

'Well, if he's got any sense at all, he'd have known he'd be the first one we'd look at if we started to ask ourselves questions,' said Sergeant Tomlinson. 'He'd have known we'd find out he had cause to be furious with his wife. My guess is he'd have done a runner by now, if he'd been guilty.'

'Was he furious?' asked Inspector Shaw.

'Well, you've got all the details, sir, about how she walked out on him after twenty-five years of marriage,' said Sergeant Tomlinson.

'On top of which, she told him he was a boring old bugger and about as useful as a doorpost,' said Constable Fry. 'That must've got right up his nose, sir.'

'I see,' said Inspector Shaw, 'you're after a crime relating to injured feelings, Fry, and Tomlinson's after something else.'

'Something not so obvious,' said Sergeant Tomlinson.

'Mystery geezer?' suggested the inspector.

'Worth making inquiries, sir,' said Sergeant Tomlinson.

'Fair point, Sergeant,' said Inspector Shaw. 'Help yourself to a good start by getting Stebbings on the track of fingerprints, and keep an open mind as far as Jones is concerned. Keep me informed on progress.'

The new door was in place, and Sergeant Tomlinson used the spare key to open it. The time was nearing five o'clock as he went up to the flat with Detective Constable Stebbings, the fingerprint specialist. They made for the bedroom. Entering, they stopped short. A very attractive young woman, stylishly dressed, was sitting on the edge of the bed.

'Mrs Way?' said Sergeant Tomlinson, recognizing her.

Olive looked at him, her fine grey eyes a little hollow.

'Oh, you're Sergeant Tomlinson,' she said.

'Can I ask why you're here, Mrs Way?'

'It's my mood,' said Olive, 'I felt I just had to come and do some thinking about my mother leaving my father to live in this place, which isn't very much compared to their house in Brixton. I haven't done much clear thinking, though, everything's still going round and round in my head, and all I can do is ask myself why she's dead.'

Sergeant Tomlinson felt a twinge of pity, pity of a very human kind. He knew she was the dead woman's youngest daughter, the daughter who, with her husband, had found the immersed corpse.

'We're asking ourselves the same question, Mrs Way,' he said.

'We all hate the thought that it might have been suicide,' said Olive, 'we'd all rather it had been a sudden heart attack. I'm sorry I was in such a state at the time, it must have been very embarrassing for you.'

'Not a bit, Mrs Way,' said Sergeant Tomlinson. Constable Stebbings looked from one to the other. Olive came to her feet and walked to the window, seeming to be lost in thought. 'I don't see how you could have taken it calmly.'

'I'm calmer now, at least,' said Olive, turning to face the men. 'Roger – my husband – has been a help. You saw him again here, didn't you?'

'Yes, he was looking for your mother's handbag,' said Sergeant Tomlinson. 'And we had one or two things to tidy up.'

'Why are you here again?' asked Olive.

'Oh, to make sure there's nothing we've missed.'

'What could you have missed, then?' asked Olive.

Sergeant Tomlinson hesitated, then said, 'Mrs Way, would you know where your mother kept her nightdress?'

'Under her pillow,' said Olive. 'Why d'you ask?'

'It's one of those things that needs tidying up,' said Sergeant Tomlinson. Olive looked at his colleague, a question in her eyes. 'This is Detective Constable Stebbings, Mrs Way.'

With a faint smile, Olive said, 'Oh, is he the tidying-up expert?'

'After a fashion, Mrs Way,' said Stebbings.

Olive, now regarding Sergeant Tomlinson a little wistfully, said, 'I wish you could find my mother had some kind of accident that led to her being drowned.'

'Mrs Way, perhaps we'll find exactly that.'

'Thanks, you're very kind,' said Olive. 'I'd better go now, I'd better get back to my husband. He doesn't know I came here, he'll think me morbid. I told him I just needed some fresh air and to do some thinking. Oh, if you want any more information on my mother before the inquest, you can always come and ask.'

'I'll remember that, and thanks,' said Sergeant Tomlinson.

'Do you know the date of the inquest?' asked Olive.

'No, not yet, but you'll be advised, of course.'

'Yes, I see.' Olive walked to the door. Sergeant Tomlinson stood aside, then accompanied her to the door of the flat. He opened it for her. She glanced at him, and he thought what exceptionally fine eyes she had, even if they were rimmed with strain and sleeplessness. 'Goodbye, Sergeant.'

'I'm damned sorry about everything, Mrs Way.'

'Are you?' The faint smile showed again. 'That helps, coming from a policeman. I need policemen to be kind to me at the moment.'

'That's not very much to ask,' said Sergeant Tomlinson.

'Did you always want to be a policeman?' asked Olive.

'A kind one?' he said, and again came her faint smile.

'If you like,' she said.

'Well, let's say even when I was at Wilson's Grammar School and most of my friends were thinking of more elevated careers, I wanted to join the force in due time.'

'Well, I hope you become Chief Inspector Tomlinson,' said Olive. 'That's fairly elevated, isn't it? Goodbye again.' She put out her hand.

He took it, and lightly pressed it. Her fingers were cold, but they lightly responded.

'Goodbye, Mrs Way.'

Olive left and he returned to the bedroom. Stebbings was already busy with his brush and powder. He glanced over his shoulder.

'Nice young woman,' he said.

'Yes, the dead woman's youngest daughter,' said Sergeant Tomlinson. 'She and her husband were the ones who found the body.'

'No wonder she's under strain,' said Stebbings.

'Yes, and I feel for her,' said Sergeant Tomlinson, and thought about her, so strangely wistful once or twice, like a young waif hoping for magical surprises on Christmas Day. He shook himself, thought about the nightdress, and went down the back stairs to the yard. There, he examined the contents of the dustbin. Everything seemed to be in it except a nightdress. Well, there'd been a faint chance it might have been rolled into a ball and buried in the bin.

He returned to the flat, where Stebbings told him he was acquiring an interesting collection of prints.

They went back to the station eventually. Inspector Shaw, however, had left. Stebbings went to the mortuary to take the fingerprints of the dead woman. Sergeant Tomlinson went home, to his quarters. He was still a bachelor, although he knew a few ladies who were always ready to be taken out, but not too ready to marry a policeman whose duties were demanding and whose homecoming times were accordingly unreliable.

Chapter Twelve

'You went to the flat?' said Roger.

'Oh, I just found myself there,' said Olive. 'I suppose it was a kind of morbid magnet, and, when I got there, I felt I wanted to sit and try to work out why Mum – well, why.'

'It's something none of us can work out,' said Roger.

'But there has to be an answer,' said Olive.

'It'll come out at the inquest,' said Roger.

'Oh, that CID sergeant turned up again, with a colleague,' said Olive. 'To finish tidying up one or two things, he said.'

'Sergeant Tomlinson?' said Roger.

'Yes,' said Olive.

'I don't trust that tidying-up business of his,' said Roger, 'and I don't trust him too much, either.'

'Why?' asked Olive.

'I think he's after making a meal of things,' said Roger.

'I think he's only trying to find out if there's a reasonable explanation for Mum's death,' said Olive.

'Don't you believe it,' said Roger. 'He's a policeman, he's not after a reasonable explanation, more like something he can really get his teeth into.'

Olive stared at him.

'What d'you mean, Roger?' she asked.

'Did he say anything to you apart from tidying up, Olive?'

'No,' said Olive. 'No, wait, he asked me where Mum kept her nightdress, so I told him under her pillow.'

'Did he look?' asked Roger.

'No, not then. Not while I was there. He simply said it was one of the things to be tidied up.'

'He's fishy,' said Roger.

'I don't think so,' said Olive. 'I think he's a rather nice man.'

'He's a policeman, and he's fishing,' said Roger.

'You said fishy a moment ago, Roger.'

'Well, one word leads to the other,' said Roger.

'Roger, what're you on about exactly?' asked Olive.

'Oh, nothing very much, Olive, just that the police have got their own way of looking at things. Are we going to try to eat some supper this evening?'

'Yes, all right,' said Olive, 'and later on I'm going to try to get a good long sleep without any bad dreams. I hope Dad does too. I'm sure he's suffering because he let Mum have her own way the one time when he knows now he shouldn't have.'

Herbert walked round to see Nell that evening. Her welcome was a warm and very friendly one. So he gave her a kiss on her smooth cheek.

'Now, Herbert, should you?'

'Just by way of a greeting, Nell.'

'Pleasure, I'm sure,' said Nell, 'and you're beginning to look a bit better. I never saw you all haggard before, like you were the morning after the police told you about Hilda. Well, sit yourself down, and I'll make us a pot of tea. Oh, the police called on me this afternoon, did you know?'

'They called on me first,' said Herbert, seating himself in a fireside armchair. 'They asked for your name and address, saying they wanted to see you about our time together that evening.'

'Yes, and they told me they had to get things clear about the circumstances, specially as Hilda didn't die of any heart attack,' said Nell. 'I suppose – well, I don't know what I suppose.'

'Myself, I suppose they were thinking I might have drowned Hilda on account of the way she walked out on me,' said Herbert, frowning.

'Well, I don't think much of that sort of thinking,' said Nell tartly. 'It's disgusting and silly as well. I told them you were here most of the evening up to some time between ten and eleven.'

'I can't remember the exact time I did leave,' said Herbert.

'Well, that's what I told the policemen, that I couldn't remember the exact time,' said Nell.

'I appreciate that, Nell,' said Herbert. 'You're not just a good woman, you're a good friend as well.'

'Well, good friends should stick together, shouldn't they?' said Nell. 'You've had enough troubles to be going on with, Herbert, you don't want more. I'll put the kettle on now.'

They were sharing the tea a little later, as well as some of Nell's home-made cake. It pleased her that Herbert hadn't let Hilda's death get him right down in the dumps. He was sad about everything, of course, but he wasn't all grey and brooding. Although he felt he was a bit to blame for Hilda's death, he was standing up to things, like a real man should. In fact, the happenings had changed him for the better, really. He'd always seemed like a man who didn't need company, which was probably one of the reasons why he hadn't had a very talkative relationship with his wife. Still, most women accepted that men just weren't as conversational as they were.

Men spent a lot of time thinking about politics and inventions and how to make money.

Anyway, it pleased Nell that he was a bit more outgoing and showed interest in her little stories about her life before she was widowed. She didn't have any children. She pointed out quite frankly that her late husband's serious war wound, which happened in France when they'd only been married a month, was responsible for that. But he'd made up for it by being a real love, and they'd had some happy times together.

'Well, you sort of spread happiness, Nell,' said Herbert. 'Not having children hasn't made you sour. People like you are worth a lot to mankind.'

'Well, bless me,' said Nell, 'what a cultivated thing to say, worth a lot to mankind.'

'Cultivated?' said Herbert.

'Yes, like you were very educated,' said Nell. Herbert smiled. 'That's it, put a smile on, Herbert. Life's treated you hard lately, and I like a man that can stand up to the kind of knocks you've had. And nothing's going to bring poor Hilda back.'

'It's hard to believe she's gone,' said Herbert.

'You'll get over it,' said Nell, 'specially as you'd already lost her. Well, you had, the day she walked out on you.'

'You're probably right,' said Herbert, 'she probably wouldn't have come back ever, but I'd still like to know exactly how she came to die in her bath.'

'Oh, won't you have to wait for the inquest to find out?' asked Nell.

'It looks like it,' said Herbert. 'By the way, about your uncle – '

'Oh, I went and saw him and put that off for a bit,' said Nell. 'Well, you need a friend just now more than he needs a housekeeper. You've always been a friend to me, Herbert. All that nice relationship we enjoyed in the shop means a lot to me. It helped to keep me going and it more than paid me rent. And it told me you're a kind man, even if you didn't say a lot. So I'm not going to housekeep for me uncle yet. I want to do more thinking about it.'

'Well, I appreciate having you around to talk to,' said Herbert. 'Did you know you dress very nice, Nell?'

'It's pleasing to hear you say so, I'm sure,' said Nell. 'I don't have much to spend on clothes, so I take care with what I do buy. You dress very tidy and respectable yourself, and that must've pleased Hilda a bit.'

'More like she saw me as a doorpost in a suit,' said Herbert.

'Oh, Lor',' said Nell, and put her teacup back in its saucer with a rattle.

'What's wrong?' asked Herbert.

'You saying what you did. It nearly made me forget respect for the dead.'

'Did it?' said Herbert.

'Yes, it nearly made me laugh,' said Nell, 'and that would've been disrespectful, wouldn't it?'

'Oh, I don't know,' said Herbert, 'it's not like chortling at a funeral. Now that would be very disrespectful.' He sounded so droll that Nell smiled, even if it was Hilda's funeral they were both thinking about.

'Well, somehow we've cheered up a bit,' she said.

'Nell, let's talk some more,' said Herbert.

'I'll be pleased to,' said Nell.

'Good,' said Herbert.

They talked some more, and in quite earnest fashion, until they were interrupted by a double knock on the street door.

'That's someone for me,' said Nell, getting up. 'Probably me neighbour Mrs Parsons. She's always popping in to borrow some tea or sugar.'

It wasn't Mrs Parsons, however. It was Madge and Winnie. They asked if their father was here. Nell said yes, he was, and she also said how terrible sorry she was about their mother's death. Would they like to come up and see their dad? He'd suffered shocking hard blows just recent, poor man.

'Yes, that's why we've come, to see how he is,' said Winnie.

'It's all very sad,' said Nell, 'you must be suffering yourselves.'

'Very much, Mrs Binns,' said Madge.

'Come on up,' said Nell kindly, 'I've been doing what I can to help your dad in his grieving.'

They went up, and Herbert came to his feet when he saw his daughters.

'Nice of you to come,' he said, and Madge and Winnie fell on him then. Awkwardly he patted their shoulders. 'Know how you feel,' he said, 'it's hard for all the family.'

Madge eyed him in moist sorrow.

'We called at the house first,' she said, 'but as you weren't at home, I thought you might be here.'

'I'm needing someone to talk to these days,' said Herbert.

'Yes, we can see you've got someone,' said Winnie.

'You both know Mrs Binns,' said Herbert. 'She's an old friend.'

'Yes,' said Winnie.

'How are you girls?' asked Herbert.

'Awful,' said Madge.

'Oh, I'm so sorry for all of you,' said Nell, sympathetic enough to ignore slightly cold shoulders. 'It must be very hard to bear.'

'It is,' said Winnie.

'I still can't believe it,' said Madge.

'Mum of all people,' said Winnie.

'Yes, of all people,' said Herbert sombrely.

'We're not interrupting, are we?' said Madge.

'You can't think you are, not at a time like this,' said Herbert. 'I've been wanting to see you and Winnie. Olive and Roger have been to see me.'

'Yes, we know,' said Winnie.

'Sit down, everyone,' said Nell, 'and I'll make a fresh pot of tea.'

'It's all right,' said Madge, 'we—'

'They'll have some tea, Nell,' said Herbert, and Nell went into the kitchen, leaving him to his daughters.

'We had to come and see how you were bearing up, Dad,' said Winnie.

Herbert said it was a shaker of a lasting kind, and that it was going to take a long time for all of them to get over it. He'd had the police call on him again, but they hadn't been able to say exactly what caused their mother to die like she did.

Madge said it just had to be something like a heart attack, except the police had told Roger no, that her heart was sound.

'So Winnie and I thought perhaps she fell and hit her head as she got into the bath.'

'Wouldn't there have been a bruise?' asked Herbert, neat shirt cuffs peeping, suit tidy-looking, and his mane of hair well brushed.

'Madge went round to the station with Roger to ask the police about that,' said Winnie.

'We didn't get any satisfaction,' said Madge. 'The sergeant there thought a bruise wouldn't have been missed during the examination, but he's going to make enquiries and let us know tomorrow.'

'Still, wasn't there any suggestion that your mum might've drowned by some sort of accident?' asked Herbert.

'As far as I know, the police haven't made any suggestion like that,' said Madge. 'Roger mentioned they weren't certain about anything, and that we'd all have to wait for what comes out at the inquest.'

'Yes, I suppose we must,' said Herbert, 'and I suppose we've got to make certain arrangements.'

'What arrangements?' asked Madge.

'Well, it's got to be mentioned,' said Herbert, 'it's – ' He fell silent and tugged self-consciously at his tie.

Winnie and Madge looked at each other.

'Dad, what's got to be mentioned?' asked Madge.

Herbert cleared his throat.

'Your mother's funeral,' he said.

Madge bit her lip and Winnie sighed.

'I don't know when's the right time for a funeral, I haven't looked at any stars lately,' she said, and she and Madge sat down as Nell came in with the tea tray.

'Here we are,' said Nell, setting the tray down on a table. She poured the tea and handed round the cups and saucers.

Winnie told Herbert that the family didn't want him to take on the worry of arranging the funeral. Madge said the husbands would to see to everything, and that she'd do the funeral breakfast herself. Winnie said she'd help, and that their dad needn't do anything except order his own special wreath for the occasion.

Nell recognized that Madge and Winnie were leaving her out of the conversation. It was obvious they didn't approve of their father being here with her. It didn't upset her, she knew they were their mother's daughters, and that only Olive had any kind of a soft spot for him. She let them talk away and didn't attempt to butt in. Herbert took all they had to say in his quiet way, and only offered a few apologetic words when Winnie said he shouldn't have let their mother go and live by herself in that flat.

'Sorry about that, Winnie.'

The sisters didn't stay long after they'd finished their tea. Madge told Herbert it was a relief to know he wasn't actually ill with shock, and Winnie echoed that. Madge asked if there was anything he wanted doing. Herbert said he was managing all right at the moment, that he was taking his washing to the laundry and getting on fairly good terms with the gas cooker.

Of course, he said, they were only very little things compared to everything else.

Madge and Winnie said goodbye very politely to Nell, and it was Herbert who went down to the street door with them and saw them off.

'You'll have to keep in touch, Dad,' said Madge.

'I know,' said Herbert, 'we've all got to keep in touch, and we'll all have to go to the inquest. Anyway, thanks for coming to see me, and take care of yourselves.'

'Are you going home now, or staying here all night?' asked Madge bluntly.

Herbert took that without flinching.

'I'll be going home soon,' he said, and they said goodbye to him then. He went back up to Nell.

'They didn't like you being here,' she said.

'Natural under the circumstances, I suppose,' said Herbert.

'Never mind, it still did you a bit of good to have them come and see you,' said Nell.

'Glad you think so,' said Herbert.

'I do,' said Nell.

'Goodnight, then,' said Herbert.

'Goodnight, Herbert.'

On their bus ride back to Streatham, Winnie said to Madge, 'I wouldn't like to think Dad has taken up with that woman.'

'If he has,' said Madge, 'he's a lot deeper than I ever realized.'

'I suppose you never know with these quiet men,' said Winnie, 'even with one's own father. I was shocked finding he was with Mrs Binns only a few days after Mum passing on.'

'And he wasn't at all embarrassed,' said Madge. 'I meant to ask him about Mum's savings, but decided not to in front of Mrs Binns.'

'Still, he can't do anything with the savings while Roger's got the book under lock and key,' said Winnie.

'Dad couldn't even if he had the book,' said Madge. 'Mum's savings have to be legally released to him. But it's better for Roger and Olive to keep the book for the time being, just in case.'

'Don't forget to go to the police station tomorrow to find out if there were signs of Mum falling and hitting her head,' said Winnie.

'I won't forget,' said Madge.

'I know I keep on saying it, but I'll never believe she committed suicide by drowning herself,' said Winnie.

'It's the last thing she'd have done,' said Madge.

'Yes, she wasn't born under that kind of star,' said Winnie.

'Do you take stars to bed with you?' asked Madge fretfully.

'No, I've got Victor,' said Winnie. 'How about you with your cats?'

'Don't be funny,' said Madge, 'I'm not in the mood.'

Chapter Thirteen

Inspector Shaw pored over fingerprint specimens the following morning.

'There's any amount of the dead woman's prints, sir,' said Constable Stebbings.

'Don't state the obvious,' said Inspector Shaw. Although he'd put Sergeant Tomlinson in charge of the case, he didn't mean to be left out of it. 'Tell me who the others belong to.'

'No idea yet,' said Stebbings. 'There's a variety.'

'How long did you say she'd been living there, Sergeant Tomlinson?' asked the inspector.

'Since last Monday week,' said Sergeant Tomlinson.

'Then I don't suppose she'd done a lot of entertaining. Find out from her daughters if any of them visited, and ask if they'd like to be fingerprinted, anyway. And you'll have to get prints from Jones himself. I've got a feeling we might find some of his among these specimens.'

'Does that mean—' Sergeant Tomlinson

checked and decided not to ask if that meant the inspector was experiencing a spot of intuition and also an inclination to take charge, after all. 'Does it mean going to see Jones again, sir?'

'Sometime today or tomorrow,' said Inspector Shaw. 'First let's try to eliminate the possibility that Mrs Jones had a lover. Go to her place of work. You might pick up the right kind of gossip there.'

'Eliminating a lover puts Jones in the frame?' said Sergeant Tomlinson.

'It could, and never mind if you think it too obvious,' said the inspector. 'Get going, Sergeant.'

Sergeant Tomlinson smiled wryly, knowing his immediate superior was going to be breathing down his neck.

Miss Simmonds, the typist, knocked and entered the boss's office.

'Yes?' said Mr Richards from his desk.

'There's two policemen who'd like to see you, sir.'

'They're after checking on my criminal record, are they, Miss Simmonds?' said Mr Richards.

'I should hope not, Mr Richards.'

'All right, send them in.'

Sergeant Tomlinson presented himself in company with Constable Fry. They were making inquiries concerning the death of Mrs Jones, he said.

'What kind of inquiries?' asked Mr Richards, mystified.

'Formal inquiries, sir,' said Sergeant Tomlinson, his impressive self making its mark on the factory boss.

'I understood the unfortunate lady was found dead in her bath,' said Mr Richards.

'So she was, sir.'

'Heart attack?' said Mr Richards.

'Did someone tell you that, sir?'

'I think it's a rumour going round the factory,' said Mr Richards.

Sergeant Tomlinson said he was trying to satisfy himself about one or two things, and would like permission to interview anyone who had worked close to Mrs Jones. Mr Richards said that would be the typist and the invoice clerk. Mrs Jones had shared an office with them. Tomlinson said he'd like to interview them one at a time, and in private, if possible. Mr Richards asked if he wanted to interview them at their homes or here in the factory. The CID sergeant said he'd appreciate here and now, if Mr Richards had no objection to their work being interrupted. Mr Richards offered immediate use of his office, as he needed to talk to the foreman of one of the workshops, anyway.

'Very obliging of you, sir,' said Sergeant Tomlinson.

'Highly convenient,' said Constable Fry.

'I'll call in the typist, Miss Simmonds, first,' said Mr Richards, and did so. Then he left the young woman with the CID men. Miss Simmonds, in her late twenties, appeared neat and efficient in a white blouse and bow tie. She was quite personable in her looks, her high cheekbones nicely symmetrical.

'What d'you want to see me about?' she asked Sergeant Tomlinson.

'About Mrs Jones,' he said.

'Oh, that poor woman,' said Miss Simmonds.

'Yes, very sad,' said Sergeant Tomlinson. 'We'd like to know if she ever talked to you about her private life.'

Miss Simmonds seemed pleased to be invited to talk, and at once said Mrs Jones often spoke to her and to Miss Taylor, the invoice clerk, about her family. She always said nice things about her three daughters, but wasn't very complimentary about her husband. She once said that he'd never properly come alive from the day he was born, except where his shop was concerned. Sergeant Tomlinson thought that since he was the father of three daughters he must have woken up three times during his married life. Miss Simmonds said Mrs Jones always seemed a very alive person herself, and had told her and Miss Taylor several weeks ago that, as all her daughters were married and settled, she was going to leave her husband before she turned into a sort of cabbage. She was very set on that, and of course it had happened in the end, and she'd said several times since how happy she was as a free and independent woman. It was an awful shock to hear she'd died in her bath.

'Um, did she speak about friends sometimes?' asked Sergeant Tomlinson.

'She spoke about her neighbours sometimes,' said Miss Simmonds, 'and what a blessing it was to have them to talk to. She said her husband hardly ever talked himself, and hardly ever listened, either.'

'D'you know if she had any men friends?' asked Constable Fry.

'She never mentioned any,' said Miss Simmonds.

'I suppose even as a lively woman, she didn't strike you as the kind who'd have broken her marriage vows?' said Sergeant Tomlinson.

'I wouldn't know about that,' said Miss Simmonds.

'Well, thanks, that's all, Miss Simmonds,' said Sergeant Tomlinson. 'Would you ask Miss Taylor to come in?'

Miss Taylor was twenty-one, thin and earnest-looking. She said she was surprised that the police had come to ask questions, because she thought Mrs Jones had simply suffered a heart attack while taking a bath.

'Not quite,' said Sergeant Tomlinson, who

wondered how many more times he'd have to listen to people talking about a heart attack. It was putting him off the subject of cardiac arrest. 'Could you tell us what you know about her private life? That is, did she confide in you?'

Miss Taylor said Mrs Jones didn't actually confide any secrets, she just came out now and again with talk about her family. She liked talking about her daughters and their marriages. She had said her own marriage would have been a mistake if it hadn't given her three nice daughters. Her husband was a sort of nothing, she said once. Sergeant Tomlinson asked about the possibility that Mrs Jones made up for that by having a special man friend.

'She was a married woman,' said Miss Taylor a little huffily.

'Not happily married, though,' said Sergeant Tomlinson.

'Thought her old man a bit of a stuffy codger, didn't she?' said Constable Fry.

'But she was still a married woman,' said Miss Taylor, looking offended.

'So there was never any suggestion of – um – an affair?' said Sergeant Tomlinson.

'She'd lately joined the Stockwell Amateur Dramatic Society,' said Miss Taylor, 'and it seemed to me that that was all she wanted in the way of outside interests. She never ever said anything about having a special man friend.'

'Thank you, Miss Taylor,' said the sergeant.

'I can get back to my work now?' said Miss Taylor.

'Yes.'

Miss Taylor left.

'You satisfied?' asked Constable Fry.

'Are you, Sidney?' asked Sergeant Tomlinson.

'Well, what about a special bloke in the drama society?'

'That's a hell of a long shot,' said Sergeant Tomlinson, 'especially as neither Miss Simmonds nor Miss Taylor ever got the impression that Mrs Jones was interested in other men. That puts a dent in my suspicions about an unknown bloke. I suppose I've got to face the fact that although Jones looks too obvious to me, he did have a bloody good reason for at least giving his wife a smack in the mouth.'

'That and a bit more,' said Constable Fry.

'On the other hand, she might have had a good case,' said Sergeant Tomlinson.

'What's a good case?' asked Constable Fry.

'Twenty-five years with a block of wood, you dummy. All the same, even a block of wood can catch fire. That's something we've already considered.'

'And which I think is a genuine pointer,' said Constable Fry.

Mr Richards returned, curious about what these policemen were after exactly. Good God, were they delving into suspicious circumstances?

'Finished, Sergeant?' he said.

'Yes, and I'm obliged for your co-operation,' said Tomlinson.

'Has it helped?' asked Mr Richards.

'To a certain extent.'

'Well, if it's of interest to you,' said Mr Richards, 'our factory manager, Mr Burnside, might also be helpful. He knew Mrs Jones well. He had a lot to do with her in her work, and he helps run an amateur dramatic society which she recently joined. I presume you're trying to find out something about her social life, that you're not happy about the way she died. There was a notorious case once, wasn't there, concerning a man called Smith who married three times and all three brides suffered a mysterious death in the bath.'

'Very interesting case, I believe,' said Sergeant Tomlinson, 'but well before my time, of course. Let's see, Miss Taylor also mentioned that Mrs Jones joined an amateur dramatic society.'

'The Stockwell group,' said Mr Richards. 'Mr Burnside's the director.'

'Is it possible to talk to him while we're still here?' asked Sergeant Tomlinson.

'That's no problem,' said Mr Richards, and phoned through to Mr Burnside, who arrived a minute later from his own office. He was carrying a black ebony ruler. Handsome bloke, thought

Sergeant Tomlinson. Getting on a bit, but still looked energetic as well as distinguished.

'Hello, what's all this?' asked Mr Burnside.

Sergeant Tomlinson introduced himself and his colleague, and told the factory manager they were making inquiries concerning the late Mrs Jones. Mr Burnside's alert expression changed to a rueful grimace.

'Can't believe that lady died the way she did, in her bath,' he said, and grimaced again, like a man disgusted with the indiscriminate hand of fate. 'She enjoyed being alive.'

'But she didn't, apparently, enjoy being married,' said Sergeant Tomlinson. 'That is, not to Mr Jones.'

'Never knew the fellow,' said Mr Burnside, 'but she did mention he was a stick-in-the-mud. She left him, didn't she? Out of boredom, I believe.'

'She confided in you?' said Sergeant Tomlinson.

'Only to the extent of saying twenty-five years of marriage were more than enough for her,' said Mr Burnside, lightly smacking one hand with the ruler. 'I didn't go into it with her. We had only two common interests, our work and amateur dramatics. She was so keen about the dramatics that I invited her to join the society, the Stockwell Amateur Dramatic Society. She enrolled a few days after she left her husband.'

184

Mr Burnside tapped his chin with the ruler. 'Incredible that she's dead,' he said, frowning.

Still interested in the possible existence of another man, Sergeant Tomlinson asked, 'Did she know any members of your society before she enrolled?'

'Not to my knowledge,' said Mr Burnside. 'Certainly, when she enrolled, she never mentioned she knew anyone there. But I'm not able to give you a definite no. People's private lives are their own affair as far as I'm concerned. I know nothing about the private life of Mrs Jones, apart from her interest in amateur dramatics. Is there something about her death that needs investigating? Here, we all thought it must have been a heart attack.'

'Point is, sir, we need a fair bit of information about her for the inquest,' said Constable Fry.

'It wasn't a heart attack, then?' Mr Burnside looked curious. So did Mr Richards.

'Her heart was as sound as a bell,' said Sergeant Tomlinson. 'That's put us in the position of having to establish certain facts, sir. I take it Mrs Jones never dropped a hint to you that made you feel her reason for leaving her husband wasn't solely to do with his faults?'

'Was there another man, you mean?' said Mr Burnside. 'I've no idea. There might have been. Although she was over forty, she was still a good-looking woman, and might have been an asset to the society. When's the inquest, by the way?'

'In a week or so, probably,' said Sergeant Tomlinson. 'Well, I think that's all, Mr Burnside.'

'You've made me curious,' said Mr Burnside.

'I share that feeling,' said Mr Richards.

'So do we,' said Sergeant Tomlinson. 'We don't have many cases of healthy women drowning in a bath.'

'Not the sort of thing that happens every day,' said Constable Fry.

'Just as well,' said Mr Burnside, 'or women would stop taking baths.'

Sergeant Tomlinson thanked the men for their help and co-operation, and he and Constable Fry left.

'What the devil was that all about?' asked Mr Burnside.

'My guess is that they're investigating suspicious circumstances,' said Mr Richards.

'Not foul play, for God's sake,' said Mr Burnside.

'Well, why else would they come here asking questions?' said Mr Richards. 'From those they asked of you, I'd say they were trying to find out if Mrs Jones had a side to her social life that her husband probably didn't know about.'

'Mrs Jones? Rubbish,' said Mr Burnside.

In the general office, Miss Taylor was buzzing with curiosity about the questions the police had asked. She thought it meant there was something suspicious about the death of Mrs Jones, and she said so to Miss Simmonds. Miss Simmonds told her she was letting her imagination run away with her.

'Well, perhaps I am,' said Miss Taylor. 'Anyway, even if I wouldn't want to say so, I sometimes thought Mrs Jones a bit deep, didn't you?'

'I wonder exactly what Mr Burnside thought of her?' mused Miss Simmonds. 'They were jolly friendly at times.'

'That's not something we ought to talk about,' said Miss Taylor.

'Of course not,' said Miss Simmonds. 'We don't want to get Mr Burnside into trouble.'

The absence of a bath towel, the unworn bath cap and the missing nightdress had enabled Sergeant Tomlinson to convince Inspector Shaw it was worth looking at the possibility of murder. Inspector Shaw said he didn't like that word, and never had. It was only a possibility, said Sergeant Tomlinson who, after the factory interviews, hadn't changed his mind about Mrs Jones. He still doubted that she'd left her husband solely because she had had enough of his wooden image. Many husbands were dull and boring, and more than a few wives overdid their prattle. But the great majority did not walk out on each other. They soldiered on. Mrs Jones, however, had become one of the exceptions, and in leaving her husband she had perhaps made the fatal mistake of letting him know too crushingly that she had no time for him. Accordingly, if she had died by enforced drowning, the first reaction of any policeman would be to point himself at her better half as the most likely suspect.

But Sergeant Tomlinson wasn't going to discount the possibility of another man, a man who represented the final reason for Mrs Jones's wish to be free and independent.

On receiving the report of the factory interviews, Inspector Shaw put some questions.

'What did you make of the office women and the factory manager?' he asked.

'The women didn't offer much in the way of anything we didn't already know,' said Sergeant Tomlinson, 'but I couldn't see they had any reason to hold anything back. Unless – ' He paused.

'Well?' said the inspector.

'The factory manager,' said Sergeant Tomlinson.

'What about him?'

'Likeable bloke,' said Constable Fry.

'So's my milkman,' said the inspector.

'Burnside helped Mrs Jones to enrol in the dramatic society I mentioned,' said Sergeant Tomlinson.

'Was there something fishy about that, then?' asked Inspector Shaw.

'Not as far as I know,' said Sergeant Tomlinson, 'but it could have meant they were on very friendly terms, friendlier than he cared to admit.'

'That sounds like wishful thinking on your part, Sergeant,' said the inspector. 'Is the bloke – what did you say his name was?'

'Burnside.'

'Is he married?'

'I've no idea,' said Sergeant Tomlinson.

'Didn't you ask? No, you didn't, did you?'

'Well, married or not, women could still fancy him,' said Sergeant Tomlinson, 'especially a woman who had no fancy for her old man.'

'Yes, handsome bloke,' said Constable Fry, 'with middle-class articulation, you might say.'

'I wouldn't,' said the inspector. 'What's it mean?'

'Educated way of talking, sir. Some women go for that.'

'Like the unfortunate deceased?' said Inspector Shaw. 'You're trying to convince yourself she fancied Burnside?'

'I'm just offering information, sir.'

'Someone talking educated is information, is it?' said the inspector.

'Not quite, sir,' said Sergeant Tomlinson. 'I think Constable Fry is only suggesting Burnside might have been the type to impress Mrs Jones. Certainly, he could have been friendlier with her than he let on.'

'Just because he helped her enrol with the dramatic society?' said Inspector Shaw. 'It's another shot in the dark. Still, it won't hurt to find out if he's married and to get hold of his fingerprints. If he's been at Mrs Jones's flat at any time, they might match some of those that Stebbings found. But don't make him suspicious, or he might come up with a cast-iron alibi for the evening in question. I don't like cast-iron alibis, they get in the way.'

'Get hold of his fingerprints?' said Sergeant Tomlinson. 'Behind his back? That'll be easy, I don't think.'

'Up to you,' said Inspector Shaw. 'This afternoon, go and see Mrs Olive Way. Of the daughters, her address is the only one we have. Let her know we need fingerprints to clear the way to a satisfactory solution of her mother's death, those of herself, her husband, her sisters and their husbands. They've probably all visited Mrs Jones's flat. Ask her if she'll arrange for all of them to come to the station.'

'Could I get Constable Fry to do that, sir?' asked Sergeant Tomlinson.

'Why?'

'I'm feeling particularly sorry for Mrs Way.'

'Don't give me that sort of stuff,' said the inspector. 'You know her well by now. You go. Constable Fry can stay here and write up the notes of the factory interviews. As for Mr Jones, I think I'd like to take a look at him myself. Stebbings and his fingerprint equipment can come with me.'

'Are you taking charge, sir?' asked Sergeant Tomlinson.

'It's still your case, Sergeant, I've got too many other things on to do more than give you some help.'

Well, if it's my case, thought Sergeant Tomlinson, I'll have to watch that the clever old fox doesn't make the arrest, if that's what the investigation comes to eventually. To keep my end up means I've got to be right in assuming Mrs Jones didn't commit suicide, didn't drown herself by accident, but was held down under the water either by her husband or some unknown geezer. The inspector did point out originally that it looked like a two-man job, but somehow I can't go along with that.

Chapter Fourteen

'Sergeant Tomlinson?' The faint smile showed on Olive's face as she beheld the CID man on her doorstep.

'Sorry to bother you again, Mrs Way.'

'I hope it won't be a bothersome bother,' said Olive.

'I hope so too.'

'There's only me,' she said. 'My husband Roger is back at work. I've managed to recover and to cope with all that's on my mind. So do come in.'

He entered, taking off his hat and closing the door for her. She led the way into the cheerful-looking living room, where they faced each other, Olive's expression of an enquiring kind, while he looked hesitant. He was, in fact, extremely reluctant to harass her in the matter of fingerprints.

'Not more bad news, is it?' she said quietly.

'No, not at all,' he said reassuringly, 'it's just

192

that we're still trying to get a clear picture of circumstances.'

'I think you mean you're trying to find out if my mother's death wasn't an accident,' said Olive.

'What makes you say that?'

'You do,' said Olive, 'you and your frequent appearances.'

'Does it upset you, an inquiry into the circumstances?'

'Yes.'

'I'm sorry,' said Sergeant Tomlinson.

'Oh, I'm not being accusing,' said Olive. 'You can begin bothering me again. What do you want to ask me?'

He explained that he required to know who might have been with her mother that evening. Various fingerprints had been found, and it was necessary to determine whose they were. Olive, still quiet, said she understood, and could say that she and Roger had been there that evening, had visited before, and so had her sisters, but not their husbands. If anyone else had visited, that was outside her knowledge. Sergeant Tomlinson asked if she could arrange for herself, her husband and her sisters to call at the station and be fingerprinted. Olive said yes, very well.

'Well, thanks,' said Sergeant Tomlinson in relief.

'It didn't hurt too much, having to ask me that?' said Olive.

'Not too much.' He gave her a smile.

'You're a very human policeman,' she said. 'Would you like a cup of tea? I was just going to make one.'

'I won't say no, Mrs Way.'

'Then sit down, while I put the kettle on,' said Olive.

Over the tea, he found her composed and resilient, much as if she had forced herself to come to terms with the tragedy. The haunted look had gone from her fine eyes. She spoke of her mother and father without any hint of breaking down. She was rueful, not tearful. He suspected she had shed an ocean at some stage, but she was in courageous control of herself now. She said how very silly it was of her parents to have come to a parting of the ways, that both of them had been old enough to realize they should have talked their way through their differences. Sergeant Tomlinson wanted to suggest it perhaps wasn't those differences that had caused the break, but something else. An affair. But he kept quiet, of course.

'Heavens,' said Olive after a while, 'I'm doing all the talking, and being tedious, probably.'

'Don't you believe it,' he said, 'but I'd better push off now. Can't thank you enough for the tea.'

'Have you seen my father since you last saw me?' she asked.

'Yes.'

'Is he bearing up?'

'He's a solid man, Mrs Way.'

'Too solid for Mum,' said Olive, then winced a little. 'It's still incredible,' she said, and he thought she looked wistful again, as if she would have given much to recapture the calm of unworried days.

'We'll see you and your husband and sisters at the police station as soon as you can arrange it?' he said.

'Fingerprints? Oh, dear,' she said. 'Yes, I'll do the arranging. Roger will help to get us all there together.'

'That'll be a great help, Mrs Way.'

'I still hope you'll find it was an accident. Goodbye again, Sergeant Tomlinson.'

'Well?' demanded Madge of the desk sergeant.

'Ah, yes,' he said.

'Yes what?' said Madge, who had fought all her demons and come out on top. She was almost aggressive in her approach.

'Your enquiry concerning the post-mortem. Miss – '

'Mrs Mrs Cooper.'

'Ah, yes. Mrs Cooper. Right. I can confirm no head bruises were found, no signs that the deceased had a fall.'

'Are you positive, Sergeant?'

'The pathologist is, Mrs Cooper, and he's not known for making mistakes. It wouldn't do, y'know, for anything to be overlooked during a post-mortem examination.'

'Then how did my mother come to drown in her own bath?'

'Ah, well – '

'It's not ah well.'

'I mean it's not for me to say, Mrs Cooper, it's for the coroner.'

'Don't you police know anything?'

'I can't say.'

'Sergeant, you're useless.'

'That's what me wife tells me occasional, Mrs Cooper.'

'Your wife is very discerning, then. Good afternoon.'

Herbert was not amused by the visit of Inspector Shaw and Constable Stebbings, but neither was he put out. He accepted the inspector's explanation that it was necessary to establish certain facts, which meant they wanted to find out who had visited the flat and could do so by examining fingerprints.

'Well, I didn't visit,' said Herbert, 'I had to wait to be invited.'

'You mean your wife discouraged you from arriving uninvited?' said the inspector.

'Yes, I do mean that,' said Herbert.

'She didn't give you a key?'

'No,' said Herbert, and the inspector thought that pointed to the possibility that his wife didn't want to risk him turning up at a time when he wasn't welcome. When she had someone with her?

'Do you mind being fingerprinted, Mr Jones?'

'I'll mind if it means I'm suspected of doing what I'm not capable of doing,' said Herbert. 'It's not in my nature to be violent. Never hit a woman in my life, nor wouldn't, nor couldn't. If I'd wanted to get my own back on Hilda for what she did to me, which ruined my self-respect, I'd have chosen my own way, which wouldn't have cost her her life.'

Here was a man, thought Inspector Shaw, who according to Sergeant Tomlinson had been seen by his wife as an inarticulate lump, but who had just come out with a bellyful of words and made each one count. Not that his protestations of innocence could be taken at face value. He was probably deeper than his wife had thought. Quiet men could be dangerous men. Mrs Binns had given him an alibi. What was that worth? On the other hand, exactly why didn't his wife want him to turn up unless she invited him?

Sergeant Tomlinson's feeling that there was another man in the frame seemed to make a little more sense now.

'I appreciate all you say, Mr Jones, and I hope you appreciate we're simply trying to work things out for the benefit of all concerned.'

'You can have my fingerprints,' said Herbert, 'and if it won't take too long I'll have time for an afternoon walk.'

It didn't take long at all, after which the inspector left with Stebbings, and Herbert took his walk. Round to Nell's.

'What a liberty, Herbert,' she said, when told the police had fingerprinted him. 'Well, blow them, I say. They're being terrible suspicious, which is daft considering I told them you were with me. Would you like a nice cup of tea?'

'Yes, I would, Nell, thanks.'

'Oh, you're very welcome, Herbert.'

'So Mum definitely didn't have a fall as she was getting into her bath?' said Olive.

'If she did,' said Madge, who had called to give Olive the negative answer from the police, 'there weren't any bruises.'

'So it really does look like suicide?'

'It might look like it, but nobody who knew Mum is going to believe it,' said Madge. 'Hell, if I have to say that one more time, I'll go cuckoo.'

'It simply must have been some kind of accident,' said Olive, and then told her sister of Sergeant Tomlinson's request for fingerprints.

Madge took a poor view of that, saying the police were out of their minds. Olive said she thought the police had an idea that the death wasn't an accident.

'That's horrendous,' said Madge, 'I can't even put words to the implications.'

'Try,' said Olive.

'My God,' said Madge, 'if they should want Dad's fingerprints too, think what that means.'

'It means they want to find out if his finger-prints are in the flat,' said Olive, and Madge stared at her.

'What are they after, for God's sake?' she asked,

'That someone drowned Mum in her bath,' said Olive.

'Did that swine of a Sergeant Tomlinson say so?' demanded Madge, horrified.

'No,' said Olive, 'and I don't think he's a swine. He was embarrassed in having to ask me to arrange for us to be fingerprinted.'

'Embarrassed?' Madge was caustic. 'Is there such a thing as a policeman suffering embarrass-ment?'

'Well, there's Sergeant Tomlinson,' said Olive.

'Olive, don't talk like a crazy woman,' said Madge. 'You're not accepting this implication that Mum's death wasn't an accident or, at the worst, suicide, are you?'

'I've just told you it must have been an accident,'

said Olive, 'and I'm not accepting anything else until the inquest.'

'Why are you so calm about it?' asked Madge. 'I'm seething.'

'I don't actually feel calm,' said Olive, 'I feel lost. Madge, I think Mum was having an affair.'

'What?'

'I've thought and thought about how determined she was to leave Dad and live her own life,' said Olive. 'Dad may have been a quiet and unexciting husband, but he never let her down, and as our father he never let us down, either. We were all a bit hard on him when we went along with Mum's complaints, we all told him he was the one mostly at fault. But I still felt Mum was out of order, that it was a bit much walking out on him the way she did. Now I think it was because she was having an affair, which could have been the main reason why she wanted her own place.'

'Having an affair?' said Madge. 'Mum, at her age? She was over forty.'

'But very well preserved, and still attractive,' said Olive.

'How can you think such things about your own mother?' asked Madge furiously.

'Only because I've given everything a lot of thought,' said Olive. 'Why, for instance, did she make it clear to Dad that he was never to visit her unless she invited him? Dad must have considered that the final insult. It was like being treated as a servant.'

'My God,' breathed Madge, 'are you trying to say that that made him mad enough to – to – '

'No, I'm not,' said Olive, 'because I don't believe Dad would ever get as mad as that. What I am saying is that because Mum didn't die from a sudden heart attack, the police are wondering exactly how it happened and looking suspiciously at Dad.'

'Did he have a key to the flat?' asked Madge.

'You know he didn't,' said Olive, 'you know Mum told us she wasn't going to give him one. That's another thing I've thought about, and it seemed to me it was another way of Mum making sure that, if Dad did turn up at any time, he couldn't actually get into the flat.'

'Olive, you're off your head,' said Madge. 'It must be the shock, it's made you lose your senses. Well, you were the most upset of all of us. For God's sake don't talk like this to Winnie, she'll faint. Look, we'll all go along to the police station tomorrow afternoon, Saturday, when Roger is home from his job, and after that we won't give the police any more help or co-operation. Let them work on the basis that it was some kind of accident. You're not to talk to Sergeant Tomlinson any more, is that clear?'

'I'll help Dad in any way I can,' said Olive,

'even if it means I'll have to put up with Sergeant Tomlinson calling every day.'

'Well, if he calls on me and Brian,' said Madge, 'he'll hear things he won't like.'

'That won't help,' said Olive.

'It'll help me, I'll tell you that,' said Madge. 'I'm going to see Winnie now, to let her know about the fingerprinting, and I just hope she won't be stargazing in the same way that you've been dreaming.'

'Request from Muscles Boddy,' said Warder Phillips to Chief Warder Brookes of Brixton Prison.

'What request?'

'To be let out for the evening.'

'Eh?'

Warder Phillips grinned.

'Says he's got to play in a darts match.'

'Is that a fact?'

'He missed out on the last one, he says, and he's sweating on making this one.'

'Don't make me spit iron filings,' said Chief Warder Brookes. 'Let him sweat.'

Inspector Shaw and Sergeant Tomlinson compared notes. The inspector's concerned his interview with Herbert Jones, which had revealed the man to be quietly but intensely resentful of his late wife's treatment of him. Yes, he could have been angry enough with her to consider doing her in. Another point to consider was that much of what he said emphasized a determination on the part of his wife to keep him out of her new way of life. Why? Because she was carrying on with some other bloke? Now, who was the more likely to do her in, a wronged husband or a lover with a mental kink who got some kind of queer satisfaction from drowning a woman in her bath?

'Have you stopped thinking it took two persons?' asked Sergeant Tomlinson.

'All right, I'll go along with one,' growled the inspector. 'Two would have been a bit of a crowd.'

'I can't help thinking a woman with an unexciting husband and a starved body might go off her head and take a lover,' said Sergeant Tomlinson.

'Along with her own flat?' said the inspector.

'Just a thought, sir.'

'Fair, Sergeant, fair. I'll accept the possibility that she kept open house for a lover while making sure her husband couldn't walk in on her.'

'Well, I favour that myself,' said Sergeant Tomlinson.

Inspector Shaw pointed out it was possible that, when she told her husband in no uncertain terms why she was leaving him, she could have included a confession that she had a lover.

Sergeant Tomlinson suggested she'd have kept quiet about that, otherwise her husband would have mentioned it during one of the interviews, wouldn't he? And she wouldn't have wanted her daughters to know. She seemed to have had a good relationship with them, the kind she'd have wanted to preserve. Her youngest daughter Olive certainly wouldn't have liked being told, and her mother wouldn't have wanted her to find out. He'd bet she hadn't been given a key, nor her sisters.

'Are you talking about Mrs Olive Way?' asked Inspector Shaw.

'Yes.'

'The daughter you weren't keen to interview about fingerprinting?'

'Yes,' said Sergeant Tomlinson.

'Are you soft in the head about her, Sergeant Tomlinson?'

'No, sir. I simply feel sympathetic.'

'Don't be bloody silly, man. What happened during your interview with her?'

'Nothing spectacular,' said Sergeant Tomlinson. 'She agreed without any fuss to arrange for herself and her husband, and her sisters, to come along to the station to have their fingerprints taken.'

'When?'

'As soon as possible.'

'You didn't suggest to her that we're very

interested in the possibility of murder?' said Inspector Shaw.

'Was I supposed to?' asked Sergeant Tomlinson.

'Did you mention it?'

'No. But she guessed we're not satisfied that it was suicide or accidental drowning. It upset her without making her break down.'

'Perhaps that young lady knows more about her mother's social life than you think,' said Inspector Shaw. 'Now, what about that factory manager, name of Burnside? Have you found out if he's married or not?'

'Not yet, but would it make any difference, one way or the other?' said Sergeant Tomlinson. 'I mean, either he was the lover or he wasn't.'

'I like to know everything, and so should you,' said Inspector Shaw. 'Get hold of his fingerprints tomorrow. Use your initiative. You've got your share of that.'

Sergeant Tomlinson asked what had happened concerning the fingerprints taken of Herbert Jones. Had they matched any found in the flat? Inspector Shaw sat up, came to his feet, walked to the door of his office, opened it and bawled for Stebbings. A relay of shouts took place, and Stebbings appeared after a while.

'Want me, sir?' he asked.

'I want the results of the check on Jones's fingerprints, don't I?' growled the inspector.

'I was about to come and see you,' said Stebbings. 'I wasn't able to match them with any found in the flat proper, sir.'

'What the hell d'you mean, the flat proper?' asked the inspector.

'Around it, sir. There's none of Jones's fingerprints on the furniture, door handles and suchlike,' said Stebbings. 'But I did find some on the luggage trunk that stood beside the bedroom wardrobe. I've just matched them with those we took from him.'

'The luggage trunk?' said the inspector.

'Yes,' said Stebbings.

'Is that helpful?' asked the inspector.

'You tell me, sir,' said Stebbings.

'It's not too helpful,' said Sergeant Tomlinson. 'We couldn't make a case out of prints on a luggage trunk. They could easily have been there before the trunk arrived at the flat.'

'My advice to you, Sergeant, is to hang on for the time being to the fact that they were there,' said Inspector Shaw.

'If we're going to produce a decent case against Jones, we've got to place him at the flat on the evening in question,' said Sergeant Tomlinson. 'I put it to you, sir, fingerprints on a luggage trunk would add up to sweet Fanny Adams in court, wouldn't they?'

'Damn it, man, you've either got to eliminate him from your inquiries or go for him,' said

Inspector Shaw, his familiar growl roughing up his tonsils. 'Eliminate him, and that leaves you looking for your unknown party. Or with the unfortunate party, the woman who took a bath, forgot to put her bath cap on, forgot to take a towel with her, mislaid her nightdress and was subsequently found drowned. Which points to premeditated suicide, or would do if there hadn't been a tablet of soap in the bath with her.'

'And if she had good reason for suicide,' said Sergeant Tomlinson. 'Oh, well, outside of her husband, a possible unknown party might get to be known if I can dig deep enough.'

Chapter Fifteen

'Roger, I'm going to see Dad,' said Olive after supper that evening.

'Good idea,' said Roger. 'I expect the old boy's well down in the dumps. Like me to come with you?'

'No, you put your feet up and listen to the wireless,' said Olive.

'By the way,' said Roger, 'find out if your dad has got to be fingerprinted, the same as us and your sisters.'

'Yes, it's food for thought, isn't it?' said Olive.

'Not the kind I like,' said Roger. 'Still, if it's going to help the police make up their minds about what might have happened just prior to your mother taking her bath, who's grumbling?'

'I'm wondering, not grumbling,' observed Olive, who had kept to herself most of what she had said to Madge. 'And I'll ask Dad if the police want his fingerprints too. I should have asked Sergeant Tomlinson while he was here.'

'That bloke's turning into your shadow,' said Roger. 'Talk about a dogged copper, he's that all right.'

'Perhaps dogged coppers get the best results,' said Olive, putting her hat on. 'Well, I'm off now, Roger.'

'Give my regards to your dad,' said Roger, relieved that Olive had recovered so well from the terrible shock, and saying nothing about where he thought fingerprinting was leading. 'Tell him I'm on his side.'

'He'll appreciate that,' said Olive. She gave her husband a kiss and left.

When Herbert answered a knock on his front door and found his youngest daughter on the step, he smiled.

'Well, this is pleasing, Olive.'

'How are you, Dad?'

'All the better for seeing you,' said Herbert, and stepped aside as she entered. 'You don't shout at me like Madge does.'

'Now, Dad, Madge doesn't shout, she's just got a strong contralto voice,' said Olive, and kissed him.

'Then there's Winnie and her thing about stars,' said Herbert.

'You're bucking up a bit, aren't you?' said Olive, going into the living room with him.

'Well, Olive, no-one can say I wasn't fond of

your unfortunate mum,' said Herbert, 'nor that her death didn't poleaxe me. But knowing, as I do now, that I didn't mean very much to her, except as someone providing her with house-keeping money, I can't sit and grieve over her. I'm sorry her life got cut off only a short time after she'd begun to properly enjoy herself, and I'm sorry for her generally, as I would be for any woman who had to pay as she did for being free. But I hope you'll forgive me, Olive, for the limitations of me grief.'

'Dad, none of that could be called nice,' said Olive.

'Sorry about that,' said Herbert.

'And after all these years of being a quiet man, you've begun to make speeches,' said Olive.

'Sorry about that as well, Olive. Has what I've just said hurt your feelings?'

'Yes, Dad. I'm still grieving for Mum myself, even if you aren't.'

'Well, you would be, Olive, you've always been a nice caring girl,' said Herbert.

'Even if I did take you for granted as a providing father?' said Olive with a little smile.

'Could you forget I said that?' asked Herbert.

'I understood why you did at the time,' said Olive, thinking he was still quite personable. It was strange, that, her mother so well preserved in her looks and her father still a fine figure of a man, yet they didn't have enough in common to prevent the separation, a fatal separation. 'Dad, have the police asked for your fingerprints?'

'They took them earlier today,' said Herbert.

'Did you ask them why?'

'Didn't need to, Olive, did I?' Herbert frowned. 'It's obvious they suspect I could have done it.'

'Done what?' asked Olive painfully.

'Seen your mother off for doing me down after twenty-five years,' said Herbert.

'Dad, oh my God, don't talk like that,' breathed Olive.

'That's what they're after, Olive, death in suspicious circumstances, as is said, with me as the prime suspect.'

'Well, I don't believe it,' said Olive, 'and I certainly don't believe you'd ever think about even harming a cat. You're not to speak like that. You didn't ever go to the flat, did you?'

'I wasn't ever to go unless your mum invited me,' said Herbert. 'Would you like a cup of Camp?'

'I'll make it,' said Olive.

'No, you won't. You do your share of chores, looking after Roger,' said Herbert, 'and you've had a bad week. You sit down and I'll see to it. I like it that you're here.'

'It's so strange, the way you've come out of your shell, Dad.'

'Well, I had to, didn't I, the day your mum left

211

and no-one was talking at me. I didn't like the silence. You know how everyone is comfortable with what's familiar. Won't be a minute with the coffee, Olive.'

Over the coffee, Olive came out with the information that her mother's savings book had been found in the flat. Herbert said he was glad to hear it, that he didn't want it to be wandering about for anyone to pick up. Olive said the savings were very high, amounting to nearly nine hundred pounds. Herbert said that proved what he'd always thought, that her mum had been a very good manager and able because of that to put money regularly into her Post Office account. Pity she hadn't lived to enjoy it, he said. Olive said she supposed it all belonged to him now.

Herbert shook his head.

'I don't want it,' he said.

'Dad?' said Olive.

'Having sold the shop, I'm not in need,' said Herbert. 'When the legalities have been sorted out, I'll see to it that you girls each get an equal share.'

So much, thought Olive, for Madge's insistence on keeping the thing dark from Dad, and Roger's agreement to that.

'You could have your own share, Dad,' she said. 'After all, I daresay the best part of the amount has come from you over the years.'

'No, once I handed your mum's allowance

to her every week, it was hers,' said Herbert, 'never mind where it came from. Fair's fair in a marriage, Olive. There's just one thing. I'd want each of you girls to start your own savings accounts, to have money that was all your own, like your mum had. It's good for women to have something at the back of them. That doesn't mean I've got anything against Roger or my other sons-in-law, only that I'd like all you girls to regard the money as your own. What d'you think?'

'I think I'm sad that you and Mum parted in the way you did,' said Olive, eyes just a little moist.

'All over now, Olive,' said Herbert. 'I've had my say about all that, and more than once these last two weeks, and that's the end as far as I'm concerned. I'll just remember her from now on as a good wife to me and an affectionate mother to you girls. I don't suppose any man could ask for more in a whole twenty-five years.'

Olive let go a few tears then, which embarrassed Herbert very much.

'Hello, love, how did it go?' asked Roger when Olive arrived home.

'Oh, the police took Dad's fingerprints today,' said Olive. 'He thinks they've got some idea that fingerprinting the whole family is going to clear up any mystery.'

'I bet they've got that idea all right,' said Roger. 'Is your dad worried at all?'

'Well, you know Dad, solid as the Rock of Gibraltar,' said Olive.

'Pity your mum wasn't an admirer of the Rock of Gibraltar,' said Roger.

'Roger, that remark was out of place,' said Olive.

'Well, excuse me, sweetie,' said Roger, 'but we could have a little bit of light relief now and again, couldn't we?'

'I'm dreading the funeral,' said Olive.

'Yes, when are the police going to release the body to the undertakers?' enquired Roger.

'We'll ask tomorrow, at the station,' said Olive.

'By the way,' said Roger, 'did your dad think to ask about your mum's savings book?'

'No, he didn't ask,' said Olive.

'Well, that helps us to keep quiet about it,' said Roger.

Madge and Brian were with Winnie and Victor, and Madge was carrying on furiously about all Olive had said to her in the afternoon. Winnie said as soon as it was dark she'd go and look at the stars. Brian asked what good that would do, and Winnie said it would make her feel more at peace with things. Victor said it wouldn't alter the fact that something odd was running about in the minds of the police. Madge said they want their heads examined, then, and as for Olive, she's gone strange. The sooner the inquest is over, she said, the better for everyone.

Sergeant Tomlinson entered the factory at ten the next morning. He avoided the general office with a sign inviting callers to knock. Running into a man in overalls, he stopped him.

'Where's Mr Burnside's office?' he asked. 'I need to see him.'

'Turn left just up there,' said the factory worker, 'and his is the first office on the right.'

'Ta,' said Sergeant Tomlinson, hatless and in a well-worn suit. 'By the way, is he married?'

'Hold on, what d'you want to know for? Got a sister who's looking for him?'

'You could say it's more to do with insurance than my sister.'

'Well, he ain't married, I can tell you that. Except to his amateur dramatics.'

'Not my line of country,' said Sergeant Tomlinson, and went on before the worker became curious about him. He found the office. It was marked 'FACTORY MANAGER'. He knocked, opened the door, and put his head in. The office was empty. He went in. He was out again in a matter of seconds. On his return to the station, he handed Constable Stebbings a black ebony ruler and told him to test it for fingerprints.

Then he went to see Inspector Shaw, to put him in the picture.

Growls were heard.

'You did what, Sergeant Tomlinson?'

'Used my initiative, sir.'

'You were well out of order. You don't enter private premises or business premises in order to do a bit of thievery, you announce yourself and ask for what you want.'

'My mistake, guv, but I thought you recommended doing it on the quiet,' said Sergeant Tomlinson. 'The idea being not to put Burnside on his guard.'

'I don't recall recommending an action that's against lawful procedure,' said Inspector Shaw.

'It seemed too good an option to turn down,' said Sergeant Tomlinson.

'If there's a complaint, don't expect my support,' said the inspector with another growl. 'Just phrase your report with care. So, Burnside's not married and you've brought back one of his rulers. Pleased with yourself?'

'Not yet,' said Sergeant Tomlinson. 'I'm waiting on Stebbings.'

The wait wasn't long. Stebbings arrived speedily.

'Well?' said the inspector.

'Prints on a certain ruler, sir, match several found in the flat.'

'Were any of those found in the bedroom?'

'Yes, a set of three prints on the mantelpiece,' said Stebbings. 'Might've got out of the bed feeling a bit weak, and held onto the mantelpiece for a couple of secs.'

'That's all your own work, that theory?' said the inspector.

'Yes, all my own work, sir,' said Stebbings.

Sergeant Tomlinson thought developments were suddenly working in favour of Herbert Jones. If they cleared him, his daughters would be spared more trauma.

'So Burnside visited Mrs Jones, and has been in her bedroom,' mused Inspector Shaw. 'Well, there are no signs that Jones was ever there, if we forget about the luggage trunk, and that puts Burnside in the lead. The factory operates on Saturday mornings, I suppose. Go down and commandeer a car, Tomlinson, and wait for me. Stebbings, you'll come as well.'

The old goat, thought Sergeant Tomlinson, he's taking over after all, never mind that it's my teeth that have been stuck into the roughest side of the investigation.

Five minutes later they were driving to the factory, and shortly after their arrival the inspector and Sergeant Tomlinson received permission from a wondering Mr Richards to interview Mr Burnside in the factory manager's office, while Stebbings remained in the car, his equipment with him.

Mr Burnside wasn't in the least happy at being asked to answer a few more questions, or to know that one of the CID men was a detective inspector.

'Damn it,' he said, 'what's the idea?'

'Something's come up, sir,' said Sergeant Tomlinson.

'And what's that?'

'Nothing we can't clear up with a little help, Mr Burnside,' said Inspector Shaw.

'And quickly, I hope,' said Mr Burnside. 'I'm busy.'

'Sorry and all that,' said Sergeant Tomlinson, 'but did you ever visit Mrs Jones after she moved into her flat in Stockwell Road?'

Mr Burnside, looking irritated, said, 'I saw her home after her first evening with the society.'

'Did you go up to the flat with her?' asked the inspector.

'No.'

'There was no occasion when you were in the flat?' said Sergeant Tomlinson.

'None.'

'You're sure, sir?' said Sergeant Tomlinson.

'Of course I'm sure.'

'That's odd,' said the inspector.

'Odd? Why?'

'We found your fingerprints here and there, sir,' said Sergeant Tomlinson.

'Bloody rubbish. You can't know they're mine.'

'Well, to confirm it, would you mind if we took yours now, sir?' said the inspector. 'It can be done here, or at the station.'

'Now look here,' said Mr Burnside, 'what's the point, anyway? What have I got to do with what happened to Mrs Jones, whether I visited her or not?'

'Well, you'll understand we'd like to know if anyone was with her on the evening she was found drowned in her bath,' said Sergeant Tomlinson.

'Why?' Mr Burnside wasn't giving an inch.

'We've reason to believe her death wasn't by suicide or accident,' said the inspector.

'Never heard such rot,' said Mr Burnside. 'Push off.'

There was a knock on his office door, and Mr Richards put his head in.

'Could you spare a moment, Inspector?' he asked.

'Take them both away,' said Mr Burnside, 'they're off their heads.'

'I don't think I can do that,' said Mr Richards, 'just hang on.'

His head withdrew and Inspector Shaw joined him in the corridor.

'Something to tell me, Mr Richards?'

'Miss Taylor, our invoice clerk, has,' said Mr Richards, 'and she'd like to talk to Sergeant Tomlinson in private. She heard Mr Burnside was being interviewed again. She's in my office, and particularly asked for your sergeant.'

'I'll send him along,' said the inspector.

'If you could hurry things up, Inspector, I'd appreciate it. There's a buzz going round the factory.'

'We'll do our best, sir,' said Inspector Shaw.

Miss Taylor, waiting for Sergeant Tomlinson, looked nervously at him when he arrived.

'Oh, good morning, Sergeant,' she said.

'Morning, Miss Taylor. I believe you want to talk to me.'

'Well, yes, I do, I feel I must,' she said.

'Go ahead,' he said encouragingly, 'I'm listening.'

Miss Taylor said she and Miss Simmonds both knew Mr Burnside had been thick with Mrs Jones, but hadn't wanted to get him into trouble, not when the poor woman had died like that, in her bath. Miss Simmonds especially didn't want to say much about Mr Burnside, as she had a soft spot for him. In fact, she'd been a bit jealous of Mrs Jones, even if she was over forty. Anyway, the day before Mrs Jones died she spent quite a bit of time looking through some files. Miss Simmonds asked her what she was doing, and she said just a bit of checking. Well, said Miss Taylor, the files contained copies of dockets, factory order dockets, and the way Mrs Jones went through them made her curious, especially as Mr Burnside was in the habit of getting Mrs Jones to make out dockets for orders he received over the phone. Or said he did. Miss Taylor then remembered they were usually for a firm called Timms, so because she was curious she did some checking herself, and soon realized there wasn't one copy of any of those dockets on either file, which meant no invoices had been made out against them. Invoices were usually made out the day after the docket copies were placed in her in-tray by Mrs Jones. There were always a lot, and Miss Taylor said she simply never noticed that dockets for Timms weren't among them. There were so many firms and every kind of name. But once she'd done her own checking of the files, it did occur to her that she'd never made out a single invoice for any Timms orders during the last few months.

She spoke to Mrs Jones about it the next day, and Mrs Jones said not to worry, she'd sorted it out with Mr Burnside, and he was going to put things right.

'Why didn't you mention this to me when I interviewed you yesterday?' asked Sergeant Tomlinson.

'Oh, just because I didn't want to get Mr Burnside into trouble,' said Miss Taylor, 'he's always been very nice and helpful. Miss Simmonds felt the same. Well, I told her what I'd found out, and she'd said to keep it to ourselves. Mind, that day, the day after, Mr Burnside seemed to be as dark as thunder, but Mrs Jones looked pleased with herself. It was awful later on to realize it was the last day of her life.' Miss Taylor went on to say she'd been worrying about it since she'd been interviewed, and when she heard Mr Burnside was being interviewed again, she decided she had to speak out. Miss Simmonds didn't want to, she still didn't want to get Mr Burnside into trouble.

Sergeant Tomlinson reflected. Burnside had been doing some fiddling and Mrs Jones had found out and spoken to him? It made him as dark as thunder? Had he decided to silence Mrs Jones? Would he do that just to make sure she didn't talk about some petty fiddling of his?

'Well, I'm obliged to you, Miss Taylor.'

'Have I done right?' asked the nervous invoice clerk.

'Of course you have. Just one point. When you spoke about Mr Burnside being thick with Mrs Jones, d'you know how thick?'

'Pardon?'

'Bluntly, Miss Taylor, were they having an affair?'

'Oh, I really don't know about that,' said Miss Taylor, slightly flushed. 'Is – is it all getting serious, Sergeant?'

'It's something that needs clearing up,' said Sergeant Tomlinson. 'Thanks very much for your help, I really am obliged.'

He returned to the factory manager's office. Mr Burnside was sitting at his desk, looking like a man whose patience was being sorely tried. Inspector Shaw glanced at his sergeant and nodded to let him know he could have the floor.

'Now what?' said Mr Burnside.

'Have you decided to let us fingerprint you, sir?' asked Sergeant Tomlinson.

'All right, get on with it,' said Mr Burnside.

'Get Stebbings, Sergeant,' said the inspector, and Tomlinson left the office to go and wake up Stebbings.

'I really don't know what you expect to get out of this farce,' said Mr Burnside.

'A few facts,' said Inspector Shaw.

'Concerning what?' asked Mr Burnside.

'The death of the late Mrs Jones, a friend of yours, sir. Can I assume she was a close friend?'

'You can assume what you like, it won't get you anywhere,' said Mr Burnside. 'You're barking up the wrong bloody tree if you think I was responsible for her death. Can't you people get it into your thick heads that it must have been an accident?'

'Like a fainting fit that made her fall into the bath?'

'Sounds feasible to me,' said Mr Burnside. 'She was a well-built woman.'

'You'd know that for sure, sir?' said the inspector.

'I'm not answering that.'

Sergeant Tomlinson returned with Stebbings in tow. Mr Burnside was silent as he watched Stebbings lay out his equipment.

'Might I have your full name and address, sir?' asked Stebbings.

'Rupert John Burnside, 14 Stockwell Park Crescent.'

'Thank you, sir.'

Mr Burnside lapsed into silence again as he submitted to the fingerprinting process, and merely looked sardonic when Stebbings compared results with existing specimens. The constable took his time before giving a nod of satisfaction.

'They match?' said Sergeant Tomlinson.

'Yes, they do,' said Stebbings.

'Well, then, Mr Burnside, here's one fact,' said the inspector. 'You did visit Mrs Jones in her flat.'

'So?' said Mr Burnside.

'Having an affair with her, were you, sir?' suggested Sergeant Tomlinson.

'I don't consider that any business of yours,' said Mr Burnside. 'In any case, can't you understand I've been trying to protect that dead lady's reputation? You'd like her family to know we made love, would you? What purpose would that serve except to give her husband and daughters a bitter pill to swallow?'

'I'd be sorry about that, sir,' said Sergeant

Tomlinson, 'but what it amounts to, as far as our inquiries are concerned, is the possibility you were with her on the evening of her death.'

'You mean I made love to her and then drowned her in her bath?' said Mr Burnside. 'That's stretching it a bit, even for you policemen. I'm not a psychopath.'

'Could I have a word, sir?' said Sergeant Tomlinson to the inspector.

'If it's necessary,' said Inspector Shaw, and withdrew, Sergeant Tomlinson following and closing the door behind him. 'Well, Sergeant?'

As tactfully as possible, Sergeant Tomlinson pointed out they were overlooking something, which was that Mrs Jones had spent that particular evening with Mr and Mrs Chance. That is, her daughter Winnie and her son-in-law Victor, who lived somewhere in Streatham. She hadn't left them until eight forty. She would have arrived home at about nine, and the time of death had been estimated between nine and ten thirty.

'So what's certain, sir, is that she didn't spend the evening with Burnside.'

'That's your problem, Sergeant.'

'But suppose the bugger was waiting for her? Let me tell you why he might have been.' Sergeant Tomlinson recounted what Miss Taylor had come up with in the way of highly interesting information. It meant Burnside might have decided to dump Mrs Jones. In her bath. Inspector Shaw didn't look too convinced. 'You don't think much of that, sir?'

'You're writing a detective story,' said the inspector.

'We might have a bit more than a story if we found a nightdress at Burnside's place.'

'Granted,' said the inspector, 'and even more if he hasn't got an alibi for the evening. One that covers him from nine until ten thirty.'

They re-entered the office. Mr Burnside gave them a glance of contempt.

'Whatever else you've now got on your minds won't help you,' he said. 'I'm not your man.'

'Well, maybe not, sir,' said Sergeant Tomlinson, 'but where were you between, say, nine and eleven on the evening Mrs Jones died?'

Mr Burnside smiled.

'Good question,' he said, 'the first good one. I was at the home of some friends, Mr and Mrs Worboys. Their daughter Felicity was also there. They're all members of the society. Felicity's our regular prompter, George Worboys in charge of props and his wife one of our leading players. I was with them from eight until eleven.'

Well, damn that, thought Sergeant Tomlinson, it's crashed a near certainty and put us back to Herbert Jones. If it's true.

Inspector Shaw chewed on his sergeant's collapsing hopes.

'We'll need to check on that,' he said.

'You're more than welcome,' said Mr Burnside. 'I'll give you their address, but you won't be able to interview them until Monday. They're in Brighton for the weekend, all of them, staying with friends.'

'Would you have the address of their friends?' asked Sergeant Tomlinson.

'Sorry, no,' said Mr Burnside. 'I'll have to wait as well, shall I, for this farce to be over?'

'It looks like it, sir,' said Sergeant Tomlinson.

'I see. Anyway, here's the address of the Worboys family.' Mr Burnside scribbled it on a slip of paper, which he handed to Sergeant Tomlinson.

'Thanks for that, Mr Burnside.'

'Good morning,' said Mr Burnside.

Chapter Sixteen

'Done in the ruddy eye,' said Sergeant Tomlinson on the way back to the station.

'Good and proper, if his alibi stands up,' said Stebbings. 'Specially if he pops down to Brighton to see the Worboys family and makes sure it does.'

'By asking a pretty dodgy favour of all three, mother, father and daughter?' said Sergeant Tomlinson. 'I've got an unpleasant feeling he doesn't need to.'

'You believed him?' said Inspector Shaw.

'I thought he made it difficult for any of us to disbelieve him,' said Sergeant Tomlinson.

'All the same,' said the inspector, 'get yourself round to see the Worboys family on Sunday evening.'

'Sunday evening?' said Sergeant Tomlinson.

'Tomorrow. Up to you, of course, Sergeant, it's still your case. I'd say Sunday evening would do nicely. Catch 'em just as they get back from

Brighton, while they've still got sand in their shoes.'

'Aside from the fact that I don't know what time they'll be back, there's not much sand at Brighton, Inspector. It's mostly all pebbles.'

'Well, hard luck for kids with buckets and spades, then,' said the inspector. 'Get to the house early in the evening, and wait for them, if necessary. Take Constable Fry with you. I'll be unavailable myself.'

So ought I to be, thought Sergeant Tomlinson, I'm supposed to be off duty tomorrow.

Roger arrived home at one o'clock from his morning's work and with a look of disgust on his face.

'What's wrong?' asked Olive.

'You may well ask,' said Roger. 'I've got to go up to Preston for three days. That's where our main works are, and there's a special project on. The blueprints relate to new railway construction in Burma. They need another draughtsman for a few days. I'll have to go up tomorrow to get in a full day on Monday, and I'm travelling back on Thursday.'

'Roger, that's four days,' said Olive.

'Yes, four days away,' said Roger, 'what a swine. Preston, of all places. It's not like Hyde Park. Wouldn't like to come with me, I suppose?'

'I would if it were Harrogate,' said Olive, 'there

are some lovely shops and hotels in Harrogate. But Preston? Have a heart, Roger.'

'Will you be all right here?' asked Roger. 'You could stay with Madge or Winnie, if you wanted.'

'I don't want,' said Olive, 'I'll be quite all right here.'

'What happens if – no, never mind.'

'Never mind what, Roger?'

'I was thinking of your mother's funeral,' said Roger. 'It's got to be soon, surely.'

'I expect it could still be delayed a little longer, until you get back,' said Olive.

'Well, I'd like to be with you,' said Roger. 'Let's see, we're going to the police station after lunch for the fingerprinting, aren't we?'

'Yes, we're meeting Madge and Winnie there at two fifteen,' said Olive.

'I've got to admire you, Olive, you've taken a bloody awful blow and come out of it still standing up.'

'I'm still hurting,' said Olive.

The police at the station were very polite, but the atmosphere was hardly cheerful for the visitors, and when Sergeant Tomlinson put in an apppearance to take charge of things, Olive looked grateful. Madge, however, took the opportunity to assert her right to express her disgust at what was going on behind the closed doors of the police station. Sergeant Tomlinson assured her nothing was going on that wouldn't be of benefit at the inquest. Madge responded to that by saying everything should be of benefit to the family and to her dead mother's good name. Brian was with her, having been asked by Madge to support her. Victor was outside, looking after his and Winnie's infant son in his pushchair. Victor was the more fortunate. Brian was rolling his eyes as Madge dressed Sergeant Tomlinson down for being so impertinent as to demand fingerprints.

'Just a formality, Mrs Cooper,' he said, 'and we're very grateful you're all here together. It won't take long.'

'You haven't been listening to me,' said Madge.

'I assure you, I'm a trained listener, Mrs Cooper, and we all understand your feelings.'

'What we all want is for you to understand my mother's death happened by accident,' said Madge.

'Which is what we're trying to prove,' said Sergeant Tomlinson with an agreeable smile, which at once caused Madge to tell him there was nothing to smile about.

'Madge, shall we get on with it?' asked Olive.

'Good idea,' said Roger.

'Good idea,' said Brian. 'I'll stand aside.'

'If I could only find my own star,' said Winnie, 'I think it would tell me all we need to know.'

'It'll drop on your head out of the sky one night, Winnie love,' said Olive.

'I object to all this,' said Madge, but gave in and the fingerprints were taken. After that, Sergeant Tomlinson saw them all out.

'Thanks a lot,' he said.

'It's all rot as far as I'm concerned,' said Roger, 'so try not to bother my wife any more, there's a good fellow.'

'My apologies for my calls,' said Sergeant Tomlinson.

'Apologies aren't necessary, Sergeant,' said Olive.

'There's one thing,' said Madge. 'When is my mother's body going to be released to the undertakers?'

Sergeant Tomlinson, who knew it wouldn't be released until the marks around the ankles had been satisfactorily explained, and the inquest over, said, 'It shouldn't be long now, Mrs Cooper.'

'It's absurd,' said Madge. 'Come along, Brian, let's get home to sanity.'

'And the cats, I suppose,' said Brian.

'I'm glad you care for them,' said Madge.

Goodbyes were spoken and a general departure effected.

The fingerprints matched various of those found in the flat, all of which had now been identified.

At one time or another, Madge, Winnie and Olive had all left their fingerprints. So had Roger, Hilda Jones herself, and Rupert Burnside. And so had Herbert Jones, but only on the luggage trunk. Nevertheless, in view of the possibility that Mr Burnside was going to be eliminated from inquiries, Sergeant Tomlinson had to turn his thoughts again on the deceased woman's husband. His daughters weren't going to like that. In a case like this, prolonged investigation could be bloody hard on a family, especially on young Mrs Olive Way.

Brockwell Park, expansive, sunlit and green, was a meeting place, a rendezvous, a playground and an escape from brick and stone. For Olive on Sunday afternoon, with Roger on his way up to Preston, it offered a slow pleasant saunter and a chance to reflect on the events of the past week. She thought about her mother, who had launched herself into the life of a free and independent woman and had had it taken away from her almost before it had begun. She thought about her father, who had failed himself as a man by not putting his foot down. But had he done that, had he failed, or had he made a splendid and selfless gesture in letting her mother go?

Reaching an empty bench, she sat down, absently watching parents and their children, young men with their young ladies, and energetic boys and girls dashing this way and that. A strolling man stopped, and his shadow fell across her. She looked up.

'Do you like the park too, Mrs Way?' asked Sergeant Tomlinson.

He was off duty, she could see that. He was casually dressed in tan-coloured slacks, brown sports shirt and brown shoes, and was without a hat. He looked a reassuring figure with his broad shoulders, his muscular frame and his pleasant smile.

'Where did you come from?' she asked.

'From my Stockwell police quarters,' he said. 'On Sundays, when I'm not on duty, I enjoy a walk in this park.'

'By yourself?' said Olive. 'Aren't you married, then?'

'I haven't met the right woman yet,' he said. 'Well, right for me as a policeman. They talk about a policeman's lot not being a happy one. The lot of a policeman's wife is a very trying one. Or so other policemen tell me.'

'Perhaps policemen's wives should persuade their husbands to change their jobs,' said Olive.

'Policemen get a bit rooted,' he said. 'Well, nice to have seen you, Mrs Way, enjoy the sunshine.'

'You don't have to run,' said Olive, 'you can do me a favour and sit down and talk to me, if you like.'

'But your husband, isn't he around?' asked Sergeant Tomlinson.

'At the moment, he's on a train to Preston,' said Olive. 'He's having to put in three days' work at his firm's main engineering works.'

'He's an engineer?'

'A draughtsman,' said Olive.

'I see.' Sergeant Tomlinson rubbed his chin. Olive smiled.

'It's against the rules to sit down with a married woman?' she said.

'It's against the rules to get drunk while on duty, but not to sit down with you,' he said, and he seated himself beside her. He detected a faint and very delicate scent. She was like that, he thought, a young woman of general delicacy.

'We don't have to talk about my mother or why you've taken my father's fingerprints,' she said.

'We don't, no, and I wouldn't be allowed to,' he said, 'that's definitely against the rules, but let me just say I admire your fortitude in the way you've stood up to everything. What recreations do you and Mr Way enjoy?'

'We have a little garden,' she said. 'He does the digging, the weeding and the lawnmowing, and I do the planting and the watering. I bring on flowers from seed. I'm not just the cook and bottle-washer. I think Roger and I have both been neglecting things lately. Just this last week, you know. But we'll get back to our routine before long. If we don't the weeds will sneak up on us and take everything over. Weeds run rampant in Brixton gardens, did you know that, Sergeant Tomlinson?'

'I think I've heard they do well even in the back yards of Walworth and Whitechapel,' he said.

'Pernicious, that's the word,' said Olive.

'They need smothering at birth,' said Sergeant Tomlinson.

'Oh, that's no good, they'll pop up through the smothering,' she said. 'You have to dig them out or pull them out.'

'Yes, so I believe,' he said. His parents, who lived in Clapham, had a garden. 'Well, then, is it a recreation or a chore, gardening?'

'Satisfying,' said Olive. 'And it's a bit creative, too. Do you have an interest outside your job?'

'Pencil sketching,' he said.

'Well, imagine that,' said Olive. 'I used to like painting with watercolours. I still do. I'm not very good, though. Are you good at pencil sketching?'

'I'm not famous,' said Sergeant Tomlinson, 'it's just a hobby.'

'What do you sketch?' she asked.

'Anything that takes my eye,' he said. 'How about your painting?'

'Oh, parks and ponds,' she said. 'You like sketching better than polishing your hand-cuffs?'

'I don't do much of that kind of polishing,' he said. 'Have you painted this park?'

'Not all of it,' she said, 'just parts of it. I don't think I could paint all of it all at once.' She smiled and sneaked in a question concerning the inquiry. 'Have you asked my father where he was last Tuesday evening?'

'Mrs Way – '

'You can tell me,' she said, 'I won't say anything.'

He shook his head at her, but said, 'A friend of his, a Mrs Binns, assured us he was with her until late.'

'I know Mrs Binns,' said Olive, 'she worked for several years in his shop. She's an honest woman. So that's all right, then. About where my father was, I mean.'

'Discussion closed, Mrs Way.'

'Still, thanks for telling me,' said Olive.

'Unofficially, of course,' said Sergeant Tomlinson.

'Is that what they call off the record?' asked Olive.

'You could say so. But the investigation isn't over yet, I'm afraid. Would you like a cup of tea at the refreshment rooms?'

'I would, but I won't, if you don't mind,' she said.

'Understood,' he said. 'Well, I'll be on my way now.'

'Thanks for our little talk,' said Olive. 'Good-bye again.'

'Good luck, Mrs Way,' he said, and left.

Olive departed herself after he had disappeared. With Roger away and the house empty, she took a bus ride to see her father. He opened the door to her knock, presenting himself to her in his shirt, tie and trousers. Since he was rarely seen without his jacket and waistcoat, Olive said, 'You're looking very casual, Dad, and on a Sunday too.'

'Well, I'm feeling a bit free and easy, Olive,' said Herbert as she stepped in. He gave her a kiss and added, 'You're looking nice yourself. Pleasing to have you call. Where's Roger?'

'He's gone up to Preston, to the firm's main works for a special job,' said Olive. 'He'll be away till Thursday.'

'Well, I'm glad you came,' said Herbert, 'I'm just about to have my Sunday tea. Stay and have some with me. Later on, I'm going to take Mrs Binns for a Sunday evening walk.'

'You're getting very thick with that lady,' said Olive.

'She's been a very good friend to me since your mother passed on,' said Herbert. They entered the kitchen. A loaf of bread and its board stood on the table, together with a dish of butter. 'I hope it doesn't hurt you, Olive, to have your mother mentioned in the same breath as Mrs Binns.'

'It's your own life, Dad,' said Olive. 'I'll stay and have tea with you. What are you going to give me?'

'Some nice bread and butter, a soft-boiled egg, some blackcurrant jam, and some scones fresh from the bakers yesterday,' said Herbert.

'Well, that's nice enough for you to have invited Mrs Binns,' said Olive.

'She's gone to see that uncle of hers today,' said Herbert, 'and won't be back till about half six.'

'The uncle she's going to keep house for?' asked Olive.

'That's the one,' said Herbert, omitting to say that Nell now had different ideas.

'I'll do the tea,' said Olive.

'I can manage,' said Herbert.

'No, let me, I'd like to,' said Olive, 'we all owe you something.'

'Nobody owes me anything,' said Herbert.

'We all turned into Mum's girls,' said Olive, 'we forgot we had a dad.' She could have pointed out that he'd been more like the Invisible Man than a husband and father, but hadn't the heart to.

'That was all my fault,' said Herbert, 'I did too much reading and hardly any talking. I've come to realize I wasn't any real company for your mother. Now it's too late to make it up to her.'

'Don't let's discuss painful things, Dad,' said Olive, 'just let me get the tea.'

Herbert gave in, and Olive prepared the tea in a way that gave distinct appeal to its presentation. They ate it in the parlour, where the family had enjoyed Sunday tea for many years. Hilda had always insisted the parlour was the only proper place for tea on Sundays. Herbert actually chatted in easy style, and Olive's faint smile was an acknowledgement of how much he had come out of his shell. They avoided any mention of the tragedy and the police investigation until Olive suddenly asked a direct question.

'Did the police want to know where you were on the evening of Mum's death, Dad?'

Herbert frowned over a scone liberally laced with butter and jam.

'They did,' he said.

'Were you upset?'

'Yes, I ruddy well was,' he said, 'seeing it was obvious what it meant, and why they took me fingerprints later on.'

'It all means, doesn't it, that they suspect it wasn't an accident or suicide,' said Olive.

'They're up the pole,' said Herbert.

'Where were you, anyway?' asked Olive.

'With Mrs Binns,' said Herbert. 'Most of the evening,' he added casually. 'It's come to something, Olive, when people you've never seen before knock on your door and suggest you might've drowned your own wife. It's put me off

Brixton and Stockwell and everywhere else here-abouts. Don't let's spoil our tea talking about it.'

'No,' said Olive, 'but could I ask if the police went round to ask Mrs Binns to confirm you were with her?'

'They did that all right,' said Herbert, 'and she confirmed it. It's very pleasing, having a friend like her. Now, how are you and Roger getting along?'

'We haven't come to blows yet,' said Olive, 'we're nicely in tune.'

'Well, Roger's a bright bloke and easy-going,' said Herbert.

Too easy-going where money's concerned, thought Olive, but a man could have worse faults.

She stayed until six fifteen and then departed, leaving her dad free to take Mrs Binns for the promised evening walk. It seemed to Olive he had really come out of his shell and, as a widower, was finding early consolation in the company of a widow.

Meanwhile, Sergeant Tomlinson and Constable Fry had entered themselves in the register for Sunday evening duty. It was for the purpose of interviewing the Worboys family after their return from Brighton.

Chapter Seventeen

It was just after seven when a man, a woman and a young lady appeared at the entrance to Stockwell Park Crescent. The man was carrying a weekend suitcase, and so was the young lady. They walked into the crescent, talking animatedly. Reaching a house, they turned in at the gate. The woman used a key to open the front door, and they all entered. The door closed behind them.

'That's them,' said Constable Fry. He and Sergeant Tomlinson had been strolling up and down, waiting.

'You're getting perceptive, Sidney,' said Tomlinson.

'You're getting sarky, like the old man,' said Fry. 'Anyway, what now?'

'As I've suggested, give 'em ten minutes to make themselves at home.'

They continued to stroll. At the end of ten minutes, Sergeant Tomlinson knocked on the door. The man answered it. He was in his forties, with thinning hair and a friendly face.

'What can I do for you?' he asked.

'Mr Worboys?' enquired Sergeant Tomlinson.

'Yes, I'm Mr Worboys.'

'Sorry to bother you on a Sunday evening – '

'I'm sorry too, I've only just got back from Brighton, with my wife and daughter.'

'I'm Detective Sergeant Tomlinson of Stockwell CID, Mr Worboys, and this is Detective Constable Fry.'

'Well, pardon me,' said Mr George Worboys, 'but what are you doing on my particular doorstep?'

'We're making inquiries in connection with a certain matter that's come to our attention,' said Sergeant Tomlinson. 'Mind if we come in, sir?'

Mr Worboys said he minded to some extent, especially under the circumstances, which included the fact that he and his family were in need of a meal, but he would yield to the principle of helping the law. He took them into the parlour, quite a pretty room with its bright colours, and asked them to go ahead with their questions, although he hadn't the faintest notion, he said, of how he could help. Sergeant Tomlinson asked if he and his family were friends of Mr Burnside, prominent in the Stockwell Amateur Dramatic Society. Mr Worboys said yes, is this something to do with the society?

'No, not the society, sir,' said Constable Fry, 'just Mr Burnside.'

'Hello, what's Rupert been up to?' asked Mr Worboys.

'Does he get up to things, then?' enquired Constable Fry.

Mr Worboys laughed.

'Burglary, you mean?' he said.

'He's not known to us for that, sir,' said Sergeant Tomlinson, and Mrs Worboys came in then. A woman in her late thirties, she was tall and attractive, and Sergeant Tomlinson could imagine she had quite a stage presence.

'George, what's going on?' she asked.

'It seems the police are interested in asking some questions about Rupert,' said Mr Worboys.

'Mr Burnside? What kind of questions, for goodness sake?'

'Apologies for disturbing your Sunday evening, Mrs Worboys,' said Sergeant Tomlinson, 'but I'm sure this won't take long. Can you and your husband think back to last Tuesday evening?'

'Tuesday? Tuesday?' Mrs Worboys reflected, and her husband did some thinking. 'Yes, we can both remember Tuesday evening.'

'Heather's always good for remembering for both of us,' smiled Mr Worboys, 'but I fancy this time I can remember for myself.'

Their daughter Felicity, a pretty young lady of seventeen, put in an appearance, and of course she too wanted to know what was going on. These policemen, said her father, needed answers to some questions about Rupert Burnside.

'Rupert?' said Felicity.

'Well, the first question was about last Tuesday evening,' said Mrs Worboys, 'and if we could think back to it.'

'That's easy,' said Felicity.

'Were you entertaining a visitor?' asked Sergeant Tomlinson.

'Yes,' said Felicity.

'True,' said Mr Worboys.

'Mr Burnside,' said Mrs Worboys.

'How long was he here?' asked Sergeant Tomlinson.

'All evening,' said Mrs Worboys.

'Until eleven at least,' said Mr Worboys. 'Why d'you ask, Sergeant?'

'Just a formal inquiry, sir,' said Sergeant Tomlinson.

'Just a minute,' said Felicity, 'is it something to do with what happened last year?'

'What happening was that, might I ask?' enquired Constable Fry.

'Nothing that's of any importance now,' said Mr Worboys.

'It was a private matter, it concerned only the Stockwell Amateur Dramatic Society,' said Mrs Worboys, delivering her words with the practised clarity of an actress who could perform well for an audience. 'We're all members. So is Rupert. Mr Burnside. He's a leading figure, in fact.'

'What did you say happened?' asked Sergeant Tomlinson.

'We didn't say,' said Mrs Worboys.

'The fact is, the takings for one of our Saturday night performances sort of disappeared,' said Felicity, 'so we had to have a meeting about it. Well, it was a lot of money in its way, and a loss to our funds. No-one could work out how it disappeared, and we decided the bag had been stolen by someone who got backstage. Some outsider. We didn't call the police in, we didn't want that kind of a fuss, but has someone reported it to you? Are you wanting to see Mr Burnside about it, because he's our president?'

'The society wouldn't wish the matter to concern the police,' said Mrs Worboys firmly.

'It doesn't, I assure you, unless we're asked for our help,' said Sergeant Tomlinson, sounding as if he understood a nod and a wink were required at this point. 'We only wish to know exactly where Mr Burnside was last Tuesday evening.'

'But why?' asked Mrs Worboys.

'Yes, why?' asked Felicity.

'It's a matter under inquiry, but nothing like theft or burglary,' said Sergeant Tomlinson. His smile made the family relax. 'It was definitely last Tuesday evening that Mr Burnside was here, and until eleven at least?'

'Quite definitely,' said Mrs Worboys. 'We entertain him regularly, usually to discuss something concerning stagecraft.'

'He's our expert on stagecraft,' said Felicity.

'I'm sure,' said Sergeant Tomlinson, smiling again, although his uppermost feeling was one of frustration. 'He's invaluable to you?'

'Certainly,' said Mrs Worboys.

'Well, that's all. Thanks for putting up with us, and sorry again for interrupting your Sunday evening.'

'I'm still puzzled,' said Mr Worboys.

'We're always hoping that some puzzles will work themselves out,' said Sergeant Tomlinson. 'Goodnight, and thanks again.'

Mr Worboys saw them out.

'I'll have to tell Rupert Burnside you called,' he said.

'That's quite all right, sir,' said Sergeant Tomlinson.

'Will he be surprised?'

'Probably not. Goodnight.'

The CID men left.

Constable Fry said, 'Dead loss, that was, except it looks to me like Burnside has got a few taking ways.'

'Perhaps his tastes are expensive, Sidney.'

'Such as women? They're expensive.'

'I suppose he appeals to women,' said Sergeant Tomlinson. 'Perhaps he appeals to Mrs Worboys.

I thought she was slightly aggressive on his behalf. Perhaps, in fact, she knows who made off with the takings, or has had a good guess.'

'If he's been doing his employers down, I don't suppose he'd lose any sleep over doing the society down,' said Constable Fry.

'It seems to me, Sidney, that it might have seriously worried him, Mrs Jones finding out about him diddling the firm, since it might have led in a roundabout way to the society asking new questions about the loss of their takings sometime last year. But damn it, how can we fit him into the frame regarding the death of Mrs Jones now that he's got what looks like a cast-iron alibi?'

'It's put him right out of the running,' said Constable Fry, 'which is making me think it might've been an accidental drowning, after all.'

'Did she forget her towel and her bath cap by accident, then?' Sergeant Tomlinson sounded as if irritation had crept up on him.

'Don't ask me, you're in charge,' said Constable Fry. 'Still, how about suicide? She wouldn't have needed to bother with the cap or the towel.'

'I still don't go along with suicide,' said Sergeant Tomlinson. 'She had no reason to do away with herself, not if it's true she was enjoying her new life.'

'We're getting nowhere fast,' said Constable Fry, 'and the old man's going to lose interest.'

'I'm not,' said Sergeant Tomlinson.

'I've got to point out, then, that that'll put you back on the doorstep of Herbert Jones,' said Constable Fry.

'Well, sod that,' said Sergeant Tomlinson, grimacing.

'I'm beginning to have a feeling I'm playing second fiddle to three fat cats,' said Brian Cooper.

'Don't be absurd,' said Madge.

'Get 'em out from under my feet, or I'll boot them through the back door,' said Brian.

'How anyone can even think of being cruel to animals horrifies me,' said Madge.

'Listen, sweetie,' said Brian, 'animals are cruel to each other. Those bloody cats think nothing of tearing birds into a pile of feathers, and come to that, if Mrs Russell's dog could have its way, it would bite Pinky's head off.'

'That doesn't excuse human beings from being cruel to animals,' said Madge.

'Even your mother aimed a smack at your cats last time she was here,' said Brian.

'Yes, and look what happened to her,' said Madge.

'What, it served her right getting herself drowned in her bath?' said Brian.

'Brian, how dare you say a terrible thing like that?'

'You asked for it,' said Brian. 'It's time you got rid of those cats and had some two-legged kids.'

'Two-legged kids?' said Madge, disgusted.

'Babies,' said Brian. 'They're more human than cats.'

Getting ready for bed, Olive thought again how empty the house was without Roger. She even had a feeling it was vulnerable, so she made sure the front and back doors were double-bolted.

On Monday morning, Inspector Shaw refrained from growling when told that Mr Burnside looked to have a cast-iron alibi and therefore couldn't be placed at the scene of the drowning last Tuesday evening.

He simply said, 'I told you I don't like cast-iron alibis. They get in the way of a solution.'

'I don't know we can break it, guv,' said Constable Fry, 'not when both parents and their daughter were all positive.'

'It's your problem, Sergeant Tomlinson,' said the inspector, 'you'll have to do some plodding. That's if you're still feeling sure it wasn't an accident or suicide.'

'You're suggesting we plod about looking for someone who might have seen a person entering by that side door?' said Sergeant Tomlinson.

'Up to you, man,' said Inspector Shaw.

'A person with a motive for murdering Mrs Jones?'

'You've only got two possibles, Burnside and Jones,' said the inspector, 'and you've as good as eliminated Burnside. I'll give you until Thursday to finish the investigation, one way or the other. Get going.'

'So what now?' asked Constable Fry, as he and Sergeant Tomlinson left the station.

'Plodding, Sidney.'

'What about my feet?' asked Constable Fry. 'I did all my plodding in the uniformed branch, didn't I?'

'It's the luck of the draw,' said Sergeant Tomlinson.

'What kind of luck is that, might I ask?'

'Making an effort to find someone who can help us place a bloke at the scene of the crime,' said Sergeant Tomlinson.

'Might I point out we can't officially call it a crime yet?' said Constable Fry.

'It's that as far as I'm concerned,' said Sergeant Tomlinson, 'so start plodding.'

Herbert took a bus ride up West again, and this time he took Nell with him. She wore her best costume and hat. When they alighted in the Strand, Herbert preceded her so that he could give her his hand as she stepped off. She said he was a natural gent, and that although she still

251

didn't want to speak ill of the dead, she felt Hilda had been too taken up with herself to realize what nice ways he had. Yes, she took you for granted, Herbert. Herbert said best if they didn't talk about poor Hilda, that she'd passed on in very unfortunate circumstances and to leave it at that. Nell said yes, all right, Herbert.

They walked along the Strand together, making quite a picture of a mature couple in their Sunday best on a Monday morning.

Meanwhile, Muscles Boddy, who considered himself a good friend to Herbert, was working out his porridge in Brixton Prison. He wasn't too happy about it, especially as no word of sympathy from his guv'nor reached him. Incarceration didn't lessen his dislike of the law. The law, he reckoned, could take liberties with a bloke who had a living to earn and friends to see.

He downed a fellow inmate for giving him lip, then trod on his breadbasket as well. Luckily, no warder noticed the incident, and the injured geezer lodged no complaint.

Muscles asked about remission.

'Remission on twenty-eight days, you berk?' said a warder.

'Ain't I a model prisoner, then?'

'So's my Aunt Fanny.'

'Sod your Aunt Fanny,' said Muscles.

Chapter Eighteen

Sergeant Tomlinson and Constable Fry spent
Monday and Tuesday in Stockwell Road in an
attempt to find someone who might have seen
a man at the door leading to Mrs Jones's flat
the previous Tuesday evening. They knocked
on neighbouring doors. All kinds of people
appeared in answer to their knocks, but none
had any help to offer. Some said they were too
busy to spend time in the evenings looking out of
their windows to see what was going on, and
others said they weren't in the habit of spying on
their neighbours, thanks very much. Inevitably,
there was the belligerent householder who said,
'So you're the bleedin' police, are yer? Well,
bleedin' bug off.' It was a fact of life that people
of a certain kind were of the opinion that a
police force existed as an interfering nuisance
and ought to be done away with.

In several cases, there were no answers to
knocks, and that meant going back again, which

in turn meant extra plodding, something that wasn't to Constable Fry's liking. Sergeant Tomlinson made him buy a packet of bath salts in which to soak his failing plates of meat.

Inspector Shaw tactfully refrained from criticism, remarking only that Sergeant Tomlinson was on the way to establishing that the police had no case. Sergeant Tomlinson said there was a case, he was damned certain of it. Well, time's running out, said the inspector.

'I need a little bit of luck,' said Sergeant Tomlinson.

'Hope it soon lands in your lap,' said the inspector.

On Wednesday, Madge, Winnie and Olive arrived at their father's house in response to postcard invitations to have a light lunch with him. Winnie brought her child, Herbert's grandson, and put him to sleep in his pushchair.

Herbert laid out a lunch of tinned salmon and salad, with bread and butter, with pineapple chunks and custard to follow. The pineapple chunks were also out of a tin.

'Who's going to make the custard?' asked Madge.

'It's made,' said Herbert. 'I did it, and it's keeping hot. I know you girls don't like cold custard.'

'Dad, are you turning into a cook?' asked Olive.

'I'm learning the ropes,' said Herbert. 'Sit down, all of you.'

They all sat round the kitchen table. The talk prior to that had all been about the police inquiries and what they could mean. Herbert had said it was best to forget what they could mean, as they wouldn't lead to anything. Your mother, he said, drowned accidental, and the police would come to realize that.

Now, as they began their meal, Winnie asked, 'Exactly why have you invited all of us, Dad?'

'You asked that when you arrived,' said Herbert.

'So did I,' said Madge, 'and, like Winnie, I'm asking again.'

'Yes, what's the reason, Dad?' asked Olive.

'What do Winnie's stars say?' asked Herbert.

'I couldn't see any last night,' said Winnie, 'it was cloudy.'

'Well, I'll tell you,' said Herbert. 'It's about your mother's Post Office savings.'

'Oh?' said Madge.

'Mum's savings?' said Winnie.

'Those that's recorded in her savings book,' said Herbert, and Olive contrived to look innocent, having kept to herself the fact that her dad intended the money to be shared out.

'Well, I think Mum would have wanted everyone to have some,' said Winnie.

'Definitely,' said Madge in her positive way.

'Well, we don't have to come to any argument,' said Herbert. 'I've got a letter on my person. It's a sort of document, actu'lly, made out by a solicitor. It's for Madge, she being the eldest, and it instructs her to see the savings are shared out equal between the three of you. I don't want any of it, it's all for you girls, and I'll give the document to Madge in the presence of you and Olive, Winnie, which'll make you and her witnesses to the handing over. The solicitor said it's always as well to be careful about money matters like these, so that there's no family arguments, which I hope there won't be among you girls. Equal shares suit you all?'

Madge and Winnie, taken aback, looked at each other. Olive smiled.

'There won't be any arguments, Dad,' she said, 'and we're all grateful. Madge and Winnie will tell you so.'

'Well, yes, thanks ever so much, Dad,' said Winnie.

'But don't you have to wait for the savings to be legally yours before you can share them out?' asked Madge.

'That's taken care of,' said Herbert.

'Well, I must say it's very generous of you, Dad,' said Madge.

'Yes,' said Winnie, 'and especially as we thought that if—'

'We won't talk about ifs and buts,' said Madge,

'it isn't respectful to Dad or to the memory of Mum.'

'Let's just be respectful to her savings,' said Olive with a hint of good-humoured satire.

'Well, your mother always treated her savings with great respect,' said Herbert with a smile. 'Lunch all right, is it?'

'I must say you've come out a lot, Dad,' said Winnie.

'I've had to, Winnie,' said Herbert. 'Mind you, it's one thing being a free man and another doing everything for yourself. I've been spoiled all these years. It's sad, y'know, your mother going off like she did and coming to such an unfortunate end. Still, it's no use harking back or letting our grief get too much hold of us. You're all looking very nice, I must say. Your cats all right, Madge?'

'You keep saying more in one go than you ever said in all your married years,' remarked Madge. 'As for my cats, they'll be missing me.'

'You sure?' said Herbert. 'Mrs Binns was telling me cats are sort of independent and can always take care of themselves as long as there's a few mice and birds around. Bit of a hard life for the birds, though.'

'And the mice,' said Olive.

Madge sniffed.

Before his daughters left, Herbert gave Madge the document in the presence of Winnie and

Olive, and they all read it. It bore the name and address of a Brixton solicitor, and it settled the matter of Hilda's savings.

'Keep in touch,' said Herbert.

'Of course, Dad, we'll see you lots,' said Olive.

'Don't forget the money's to be your own savings, and try to add to them like your mum did, so that you'll all have something behind you,' said Herbert. 'By the way, I might be going on a sea trip sometime.'

'A sea trip?' said Winnie.

'Yes, I might treat myself to some ocean breezes,' said Herbert. In company with Mrs Binns, he had visited the offices of a shipping company on Monday. 'I'm thinking serious about it.'

'Do it, Dad, enjoy yourself,' said Olive.

'Dad, you're getting quite adventurous,' said Madge.

'Well, I'm a free man,' said Herbert. 'So long now, all of you. '

Sergeant Tomlinson and Constable Fry were close to Herbert's home early that afternoon, trying to find out if any neighbour of his had seen him last Tuesday evening. They discovered one lady, a former customer of his shop, who had run into him in Saltoun Road at about half past eight. They'd said good evening to each other, and the lady had asked him jokingly if he was going out on the tiles. He said no, that he was going to call on Mrs Binns, the woman who'd worked for him in his shop, and who lived in Saltoun Road. The lady thought my, and her a widow too, did his wife know? Mr Jones, apparently, hadn't informed the lady his wife had recently left him.

The lady wanted to know why they were asking questions about him, and the CID men said it was a private matter, and the lady said well, Mr Jones was a sort of very private man.

'We're still up a bleedin' gum tree,' said Constable Fry after they'd parted from her. 'We can't place Burnside at the scene, nor Jonesy. Sarge, we've got nothing that means anything. Inspector Shaw's going to tell you to drop the case.'

Sergeant Tomlinson, not keen to accept that, said they'd have to hope for some positive clues to turn up before the inquest took place. Constable Fry said that that could happen on the day a cow jumped over the moon.

'Let's go one more time to Mrs Jones's flat,' said Sergeant Tomlinson. 'Let's see if we overlooked any kind of clue.'

'It'll be giving my feet a hard time,' said Constable Fry. Nevertheless, he accompanied his sergeant to Stockwell, and they let themselves into the flat with the spare key.

While Fry gave the living room and bathroom

a thorough examination. Sergeant Tomlinson concentrated on the bedroom and kitchen. Neither man found anything that had not been noticed before, although Sergeant Tomlinson did come across a bunch of flowers in a vase on the kitchen table, with a card propped against the vase. Curious, he read what was written on the card.

'Sorry, Mum. Love, Olive.'

Sorry? Strange, very strange.

He left the kitchen, giving the flowers another glance on his way. He bumped into Constable Fry. They compared notes. Neither offered the other anything in the way of a fresh pointer.

'It's like the old man says, we've got no case, then,' said Constable Fry.

'Which gets up my nose,' said Sergeant Tomlinson.

'Ten to one the coroner's going to conclude it's death by accident,' said Constable Fry, 'which'll mean my feet have been hurting for nothing.'

'We're both suffering,' said Sergeant Tomlinson.

They left.

At eight o'clock that evening, Olive answered a knock on her front door. Sergeant Tomlinson doffed his trilby hat.

'Good evening, Mrs Way, am I disturbing you?'

'Well, yes, you are, Sergeant,' said Olive, 'I'm listening to a play on the wireless.'

'Oh, sorry. Shall I go away and come back again?'

'No, not now you're here. But I'd like to know why you've called.'

'May I come in and tell you?'

'Very well,' said Olive.

The first thing she did in her living room was to turn off the wireless. The second was to invite him to sit down. The third was to touch her hair and lightly fluff it. Sergeant Tomlinson, seating himself, thought she looked charming in her summer dress, and quite at ease with herself.

'Mrs Way – '

'Yes?' Olive sat down opposite him.

'I was at your mother's flat again this after-noon.'

'Were you?' she said. 'Why?'

'In connection with completing our inquiries.'

'Oh, inquiries.' Her faint smile showed. 'I'm glad to hear you say they're nearing completion. Are you going to tell me what your conclusions will be?'

'We haven't arrived at any yet, Mrs Way.'

'I should think that's because you're looking for something that's not there,' said Olive. 'You should accept my mother's death was suicide or an accident.'

'There were one or two things that puzzled us,

though,' said Sergeant Tomlinson. 'What I want to say now is that I noticed you'd placed a vase of flowers on the kitchen table in the flat.'

'Oh, just as a gesture after she'd died,' said Olive.

'You left a card saying you were sorry, Mrs Way. Sorry about what?'

'It meant I was sorry that none of us, none of the family, did anything to stop her leaving my father, sorry that this led to her death, sorry that none of us were there at the time, which might have prevented the accident. I believe, you see, that it was an accident.'

'I see.' Sergeant Tomlinson was thinking about her husband, Roger Way, and how he had found him in the flat looking, so he said, for his mother-in-law's handbag, which happened to be plainly visible. Then there was the fact that although this very pleasant young woman had suffered physical collapse at discovering her mother's body in the bath, she had made a remarkable recovery within a day or so. 'I don't want to upset you, believe me, but could you tell me where you and your husband were on the evening of what you feel was an accident?'

'My word,' said Olive, eyes opening wide, 'aren't you a demon, Sergeant Tomlinson? And a shocker as well.' She shook her head at him. 'It's all very well, only doing your job, as they say, but really, making suspects of Roger and me is the giddy limit. Never mind, I forgive you, and can tell you Roger and I were working in the garden until dusk. Our neighbours were in their own garden, we chatted a bit with them, and when we'd finished our outdoor chores they invited us in to have a drink with them, which we did, and were with them until about ten thirty. Your next move is to go next door and check, I suppose. Knock and ask to see Mr and Mrs Gibson.'

Sergeant Tomlinson knew he'd arrived at another negative.

'No, I'll take your word for it, Mrs Way,' he said.

'That's very nice of you,' said Olive, 'and makes up a little for thinking dark thoughts of Roger and me, although I'm astonished you could have such thoughts. You actually suspected Roger and I might have contrived my mother's death? How utterly rotten of you, Sergeant. What would have been our motive?'

'I haven't the foggiest idea, Mrs Way, and can only apologize for being the heavy policeman.'

'At the moment, you look more like an embarrassed one,' said Olive. 'And you should be. I ought to be furious with you. I'm me, my mother's daughter.'

'So sorry to have upset you,' said Sergeant Tomlinson.

'It's cost you the offer of a cup of tea,' said Olive, and he rose from his chair.

'I think my best bet is to disappear,' he said.

'Yes, I think so too,' said Olive, and saw him out. 'There's nothing suspicious about my mother's death, you know. Goodnight, Sergeant Tomlinson.'

'Goodnight, Mrs Way.'

Chapter Nineteen

'That's it, then,' said Inspector Shaw the follow-ing morning.

'I still don't think it was suicide,' said Sergeant Tomlinson.

'No?'

'Or an accident.'

'Look, man, if it was murder, you've eliminated the only two possible suspects and found no other, haven't you?' growled the inspector.

'I'll admit we can't place either of them at the scene,' said Sergeant Tomlinson, who hadn't mentioned his latest interview with Mrs Olive Way. He felt he'd made a fool of himself.

'You can't place anyone else, either,' said the inspector. 'Call it off. There's the obvious fact that if she was going to commit suicide, she wouldn't have bothered about a cap or a towel. We can't offer the coroner anything to sub-stantiate murder. Well, don't let it get you down, Sergeant, I'm satisfied you conducted a thorough

265

investigation, but we've got nothing to justify any further inquiries.'

'Just one thing, sir,' said Sergeant Tomlinson, 'there's still no explanation for the marks around the ankles.'

'Didn't we decide they were made by shoe straps?'

'Dr Strang's opinion was no.'

'Some other explanation, then,' said the inspector, who'd lost interest. 'Inquiries closed. Sergeant, unless the coroner finds we've got some work to do, after all.'

Sergeant Tomlinson still wasn't happy.

Olive received a letter by the midday post. It was addressed in Roger's handwriting. He was due back home today. Had he written to tell her his return was being delayed?

She opened the letter and read it.

'Dear Olive,

'I'm afraid this is going to be a shock to you, and I thought it only fair to write instead of leaving you wondering what was happening. The fact is, I'm going abroad. I can't tell you where, and I'll have sailed by the time you get this letter. I'm going with two artesian well engineers who have formed a company, and have an overseas contract. But they need a draughtsman and more capital, and I'm providing the extra, seven hundred and fifty quid, in exchange for thirty-three per cent of the shares. Well, of course, I didn't have that kind of money, not until this morning when, after giving the Post Office proper notice in your mother's name, I cashed all her savings. Yes, I had to forge her signature on the withdrawal form. You'll think me a bloody bounder, I know, but I couldn't turn down the chance of a lifetime, and your family would never have loaned me your mother's savings. But I'll pay it all back as soon as this company is in handsome and expected profit, and then I'll ask you to come out and join me. Don't gnash your teeth and curse me, just bear with me. I couldn't tell you my plans as I know you'd have scotched any attempt on my part to cash your mother's savings. Sorry about giving you a new shock on top of the other, but it'll all work out fine for us in the end. Love, Roger.

'PS. I'll be writing from time to time, if poss.'

Olive stood rigid, then read the letter again, to make sure that her husband's infamy really was evident in black and white. She placed it on the table and examined the postmark on the envelope. Southampton. She walked on stiff legs to the bedroom. There she opened one of the bottom drawers in her dressing table, and turned over the items it contained. Her mother's savings book had been put beneath them. It was missing now.

She put her hat on, returned to the living room, placed the letter and envelope carefully in her handbag, then went out to the nearest public phone box. She called the Stockwell police station and asked to speak to Sergeant Tomlinson. She gave her name, and after a minute's wait she heard his voice.

'Mrs Way? Sergeant Tomlinson here.'

'I want you to come and see me immediately, Sergeant Tomlinson. I've something to tell you.'

'Something important, Mrs Way?'

'You can judge for yourself. It's very important to me, I can tell you that.'

'I'll be with you as soon as I can.'

'Come by yourself, please.'

'If you're going to make some kind of statement – '

'For this interview, I'd prefer to speak to you privately. Any statement can come later.'

'Very well, Mrs Way.'

When Sergeant Tomlinson arrived, she did not beat about the bush.

'It's my husband,' she said, her voice ominous.

'Your husband?' Sergeant Tomlinson regarded her with intense curiosity. Was she going to tell him the unbelievable about her husband? Her face was slightly flushed, and he had a feeling she was on fire.

'I find I'm married to a swine,' she said.

'Then I'm sorry, Mrs Way, but is that anything to do with the police?'

'It's everything to do with the police,' she said. 'He's stolen my mother's life savings. He's aboard some ship that I think sailed yesterday. I want him arrested and brought back.'

'Mrs Way—'

'Read that,' she said, taking the letter out of her handbag and thrusting it at him. He took it. 'Read it and see what he's done to me and the family.'

Sergeant Tomlinson read the letter. His first reaction was to wonder if Roger Way had murdered his mother-in-law in order to get his hands on her savings book. The book, yes, that was what he had really been looking for in the flat that day. He had obviously already searched the handbag and not found it there. But would he seriously have considered murder when there were other ways of getting hold of the book, the ways of a petty thief?

'Mrs Way, what was the amount of your mother's savings?'

'Nearly nine hundred pounds.'

'I see he mentions he needed seven hundred and fifty.'

'Yes,' said Olive, struggling to control her fury. 'Are you going to stand there and ask questions? Shouldn't you be telling me that you're going to check ship sailings and passenger lists immediately?'

'No, I don't think so, Mrs Way.'

'You don't think so?' Olive's flush deepened. 'Why don't you think so?'

'Because I doubt if he's aboard any ship.'

'But he makes it quite clear he is. I asked for you to come and see me so that as a humiliated woman I wouldn't have to suffer a whole roomful of police.'

'We wouldn't have sent a roomful, Mrs Way. I take it as a compliment that you asked for my help. Well, let me suggest to you that this letter is an act of deception. I don't mean that he hasn't withdrawn the savings, I'd say that's all too true. But the set-up. A newly formed company with a contract to sink artesian wells somewhere overseas needs a draughtsman and extra capital? How would a new and under-capitalized company have secured a contract? And how would your husband in a very short space of time have secured his place in that company and a place aboard a ship? He had no money to show until yesterday. He needed a passport, a ticket, and other things. Mrs Way, a company with an overseas contract could have raised extra capital quite easily.'

'Sergeant Tomlinson, are you telling me that, apart from the withdrawal of my mother's savings, that letter is a lie?' demanded Olive.

'I'm suggesting it is, yes,' said Sergeant Tomlinson. 'In fact, I'm suggesting your husband is still in this country, but that he's hoping you'll believe he's on his way to the moon. That is, somewhere far away. Is he fond of money?'

'Very,' said Olive, 'and he's never had enough of it. My God, the swine.'

'Do you want him found and charged, Mrs Way?'

'You feel sure he's still in this country, Sergeant Tomlinson?'

'I'd bet on it,' said Sergeant Tomlinson.

'Then, yes, I want him found and charged,' said Olive.

'Um – ' Sergeant Tomlinson hesitated.

'Um what?' asked Olive.

'There's no possibility that he was responsible in some way for your mother's death?'

'That again?' said Olive. 'You're a bulldog, aren't you? No, Roger may be a swine, but not of that kind. As I told you, he was with me from the time he came home from work that evening until we went to bed, and that includes the time we spent with our neighbours. I hope you find him before he's spent my mother's savings.'

'We'll circulate his description, and if you've got a photograph, that will help, Mrs Way.'

'Yes, I'll give you a photograph,' said Olive.

'Do you know where he was when he wrote

this letter?' asked Sergeant Tomlinson. 'That is, where was the stamp franked?'

'Southampton,' said Olive, and produced the envelope. The sergeant inspected the postmark.

'Southampton, yes, very appropriate,' he said, 'and it wouldn't have cost him much to get there and make you think of ships.'

'I'm going to have a drink,' said Olive, 'a strong one. Would you like something, Sergeant?'

'Not for me, Mrs Way.'

'You're on duty, of course.'

'Yes. I'll take the photograph and also this letter, if I may.'

She found a framed photograph. She took it out of the frame and handed it to Sergeant Tomlinson.

'There,' she said. 'You won't mind, will you, if while you're setting the wheels in motion, I get drunk?'

'I think you're overdue, Mrs Way, for that kind of medicine, but don't empty the bottle.'

'You're a sympathetic policeman, aren't you?'

'Sometimes,' he said. 'I'll see myself out, and I'll be in touch.'

'Go ride your horse, Sergeant, and let me know when my husband's been arrested,' said Olive.

'By the way,' he said, 'our inquiries concerning your mother's death are being called off, and her body will be released to the undertakers. Your father was told this morning.'

'Then why did you ask me a little while ago to confirm where Roger was that evening?'

'Forgot myself,' said Sergeant Tomlinson.

'It's your bulldog streak,' said Olive.

When he had gone, she poured herself just a little brandy. She steeled herself and drank it at one go. She made a face, then thought about telling her father and sisters of Roger's infamy. But instead of doing so, she went out into the garden and used a hoe. She took her fury out on the weeds.

It would have pleased her to know that the police at Stockwell were setting in motion the procedures that they hoped would lead to the apprehension of one Roger Way. The wheels began to turn, the Post Office Savings Bank department consenting to help in a check that would establish at which branch the withdrawal was made.

Sergeant Tomlinson was particularly active on Olive's behalf. It took his mind off the frustrations brought about by his stubborn belief that Mrs Jones's death was neither the result of suicide nor accident.

Herbert had enjoyed a nice lunch at Nell's flat. He'd also enjoyed another satisfying chat with her, during which Nell had remarked that he'd turned into quite a talking man.

'Well, y'know, Nell, looking back, I can't help thinking Hilda had good reason to see me as unsociable, though I wish she hadn't called me so many names in the end. I always thought it was best to let her do all the talking, she being the kind of woman who hardly ever stopped. Real gift of the gab, Hilda had. Anyway, I don't want you to find me unsociable, which I hope I'm not at this here moment.'

'Oh, you're very sociable these days, Herbert. It's been very nice listening to you, and being told just how you're arranging everything.'

'Yes, shouldn't be long now, Nell. Say in two or three weeks.'

'Lor', by then I won't know if I'm on me head or me heels, Herbert. And all them new clothes, goodness me, I'll look like a duchess.'

'You liked going round the shops with me, Nell?'

'Best time of me life, Herbert. Ain't you a love?'

'Well, I'm hardly that, Nell, but I pride myself I've never minded putting my hand in my pocket. Anyway, I'll be off now. See you again tomorrow.'

'All right, Herbert. Oh, and I want to say again I'm pleased you've heard from the police that Hilda's funeral can take place. I hope she rests in peace, poor Hilda, and it must be a relief to you that the police aren't going to fuss any more.'

'There'll be the inquest soon, Nell. Me and the girls will have to face up to that. Well, goodbye now, thanks for the nice lunch.'

'Oh, you're always welcome, Herbert.'

Gritting her teeth, Olive called on her father during the afternoon. Herbert was surprised to see her again so soon, but it didn't take him more than a minute to realize she was far from her usual self.

'What's up, Olive? Not still worried about things, are you? I've heard from the police that the undertakers can collect your mother's body.'

'Yes, I've heard too, Dad, from Sergeant Tomlinson,' said Olive. 'It's something different from that, something you'll hardly believe.'

Herbert listened as she talked to him at length about what Roger had done to her and the family. He was thunderstruck. Olive went on to tell him she'd spoken to Sergeant Tomlinson.

'Well, he's the right kind of policeman to talk to,' said Herbert.

Olive said Sergeant Tomlinson believed that most of what Roger had put down in his letter was a lie, that there was no company, no nothing except a rotten swine of a husband absconding with her mother's savings. Herbert asked if that was what Sergeant Tomlinson had called Roger, a rotten swine.

'No, I did,' said Olive. 'Sergeant Tomlinson is

sure he's still in this country. He's promised the police will do their best to find him and arrest him.'

'You're going to have him charged, Olive?'

'Yes,' said Olive.

'So you should, even if he is your husband,' said Herbert. 'Any bloke who does that kind of thing to his wife needs a dose of hard labour. Did I have a feeling once that Roger was easy come, easy go about money?'

'If you did, you were right,' said Olive.

'This needs thinking about,' said Herbert. 'I'll make a pot of tea and we'll talk some more.'

Over the tea, he pointed out that Roger's deed was even worse than he'd first thought. He had left Olive with nothing, with no housekeeping money coming in, and probably nothing with which to pay the rent. Was that so, was she broke?

'All I've got is what's in my purse,' said Olive, 'about twenty-five shillings.'

'No savings, Olive?'

'Savings? Don't make me laugh, Dad.'

'Didn't he give you enough so that you could put a bit aside each week?'

'No,' said Olive. 'He always seemed to be in debt.'

'Well, some marriages turn out to be a mistake,' said Herbert soberly. 'You've found yours out early, I found mine out after twenty-five years. At least, your mother did.'

'Don't go on about her, Dad,' said Olive.

'I was thinking about selling this house,' said Herbert. Actually, the landlord who owned adjacent houses had already made him an offer. 'I won't now. Well, you'll get notice to quit as soon as you can't come up with the rent, Olive. You can move in here, and bring your furniture. Say in a few weeks, when you've had time to get over this new shock and you're able to think straight about what you're going to do. I'll see you can pay your rent till then.'

'Dad, that's so good of you,' said Olive.

'Part of me obligation as your father,' said Herbert.

'Don't spoil it by saying that.'

'Let's say due to me paternal affection for you, then.'

'That's better.' Olive smiled wanly. 'I'll have to get a job.'

'Go back to being a typist?' said Herbert.

'I don't like the idea,' said Olive, 'I like growing flowers and having a house to look after.'

Herbert said he understood. Women, he said, had to look out for themselves if they wanted to do what best suited them. And there were always some men willing to go along with that in return for what women could do for them, such as putting their meals on the table regular and doing their washing. And other things.

'You get rid of Roger,' he said, 'and look out

for some other bloke, a bloke who'll give you a house and garden and a decent amount of housekeeping. But find out first if he'll put his hand in his pocket for you. You don't have to be in love with him, though you've got to like him. You've got to consider what you want and go for it, especially if you don't fancy being a typist day in and day out. You'll be happy enough, Olive, with a husband who'll give you what you want.'

'Dad, you're the surprise packet of the year,' said Olive, 'you're talking like a wise old owl instead of being as quiet as a mouse.'

'I've learned a lesson, I daresay,' said Herbert. 'Now, seeing you've been knocked for six and left with nothing, I'm going to give you fifty pounds. That'll keep you going for a few months, especially as you won't be paying any rent here, and I should think, if you use your noddle and get rid of Roger legal, you ought to have found the right kind of bloke in that time. What d'you think, will that look after your problems?'

'Dad, what can I say?' Olive looked emotional. 'Only that if Mum were still alive she'd realize she'd badly misjudged you. The poor dear paid for that, didn't she?'

'God rest her soul,' said Herbert.

'There's one thing I can do,' said Olive, 'I can keep house for you.'

'You could do something with the back

garden,' said Herbert, 'turn it into something a bit pretty, perhaps, while I'm on my sea trip.'

'Oh, I'll be pleased to,' said Olive. 'You're really going?'

'Yes, do me good, I thought, after what's happened,' said Herbert. 'Australia.'

'Australia?'

'It's a long way,' said Herbert.

'Australia, for goodness sake, you'll be away ages,' said Olive.

'I should think I will,' said Herbert. 'I'll leave you to look after things here. Mind you, don't let that stop you looking out for another bloke. And keep your fingers crossed that Roger gets nabbed before he's spent too much of your mother's savings. By the way, have you told Madge and Winnie about him?'

'Oh, Lord, I'm not going to like having to confess to them that I married a rotter, and that he's thieved Mum's savings,' said Olive.

'They're all right, they've got husbands to look after them,' said Herbert. 'I'll let you have the fifty pounds on Monday, but here's a couple of quid to keep you going till then.' He took two pound notes out of his wallet and handed them to her.

'Well, bless you, Dad, I'm not in a position to refuse,' she said.

'You'd better go and talk to Madge and Winnie,' said Herbert. 'Tell you what, I'll call for

you this evening and we'll go together. I know
you've got backbone, but you've got a bit of
misery as well, so you need some support. I'll be
with you about half seven.'

'Thanks, Dad, you're a brick,' said Olive.

'I take it that's one step up from a doorpost,'
said Herbert.

Chapter Twenty

Madge was furious, of course. Brian was stupefied. Madge said Olive could have done a lot better for herself and the family by marrying a postman. Postmen had to be honest and reliable men. Herbert said he didn't think every woman asked a would-be husband if he was honest and reliable. Madge said Olive should have made sure the savings book was put where it couldn't be found. Herbert said Olive wouldn't have known she had reason to distrust Roger to that extent. Brian said it wasn't Olive's fault. All that money, said Madge, gone like a puff of smoke unless the police get it back. Olive said she was utterly sick about it, especially when she was still in shock about their mother. The police, she said, were releasing the body to the undertakers at last, and the inquiries were over.

'What with a thief in the family, and the funeral and inquest to attend,' said Madge, 'I'm not in a fit state for any more conversation.'

However, she did manage to say that cats didn't give a woman trouble as some men did. Brian muttered something uncomplimentary about all cats.

'Dad and I will go and see Winnie now,' said Olive, and she and Herbert left before Madge found new voice.

Winnie was aghast. Victor couldn't credit it. However, they refused to attach any blame to Olive or to suggest she ought to have kept her eye on Roger. They both gave her a great deal of sympathy, and both were pleased to know the police were going after her worthless husband. Winnie hoped they'd get most of the money back, and Victor said Roger ought to be boiled in oil for what he'd done to Olive. Finally, they expressed relief when told that Hilda's funeral could take place at last.

Herbert took Olive to her home and then insisted she ought to stay at his place for the night. Olive shed a tear or two at that point. She packed a few things and Herbert took her home with him.

The funeral took place the following Monday. The family attended, and so did certain relatives and some friends, including Mrs Nell Binns. Madge, Winnie and Olive were all in black, Herbert, Brian and Victor in sober grey. At the church service, the vicar spoke some gentle words of praise about the deceased, and besought the family to bear with their loss.

At the cemetery, Herbert watched sombrely as the coffin was lowered into the grave. It was a certainty, he thought, that Hilda never expected her life as a free woman to be as short as this.

Nell, standing apart from the family, thought what a shame for poor Hilda, coming to her end so sudden, and in her own bath too. Still, Herbert was standing up to the burial with a straight back and a lot of dignity. His girls looked very mournful.

Brian thought, well, there you go, mother-in-law, ruddy hard luck that your bath was an oversized one. As for your eldest daughter, I know now why she hasn't conceived, having dipped deep into one of her dressing-table drawers. I'll give her Dr Marie Stopes. I'll give her a surprise. No, not tonight, on account of this being the funeral day. Tomorrow night.

Madge herself thought the occasion a suffering one for all concerned. And it was a suffering made worse by what Roger had done. The swine ought to be hanged and given a burial of his own.

Winnie thought poor Mum, there must have been one of her unlucky stars hovering about that night.

Olive simply hoped that her unlucky mother would rest in peace.

A representative from the factory was present.
Mr Rupert Burnside. And he thought what a pity,
a body like yours, Hilda, along with all your
hidden fires. Not many women of your age look
no more than thirtyish when they're all undone.
Damned if you weren't a positive eye-opener.
Still, I think you'd have turned into a nuisance as
time went on. Wanting to play the part of Lady
Bracknell was your opening shot. Well, perhaps
St Peter can find you a suitable part. As one of his
full-bodied angels with a touch of the seven veils.
Enjoy yourself.

The funeral breakfast took place at Herbert's
home. Madge, Winnie and Olive had all helped
in the preparation of food, but Herbert had
turned down an offer from Brian and Victor to
supply the drink. Good of you lads, he'd said, but
it's up to me.

Nell kept a low profile. Well, she knew it
wouldn't do to give the impression she was step-
ping into Hilda's shoes.

There were some awkward moments, oc-
casioned by friends or relatives asking exactly
how Hilda came to drown. Herbert got over that
by saying to each enquirer that the family
couldn't give an exact answer, and wouldn't be
able to until after the inquest.

Nell, standing in the passage and talking to
one of Herbert's neighbours, was closest to the

front door when its knocker sounded. So she opened it. An impressive-looking gent in a grey suit and trilby was on the step. She recognized him.

'Here, excuse me,' she whispered, 'but you shouldn't have come on the day of the funeral.'

'Perhaps not,' said Sergeant Tomlinson, 'but I do have some news which I think Mrs Way would like to hear, despite the occasion.'

'You sure?' said Nell.

'Yes, I'm sure, Mrs Binns.'

'Oh, you recognize me, do you?' said Nell.

'Yes, you're a close friend of Mr Jones. Would you tell Mrs Way I'm here?'

'Well, I suppose I should,' said Nell, 'but you'd best stay there while I go and find her.'

She found Olive and whispered to her.

'Oh, I'll see him,' said Olive, and joined him on the step, with the door pulled to behind her. 'Sergeant Tomlinson, you've something to tell me?'

Because she was dressed in mourning black, Sergeant Tomlinson took his hat off in a gesture of deference.

'I know I might be interrupting a very private family occasion,' he said, 'but I was sure you'd want to know your husband has been found. In Torquay, at the Palace Hotel. A constable spotted him coming out of the hotel this morning, recognized him from his description and arrested him.

He's now at the Torquay police station. His room at the hotel has been searched and a large wallet containing exactly eight hundred pounds in notes was found. It's now in the possession of the police. There were also twenty-two pounds in his pocket wallet.'

Olive's mouth tightened for a moment, and her lashes flickered. She'd spent the last few days feeling utterly sick about Roger. That feeling was gone now, replaced by contempt.

She said, 'Yes, I'm glad you came to tell me, Sergeant, I would have wanted you to. Thank you.'

'Damned rotten for you, though, your own husband failing you so badly on top of your mother's death, Mrs Way. You've had a rough time and I feel for you.'

'How did you know I was here?' asked Olive.

'I went to your house and was told by your next-door neighbour you'd be at your father's after the funeral,' said Sergeant Tomlinson. 'I don't want to worry you, but could you and your father come to the station sometime and make an official statement on which we'll base our charge when we have your husband in our custody? He's being brought from Torquay under escort.'

'I don't wish to see him or to be near him,' said Olive. 'And why do you need my father?'

'We presume he has first claim on the money

unless your mother left a will in favour of someone else.'

'Yes, I see,' said Olive. 'I'll speak to my father.
My mother made no will. My father means my
sisters and myself to have equal shares. I'll let
you know about making the statement. Thank
you again. Goodbye, Sergeant.'

'Goodbye, Mrs Way.'

'We've said a lot of those, it seems.' Olive's
little smile came and went.

'A lot of goodbyes?' he said.

'Yes,' she said, and he smiled and left.

Not until all friends, neighbours and relatives
had finally departed did Olive tell the family that
Roger had been found and arrested in Torquay,
where he'd been staying at the Palace Hotel.

'Good,' said Madge, vibrant with satisfaction,
'his crafty little ruse to make us think he was
somewhere on the high seas didn't come off, did
it?'

'His star fell out of the sky,' said Winnie.

'You saw it, did you?' said Brian.

'It was a figure of speech,' said Winnie.

'Sounded all right, though,' said Herbert.

'Olive, what about the money?' asked Madge.
'Did Sergeant Tomlinson mention it?'

'Yes,' said Olive. 'The Torquay police found
eight hundred pounds in one wallet, and twenty-
two pounds in another.'

'Well, that's a piece of glad tidings for you

287

girls,' said Victor, 'but the sod still managed to spend all of sixty quid living it up at the Palace Hotel in Torquay.'

'I expect he used some of it to pay off the kind of debts he always built up,' said Olive.

'Olive, d'you still want him put away?' asked Herbert.

'Must we talk about that when Mum's only just been buried?' asked Winnie.

'All the same, there's one point that ought to be mentioned,' said Herbert, 'which is, will Olive be able to charge Roger? Well, it's just occurred to me that she can't charge anyone for stealing money that didn't belong to her. I think I'd have to do it.'

'Sergeant Tomlinson asked if we could go to the station and make an official statement, Dad,' said Olive. 'He mentioned the money would be legally yours.'

'I'll talk to you a bit later.'

'Roger's got to be charged,' said Madge.

'Well, yes,' said Winnie, 'but I'd let Olive decide. She's the one who's been hurt the most.'

'That's my advice too,' said Brian.

'And mine, even if it's not my business,' said Victor. 'Leave it with Olive. That's if your dad agrees.'

'I'll do what Olive wants,' said Herbert.

He had a little chat with Olive later.

*   *   *

288

The following morning she appeared at the Stockwell police station and asked to see Sergeant Tomlinson. She spoke to him in an interview room. His eyebrows went up.

'Your father doesn't want to press charges, Mrs Way?'

'No.'

'Well, damn it, we—'

'I beg your pardon, Sergeant?'

'Damn it, I said, we had all the wheels set in motion, police up and down the country alerted, time and money spent, and your husband brought here all the way from Torquay. Dropping the charge is making a monkey of us, and I'm not sure we can do it, anyway.'

'Sergeant Tomlinson, are you shouting at me?'

'Nearly, but not quite, Mrs Way. I'm angry.'

'I'm sorry,' said Olive, 'but neither my father nor I want to appear in court and give evidence against my husband. Anyway, only my father can do that, isn't that right? Wives are excused, aren't they? My husband, Sergeant, is a worm and a snake, and I never wish to see him again, in court or anywhere else. He can go on his way to the devil, as far as I'm concerned.'

'On behalf of your father, you're asking the chief inspector here to let your husband off with a caution?' said Sergeant Tomlinson. 'He'll raise hell.'

'I'm sorry,' said Olive again. 'Will it mean embarrassment for you?'

'Embarrassment?' Sergeant Tomlinson fixed her with a glowering look. 'It'll mean I'll get a rocket that'll blow my head off.'

'Oh, I am sorry,' said Olive.

'Don't keep saying sorry. I suppose you realize your husband has already been charged?'

'Well, I hope that's frightened him to death,' said Olive.

'It has.'

'Good,' said Olive.

'Now look, Mrs Way, he's a cheap thief and an unpleasant one in what he did to you.'

'I know,' said Olive, 'but my father and I don't want to go to court.'

'Well, I'm damned if I could be as forgiving as that,' said Sergeant Tomlinson.

'No, I haven't forgiven Roger,' said Olive, 'and I don't think I ever will. I simply don't wish to have anything more to do with him.'

'It's an offence, wasting police time, Mrs Way.'

'Am I going to be arrested, then?'

'You should be,' said Sergeant Tomlinson, almost as growling in his mood as Inspector Shaw was on occasions. 'Your mind is definitely made up, is it?'

'Yes. I'm sorry, but—'

'If you say sorry again, Mrs Way, I'll catch fire.'

'Oh, I'd better just say goodbye, then. Will I see you at the inquest?'

'Yes.'

'Well, I hope you'll have forgiven me by then, Sergeant,' said Olive.

Sergeant Tomlinson managed the ghost of a smile.

'I think you can bet on that,' he said.

Subsequently he was forced to suffer a very awkward and harrowing session with the superintendent, who threatened to have Olive and her father arrested for wasting police time. Inspector Shaw helped to cool things down. In the end, there was no alternative but to drop the charge. The following morning, Roger Way was released with a severe caution.

Roger at once made tracks for home. Olive, anticipating this, had her father staying with her for a few days before she finally moved out. It was Herbert who confronted Roger when he arrived, and it was Herbert who delivered defamatory words, the kind of words of which neither his family nor his neighbours would ever have considered him capable.

Finally, 'And if you ever try to see Olive again, you bugger, you'll wish you'd never been born. On top of which, you'll find yourself in court, after all. Now get out of here before I knock your bloody head off.'

*　　*　　*

Muscles Boddy, fuming and fidgeting in Brixton Prison, heard from his guv'nor eventually, through the grapevine. The message was short and terse. You're fired. Muscles considered that the height of spiteful ingratitude. It put him into the position of needing the help of a friend.

Chapter Twenty-one

The inquest was held two days later.

The coroner listened to the pathologist expounding on the cause of death. Drowning, with no signs to indicate the deceased could have suffered a heart attack. Her heart, in fact, had been sound. There was, however, a faint bruise around each ankle, but the pathologist could not say how they came about.

Sergeant Tomlinson, representing the police, spoke next. He told the coroner that he and Constable Fry had been called to the scene by a Mr Roger Way, son-in-law of the deceased. Mr Way and his wife had discovered the body. Following that, inquiries had been made to establish whether or not suspicious circumstances obtained, by reason of the marks around the ankles, and the fact that the deceased had not been wearing her bath cap and had, apparently, not taken a towel with her into the bathroom. Further, her nightdress was missing. However, after an exhaustive investigation, the police could offer no evidence that the deceased had been forcibly drowned.

The coroner asked if he might put some questions to the husband. Herbert stood up, looking entirely respectable in a navy blue suit, white collar and black tie, his mane of hair as well brushed as ever.

'Mr Jones,' said the coroner, 'I understand you and your late wife had recently separated.'

'That's correct, sir,' said Herbert.

'You and your wife had been on bad terms?'

'No, never,' said Herbert.

'What, then, was the reason for the separation?'

'My wife felt that after twenty-five years of marriage, it was time to live her own life.'

'But you weren't on bad terms, you said?'

'No, but my wife considered life on her own would be – well, more entertaining,' said Herbert, and Olive bit her lip, Winnie made a face, and Madge fidgeted.

'Are you saying, Mr Jones, that your wife left you in order to be entertained?'

'Well, the fact is, I'm not very entertaining meself,' said Herbert, 'being a bit quiet and conservative in my ways, whereas Hilda liked things a bit lively.'

'For that reason, Mr Jones, you agreed to a separation?' said the coroner.

'I wouldn't say I agreed, sir,' said Herbert. 'It was more that my wife made up her mind to leave and she upped and went. It upset me considerable.'

'Did you quarrel with her at that point, Mr Jones?'

'No, I didn't, I don't like quarrels,' said Herbert, 'they're too disturbing and never make anyone feel better – well, that's my opinion.'

'I must ask you, Mr Jones, if your wife had another reason for leaving you.'

'Pardon?' said Herbert, upright, solid and square-shouldered.

'I'm suggesting, Mr Jones, that perhaps she was looking forward to being entertained by a third party.'

'A what?' said Herbert.

'Come, Mr Jones, it happens,' said the coroner.

'Not with Hilda, no, she wouldn't have done that to me,' said Herbert. 'She just meant that life gen'rally would be more entertaining without me.'

'I frankly find it difficult to believe that after twenty-five years of marriage a wife would leave her husband in the hope of finding life was a kind of circus,' said the coroner.

'Hilda liked a circus,' said Herbert, 'I took her to one once. But I'm refuting any suggestions that there was another man in her life.'

'Well,' said the coroner, 'you must have known

her better than anyone, Mr Jones, and on this
point I therefore go along with your feelings. I
come back to the separation. I can't help suspecting that after so many years this would have had
a drastic effect on her emotions, whether it was
instigated by her or not. I wonder, would any of
your daughters care to say something? I believe
they're all here.'

Madge stood up.

'I'm the eldest daughter, Mrs Madge Cooper,'
she said.

'Yes, Mrs Cooper?' said the coroner.

'I'd like to say yes, that my mother was very
upset,' said Madge. 'She naturally hoped my
father would fight to make her stay.'

'Did she tell you that?' asked the coroner.

'Yes, in so many words,' said Madge. 'My
sisters will confirm it.'

The coroner consulted a slip of paper.

'Mrs Winnie Chance?' he said, and Winnie
stood up.

'Yes, my mother was in quite a state about Dad
letting her leave, sir.'

'But she need not have left, surely?' said the
coroner.

'It was her pride,' said Winnie, 'she didn't want
to back down, she just wanted my father to let
her know he couldn't do without her. But he had
his own pride.'

Herbert was agape by now. And Brian and

Victor were dumb-founded about the way their wives had spoken about their old man.

Olive stood up.

'I'm Mrs Olive Way,' she said. 'It's quite true, my mother was very emotional about it all. She wouldn't let everyone know she was, but she confided in me and my sisters. But I don't think she wanted my father to oppose the separation. She made it clear to us that it was what she wanted, the chance to make a new life for herself.'

'Yes,' said Madge, 'but you know how it all upset her.'

'And how it grieved her,' said Winnie.

Herbert addressed the coroner. 'I wasn't aware my wife had regrets about leaving, it struck me it was more the reverse,' he said.

'Perhaps you mistook her attitude,' said the coroner.

'Excuse me, sir,' said Olive, 'there's nothing to be held against my father. He was shocked out of his mind by everything. I want you to know he was always a good providing husband to my mother and a quiet and affectionate father to us. He was very good and kind always, but not very outgoing, and my mother was restless at times.'

'But it was a shock to her that your father made no effort to repair the break?' said the coroner.

'Yes, very much of a shock,' said Madge.

'Did he ever go to see her after she moved into the flat?'

'No,' said Madge.

'That is correct, Mr Jones?'

'Yes,' said Herbert. 'But that was because she wanted me to visit only when she invited me.'

'Surely that showed her state of mind was unusual?'

'It didn't seem so to me,' said Herbert, 'but I know mine was. Well, after twenty-five years, I was hardly meself, was I?'

'Your elder daughters seem convinced your wife was in a distressed state,' said the coroner, and looked at Madge.

'Yes, she was,' said Madge positively.

'Yes,' said Winnie.

The coroner glanced at Herbert.

'And your youngest daughter,' he said, 'has declared that your wife was in a very emotional state.'

'She was in a state all right, and so was I,' said Herbert.

'Of course,' said the coroner. 'Thank you, ladies, and thank you too, Mr Jones. I don't think there's any necessity for further evidence.' He deliberated for a short while, then said, 'I find the deceased took her own life while the balance of her mind was disturbed.'

'Drowned herself?' breathed Brian to Victor.

'Off her head, poor old girl,' murmured Victor.

The court rose.

Outside in the street afterwards, Herbert, still looking as if he'd walked into a brick wall, regarded his daughters helplessly.

'What happened, eh, what happened?' he asked.

'Oh, short and sharp, Dad,' said Winnie.

'No going on and on, and round and round,' said Madge.

'Best thing, Dad,' said Olive.

'But your mother was never upset about leaving me, then or afterwards, I'll bet my life on it,' said Herbert. 'Look what you've done, you've made her a suicide, which I thought was the last thing any of you wanted to believe.'

'We didn't, of course,' said Madge, 'but we had a serious talk about it just before the inquest opened, and realized that if the coroner decided it must have been some kind of accident, the police would never have let go of trying to find out what, why and wherefore, and everything else. So we decided to help the coroner settle for suicide.'

'You and Winnie went for that, did you, with a little backing from Olive?' said Herbert. 'Well, thanks a lot. Mind, I'm not forgetting that Olive managed some kind words on me behalf, even if she did talk about her mother being very emotional about everything, which you all know she wasn't. Well, the result hasn't done me much good, it's left me looking as if I'm to blame for not bringing her back home. She'd never have come, anyway. You girls did it on me.'

'Only to get it all settled once and for all, Dad, really,' said Winnie. 'It was for your peace of mind.'

'Yes, really,' said Olive, 'and nobody will put any blame on you, Dad. Let's be glad it's all over, and that Mum's resting in peace. No more calls from the police, no more of that.'

'I know now why they made such frequent calls,' said Madge, frowning. 'I mean, did you all hear Sergeant Tomlinson say Mum wasn't wearing her bath cap and that there was no towel in the bathroom?'

'Yes, that helped to point to suicide,' said Olive. 'The coroner would have told himself she wouldn't have bothered. Lord, perhaps she didn't. Perhaps she really did let herself sink under.'

'Might I remind you again that none of you liked the idea of your mum committing suicide?' said Herbert.

'We still don't like it,' said Winnie, 'but it was the only verdict that would settle things.'

'Winnie's right,' said Victor.

'Yes, I'll go along with that,' said Brian. He was quite willing to, since something else needed his attention following a serious talk he had had with Madge, a talk that was intimidating enough to make her promise to dispense with the con-traceptive measures recommended by Dr Marie Stopes.

'I'd have liked it if I'd been consulted,' said Herbert.

'You didn't get here in time,' said Madge.

'All over, Dad,' said Olive. 'Now you can enjoy your cruise to Australia.'

'Australia, for God's sake,' said Madge, 'it'll be like going round the world.'

'Lovely,' said Winnie, 'think of all the tropical nights and the stars.'

'Perhaps he'll find yours hanging about over Sydney,' said Victor.

'Oh, excuse me a moment,' said Olive. She had seen Sergeant Tomlinson. She broke away and detained him on his walk to a police car. 'Sergeant, is that satisfactory to you, a suicide verdict?'

Sergeant Tomlinson was tempted to say no, it wasn't. But that would have invited questions he couldn't answer. He could only have offered suspicions.

'Was it satisfactory to you, Mrs Way?'

'I don't think any of us wanted to believe that of our mother,' said Olive, 'but I couldn't see how the coroner could have given a different verdict.'

'Yes, it did seem like that,' said Sergeant Tom-linson. 'By the way, your father can collect that money now, if he'd like to call in at the station sometime.'

'I'll tell him,' said Olive.

'And now, I suppose, this is our final goodbye, Mrs Way.'

'Do you think so?' said Olive. 'But I'm going to divorce Roger, I have the right grounds, I'm told. So if you brought your pencil and sketch block, and I brought my watercolours, perhaps we could go to Richmond Park together next Sunday. That is, if you're not on duty.'

'Are you serious?' asked Sergeant Tomlinson.

'Of course,' said Olive, who, on her father's advice, was looking out for herself with the right kind of bloke.

'You're on, then,' smiled Sergeant Tomlinson.

'Oh, that's good,' said Olive. 'Goodbye until next Sunday, then. I'll be ready at two o'clock.'

'I'll call for you.'

'Suicide, would you believe,' said Nell a little later, when Herbert was taking her home. She'd sat at the back of the court, and had thought she might be called.

'Beats me, those girls of mine saying what they did,' brooded Herbert.

'Well, p'raps Hilda did tell them things she didn't tell you,' said Nell.

'They cooked it up, to get it over with,' said

Herbert. 'Oh, well, it's done now, and the blame's mine.'

'Oh, I wouldn't say that, Herbert, and anyone that knows you wouldn't even think it was. Mind, it was a bit queer, wasn't it, that Hilda didn't take a bath towel with her to the bathroom. No wonder the police got suspicious. It got me agitated when they asked me questions about you being here that evening. Still, I was able to think straight and tell them you didn't leave till late. It was late, wasn't it?'

'Late enough, Nell.'

'Yes. Lor', Herbert, now I can't think of much else but Australia.'

'Life on the ocean wave, we'll enjoy that, Nell, all the time it'll take to get there.'

'I hope I don't get seasick,' said Nell.

Chapter Twenty-two

Herbert invited his daughters to lunch again a few days later, and over the meal he announced he was taking Mrs Nell Binns to Australia with him.

'You're doing what?' said Madge.

'Taking Mrs Binns with me,' said Herbert, looking his usual formal self, but implying from his announcement that he was chucking respectability out of the window.

'Dad, you can't, it's not decent,' said Winnie.

'Well, it's not half bad,' said Herbert, 'considering we're going cabin class.'

'My God,' said Madge, 'you're actually sharing a cabin with her? That's disgusting.'

'I'll thank you not to talk like that,' said Herbert. 'We'll have separate cabins, which is only right and proper, like I've always done.'

'It's not right and proper when it's not paying respect to the dead,' said Madge. 'Mum would turn in her grave if she knew you were going on a sea trip to Australia with a widow.'

'Dad, it's far too soon for you to take up with any woman,' said Winnie.

'I think Dad sees himself as a free man,' said Olive, 'and I have to admit I now see myself as a free woman, even if it'll be some time before my divorce comes through.'

'Being a free man doesn't entitle Dad to make eyes at Mrs Binns so soon after Mum's death,' said Madge.

'I'm free to reward Mrs Binns for all the years she worked for me in the shop,' said Herbert. 'She was a great help to me every day she was there.'

'But the cost of taking her all the way to Australia,' said Winnie, 'that's being a lot too grateful, I should think, and so would most people.'

'Well, never mind about most people, Winnie, it's all arranged,' said Herbert. 'We're sailing from Southampton on Friday, and we're going there tomorrow, Thursday, by train and staying in a hotel overnight. Olive, you can move in here now, any day you like.'

'I will, Dad, thanks very much,' said Olive, who had delayed her move until her dad was on his way. She was appreciative of the prospect of living rent-free. She had applied for an office job with an insurance company, and was waiting to hear. Of course, if Sergeant Tomlinson became very fond of her, well, things might happen that would enable her to give up any job and grow roses again. 'I'll move in definitely at the week-end.'

'It'll make up a bit for what Roger did to you,' said Herbert. 'Mind, I'm still sore that all you girls laid it on thick with the coroner over your mother's feelings. It was news to me that she had those kind of feelings.'

'Dad, we're all sure it must have upset her that you just let her go without doing a thing to stop her,' said Winnie.

'Anyway, that's all over, and a good thing too,' said Madge. 'It's sad enough to know we've lost her, and that we've got the grief to bear. But you can't be grieving much yourself, Dad, if you're going to enjoy a cruise all the way to Australia with Mrs Binns.'

'What I'm grieving about is that twenty-five years of marriage didn't count for anything in the end,' said Herbert. 'It's my opinion your mother danced out of all that like a happy sixteen-year-old.'

'That's an unkind thing to say,' said Winnie.

'Bitter, I call it,' said Madge.

'Still, Dad was badly hurt,' said Olive.

'Best not to chew over it,' said Herbert. 'Let's leave it now and for ever.'

Later, when his daughters were departing, he wished them luck and said he'd send them a picture postcard each time the ship touched port. Madge managed to say a fairly friendly goodbye to him, Winnie a forgiving and affectionate one, and Olive gave him a hug and a kiss.

After they'd gone, Herbert checked that certain items necessary to his voyage were at the ready in the top drawer of the dressing table. Passport, tickets and immigration document.

Nell had her own passport and immigration document securely lodged in a new handbag. Herbert had been so good, buying her all kinds of clothes and accessories.

Muscles Boddy was released from Brixton Prison the following day, having served his twenty-eight days in fairly fractious fashion. He was enjoined by the chief warder to behave himself from now on.

'Do me a favour,' said Muscles, 'fall under a bus.'

He busied himself as soon as he was out of jail.

The SS *Pacific Star* steamed out of Southampton at seven in the evening, on the turn of the tide. By half past ten it was well on its way, heading for the Bay of Biscay. The night was refreshingly cool, the stars visible in the inky sky, and Herbert was on the promenade deck, contemplating the faintly perceptible wash of the ship from the stern rail. He and Nell had enjoyed their first dinner aboard, in the cabin-class dining room, and Nell was now in her cabin. He'd taken her down after she'd spent a little while on the deck with him. She'd said she was a bit tired and would like to prepare for her first night's sleep at sea. Herbert had come up again, wanting to take in lungfuls of the night breezes before turning in himself.

Well, he thought, this is the life. What a dinner, as good as a bloke could get at the Ritz, he'd bet on it. And having Nell enjoy it with him had been highly satisfying. Nell was a warm-hearted and affectionate woman, that she was. She'd make a warm-hearted and affectionate wife once they were married. The wedding would take place in Australia. The people at Australia House had been nice and helpful, especially when shown that he had enough funds to ensure he would not be a liability as an immigrant. He intended to buy a shop and its goodwill, and run it with Nell for about ten years, say, and then retire with her. Nell had been in agreement, saying it was best to have something to do, like running a shop, instead of sitting around and doing nothing. Herbert ought to have some spare time to grow things, she said, if they bought a nice little house with a garden. She thought flowers probably grew lovely in Australia, and perhaps oranges too. Imagine if we could have an orange tree, she said. That, thought Herbert, was very promising kind of talk. She hadn't said anything about hoping he would be lively and entertaining once they were married, she seemed happy to take him on just as he was. Madge, Winnie and Olive, well, his intention to stay in Australia would come as a surprise to them, but there it was, he'd given them many years as a father, and didn't owe them anything, any more than they owed him.

He jumped as a beefy hand clapped his shoulder and a voice reached his ear.

'Hello, 'Erbert old cock, ain't leaving yer best friend in the lurch, are yer?'

He turned. The lights of the promenade deck silhouetted the large bulky figure of Muscles Boddy. Herbert gaped.

'Eh?' he said.

'I been looking all over for you, 'Erbert. Caught a train to Southampton this morning, didn't I, after finding out yesterday from a neighbour of yourn that you was off to Australia today. What a bleedin' chase I've had to catch up with yer. Lucky I found this was the only ship going to Ossie, or I might still be looking for yer. Saw you up here a bit ago with a lady, saw you go down with her, and then up you come again. Might I ask if the lady's a welcoming widow that you're taking with you all the way?'

'None of your business,' said Herbert.

"Erbert, I wouldn't like to think you was after buggering off without me.'

'Now look here – '

'Don't come the old acid, 'Erbert. We're friends, ain't we? And I done you a good turn, didn't I, like a friend should. I scratch your belly, and you scratch mine, that's fair, ain't it? Australia'll suit me fine. Well, I lost me job with the guv'nor on account of a couple of lousy coppers laying an unfair charge on me, which cost me twenty-eight days in Brixton, which got up the guv'nor's nose.'

'Well, hard luck,' said Herbert, recovering a bit, 'but it's nothing to do with me. As for doing me a good turn, what good turn?'

Muscles took a look along the promenade deck. There were a couple of people leaning on the rail at a distance that was well out of earshot, but the coolness of the sea breeze had sent most promenaders down to their cabins. He edged close to Herbert, and from the corner of his mouth came confidential words.

'Now then, 'Erbert old matey, you know what good turn all right, don't yer? I'll grant your ungrateful missus didn't get pushed under a bus, but all that bathwater did the trick very nice, didn't it?'

'What the hell d'you mean?' asked Herbert, stiffening.

'Don't you worry, 'Erbert, it's just between you and me, like we agreed. Remember we talked about how you needed a friend that would do you a good turn? Well, I done it.'

'Jesus Christ,' said Herbert, 'you drowned my wife in her bath, you bloody fiend?'

'Not me, 'Erbert, not me personal.' Muscles turned his head and took another look along the deck. The couple had gone. A little deep chuckle found its way up from his large chest, and he told Herbert then that he'd used the services of an old East End mate of his. Herbert listened paralysed as Muscles relayed details. He'd found Hilda's address on Herbert's mantel-piece, having entered the house by way of the kitchen window. He was a dab hand, he said, at opening kitchen windows. He begged Herbert's pardon for doing that off his own bat, but it was always best not to let the client know too much beforehand.

'Client?' said Herbert, shivering. 'What d'you mean, client?'

Muscles said when a job was being done for a friend, the friend turned into a client. Herbert pointed out in a strangled voice that he hadn't asked for any job to be done.

'I'm talking about a good turn, ain't I?' said Muscles. 'Same thing, y'know.' Well, he went on, having got the ungrateful wife's new address, he did a recce on the flat and soon found it was easy to get into the yard and through the back door. He informed his old mate, and told him what was required. See the lady off nice and quick, but don't draw blood, don't get messy. So his mate said right, and put himself under contract.

'Contract, what's that mean, you bugger?' asked Herbert hoarsely.

'It's a trade term, 'Erbert,' said Muscles. His mate reported to him after the job was done. He'd got into the flat when Herbert's wife was out, and having already thought of a nice quick and clean way to see her off, he filled the bath with water and waited. Out of sight, of course. When the lady returned, she undressed, then entered the bathroom in her nightie. Of course, as soon as she saw the bath was full of water, she bent over to pull the plug out. Which was just what Cabbage Ears was waiting for.

'Cabbage Ears?' said Herbert from out of his nightmare.

'Best not to give no names,' said Muscles. 'Anyway, 'Erbert mate, he was wearing thick fur gloves and not leaving no careless fingerprints around. He took hold of her ankles from behind and upended her. Down went her napper in the water, where it rested very convenient on the bottom. She was no problem at all, not with her napper taking her weight, and all he had to do was keep hold of her ankles, which he did, and as gentle as a baby, with just a finger and thumb round each one. Mind, she waggled a bit under the water, but only for a few ticks. Well, the surprise and the shock helped to make it nice and quick, which I fancied you'd be in favour of, eh, matey?'

'In favour?' breathed Herbert.

'Well, she had been yer wife for a good many years, 'Erbert, and I know you've got feelings,' said Muscles. 'Just a bleedin' pity she didn't appreciate you. Still, all's well that ends well, she's gorn now. Me friend, yer contract man, laid her out in the bath with a cake of soap, took 'er nightie off, and off he went with it. Didn't want to leave it on her, yer see. Might have looked suspicious. He took it home to his missus, and I daresay she hung it on her yard line to dry out. Of course, he met me in a pub later to let me know the job was done. Well, we had an appointment there, anyways, with the landlord at chucking-out time. By the way, I paid Cabbage Ears on your behalf. Forty quid.'

'What?' said Herbert, aghast.

'No, I told a lie, blowed if I didn't,' said Muscles. 'Forty-five quid. Well, five for travelling expenses.'

'Travelling expenses?'

'Give or take a bob or two,' said Muscles. 'Still, all that can come out of me share of what you sold yer shop for. Say a half-share, 'Erbert, as soon as we get to Ossie. I'm stowage aboard this here ship, by the way, I'm tucking meself down in that there lifeboat at night.' He pointed. 'I ain't exactly comf'table, but you bring me some rations each night when it's dark and I'll put up with the inconvenience. In Australia, I'll be the first off the ship, I know how to manage that, and I'll be waiting for you, old cock, for you and yer welcoming widow. And yer bank balance. Well, half of it.'

'You ought to be hung up on meat hooks,' breathed Herbert. 'I never at any time asked you to have my wife murdered.'

'Now then, 'Erbert, you didn't say no to me offer to do you a good turn, and when a friend don't say no, it means yes, don't it? Course it does.'

The ship was steaming on through the night, churning water, and Herbert was sweating all over. He turned to the rail, put his arms along it and stared down again at the pale wake. Muscles turned with him, put his elbows on the rail and dropped his large chin into his cupped hands.

'I've got you on my bloody back,' said Herbert.

'Course you ain't, 'Erbert, you got me for your best friend,' said Muscles, and chuckled again.

Herbert moved like lightning then to put

himself behind Muscles. He stooped, took hold of him by his ankles, and heaved upwards. Despite his size and his weight, Muscles parted company from the deck, and because his elbows were on the rail and he was caught completely off guard, he cartwheeled over the side. Herbert let go and there was a choking gasp of maddened panic as Muscles plunged down and hit the foaming wake.

Man overboard, thought Herbert, and turned to examine the promenade deck. It was empty. Well, hard luck on Muscles Boddy. A stowaway, he wasn't on the passenger list. He wouldn't be missed because his presence aboard hadn't been registered.

Herbert walked towards a companionway. A ship's officer appeared.

'A fine night, sir,' he said.

'There's an ocean of fresh air out here,' said Herbert, 'and it's been doing me the world of good.'

'And there's a lot more to come,' smiled the officer.

'I suppose there is,' said Herbert, 'it's a long way to Sydney. I'm turning in now. Good-night.'

'Goodnight, sir.'

Herbert went down to his cabin.

The ship steamed on.

Muscles Boddy, having escaped being sucked

into the mincing machine of the propellers, was nevertheless dead from drowning. He had come to the surface, however, and was floating like a large porpoise on a gentle swell.

THE END